THE COACH HAD PULLED INTO A NAR-
ROW ALLEY. MY STOMACH RECOILED
AT THE SIGHT THAT GREETED US. . . .

Approaching silently and sealing off any
retreat to the street was a group of six
burly Chinese. They were all dressed in
a mixture of Oriental and western garb.
Three wore close-fitting caps and loose-
sleeved, silk tops and had long queues
down their backs. Two had ordinary felt
hats. They were all short and blocky,
with impassive features. But what drew
my attention immediately were the short,
curved swords they carried.

"What the hell is this?" Carlyle yelled. But
the driver just gave him a snaggletoothed
grin. Infuriated, Carlyle leaped for the
driver on the box. . . .

GREAT
TIMBER RACE

Tim Champlin

BALLANTINE BOOKS • NEW YORK

For Father Ed Steiner
With Many Thanks

Library of Congress Catalog Card Number: 86-90930

ISBN 0-345-33630-5

Manufactured in the United States of America

First Edition: October 1986

CHAPTER 1

IT was with a strange mixture of curiosity and dread that I stepped from the plush four-horse carriage and looked up at the huge Nob Hill mansion before me. I was interested to find out what would take place at this meeting. I also had the strangest premonition that the events of this day were going to draw me into a dangerous situation I would be better advised to steer clear of.

These thoughts were only fleeting as I turned to watch a uniformed liveryman hold the coach door for my four traveling companions—Phineas "Fin" Staghorn, the stocky blond sailor who had talked me, Matt Tierney and Wiley Jenkins into coming here. Wiley, a young southerner of thirty, and I had shared several adventures in the past. Asa Carlyle, a slim man in his late forties who was a Puget Sound lumberman and Fin's boss, was next out of the coach. And lastly came William Rust, a small man in wire-rimmed spectacles who was representing the firm of Rust and Barrett, the most powerful lumber company on the West Coast.

The early morning fog of San Francisco had burned away, leaving in its place the clearest, most invigorating air I had ever breathed, even though I shivered in the unaccustomed chill of the sea breeze. The hills of the city were spread out below us in a grand panorama, and farther out the blue waters of the bay sparkled brilliantly in the morning sun.

1

But I had no time to enjoy the scenery, as we were ushered quickly up the steps and into the house.

"One moment, gentlemen," the tall butler said as he took Mr. Carlyle's hat, hung it on the hall tree, and disappeared noiselessly into the next room.

I tried not to gape at the magnificence of this house. The double front doors we had entered contained stained glass windows and the carpeted hallway where we stood was done from floor to ceiling in ornately carved redwood and some strange wood I couldn't identify.

"Primavera wood. It's from South America," Asa Carlyle remarked as he saw me run my hand over the polished surface.

A grandfather clock ticked loudly in a corner. As I turned toward Wiley, I caught a glimpse of my reflection in a full-length beveled mirror set into the wall by the umbrella stand.

"If all this was meant to impress us, it's sure working on me," I said in a low voice. Wiley nodded, but before he could reply, the butler reappeared. "This way."

We followed him back into the hushed interior of the big house and were shown into a high-ceilinged library with three walls lined from bottom to top with books. The fourth wall contained bay windows that gave a magnificent view of the city. Marble busts of Roman emperors stood on pedestals here and there and a huge crystal chandelier hung over an oval conference table in the center of the room.

A big deep-chested man in black broadcloth got up from behind the table.

"Welcome, gentlemen!" he boomed, his voice filling the large room. "Please be seated." His snow-white hair and beard and clean-shaven upper lip, as well as his size and vitality, gave him the appearance of a New England whaling captain.

"I'm glad you accepted my invitation to meet here instead of in our company offices downtown. If you don't mind, we'll get right down to business," he continued briskly as we sat ourselves on the damask-covered armchairs on either side of the table.

"The members of my board of directors are not here, but they have authorized me to make any decision I see fit to resolve this impasse. As you know, Mr. Rust and Mr. Carlyle, we have been dickering for several months in the awarding of this contract.'' He nodded toward each of these men, without even glancing at Wiley, Fin or myself. He had not given time for any introductions and apparently assumed that we knew we were in the presence of Caleb Hale, wealthy entrepreneur who had risen from common laborer to foreman, from manager to owner of the largest contracting company in California.

''I have little patience with the intricacies of business. I am known for doing things with broad strokes and, I daresay, with a little flair.'' He smiled as he spread his big hands on the table in front of him. ''How dull life would be if business had to be conducted by strict, inflexible rules. If that were the case, I never would have arrived at the position I find myself in today.'' He gestured at our sumptuous surroundings. ''I have always operated on my instincts—hunches, if you will—and these instincts have steered me more right than wrong. That's why my more timid colleagues on the board have rather reluctantly allowed me to proceed on my own. So''—he paused to select a cigar from the humidor on the table—''since your two mills have submitted virtually identical bids for the amount of lumber we figure to need over the next five years and you both seem to have the capability of delivering this lumber to San Francisco safely and on schedule, there is virtually little else to look at in determining who should be awarded this contract. True, the firm of Rust and Barrett is larger by far and older, but I don't feel they should be given preference just for that reason. Instead, I wish to propose a solution that is certainly more interesting than drawing straws or tossing a coin. I propose a race, with the winner getting the contract.''

Carlyle and Rust glanced at each other, bewildered.

''It will be a race from Puget Sound to our docks here in the bay with vessels of your choice loaded to capacity with sawed lumber, either fir or pine or a mixed load of anything but hardwoods. It will be a great competition for your companies as well as for mine. The date of the contest could be set for a few weeks from now to allow for adequate planning and hopefully at a time when the

3

late summer weather would be reasonably stable. Well, what do you think?" He sat back and looked from one to the other of the two principals at the table.

"Well . . ." William Rust glanced across at Asa Carlyle, waiting for him to speak first. When he gave no indication of it, the small man continued. "This is not exactly what I expected. If you are serious, I may have to withdraw our bid."

"Where's your sporting blood, Bill?" Carlyle said, arching his brows at his bespeckled counterpart. "Afraid of a little challenge?"

Rust colored slightly but held his composure. "I'll have to consult my partners. We are an old, established firm, and this is not our way of doing business. We have a reputation to maintain. We have submitted our sealed bid. If that is not adequate to secure the contract, then Rust and Barrett will have to withdraw."

"Don't be so stuffy," Caleb Hale said. "There is nothing degrading about this contest. It won't hurt Rust and Barrett's dignity.

"As you know, the industry is in a slump right now, and I'm sure this contract would mean a great deal to your company. Especially since"—he paused to strike a match and puff his cigar into life—"I happen to know that your family business back in Maine has been put under a rather severe financial strain lately to subsidize losses on your West Coast operations. Of course, if you still want to withdraw, I'm sure Mr. Carlyle here will have no objections." The white-bearded tycoon leaned back in his chair and blew a cloud of smoke at the ceiling.

William Rust shifted uncomfortably in his chair and appeared to examine his perfectly manicured fingernails. His black hair was cut very short and plastered to his head and his ears protruded slightly, giving him the appearance of a somewhat ludicrous mannequin. There was a long silence that stretched to an embarrassing length.

"All right, Mr. Hale," the slender, formally dressed man said at last. "On behalf of Rust and Barrett, I will agree to this . . . this sporting event if that's what it takes to win this contract. Obviously you have done your research to know something of our company's finances. But we will prove to you that we are the best and will be able to deliver the lumber in our company ships faster than anyone else, including Mr. Carlyle." His voice had risen slightly as had the color in his face while he talked.

"I'm glad you accept the challenge." Caleb Hale smiled. "I think the contest will prove beneficial to us all.

"Now to the details. My associates and I, many of whom are former sailors, as I am, have already given considerable thought to this race. I was hoping that both of you would agree to it. Both vessels will be loaded under the eye of an inspector; both will be loaded at your respective mills and be towed to the mouth of Puget Sound, where they will drop their tugs on a signal from a boat stationed there. From then on it will be up to the seamanship and ingenuity of your two crews. There is no requirement that you pick up a steam tug to enter the Golden Gate, although you may do so if you wish. The first vessel to throw a mooring line at our company docks will be declared the winner and be awarded the contract.

"One further requirement—if there is any evidence of interference by either side, the other will be declared the winner by default. Any questions?"

No one had any.

"In that case, why don't we have a champagne toast?"

The butler appeared, on some unseen signal, bearing a tray, an iced bottle of wine, and several crystal goblets. Hale took the green bottle in his huge hands, worried the cork from it and poured six glasses of the sparkling liquid. He set the bottle down and stood up, raising his glass. "To our good health and to the success of the upcoming race. May the best company win!"

Over the lip of my goblet, I noticed the sour look on Rust's face across from me as he took a tentative sip. Either he was a teetotaler, or he was thinking of something else he was being forced to swallow that was much more bitter than the expensive French champagne.

Rather than take Caleb Hale's coach back to our hotel and ride with the dour William Rust, Asa Carlyle made some excuse about us wanting to get some exercise, and

5

the four of us started afoot back down the hill away from the mansion. The clear air was even headier than the champagne. I started to discuss the upcoming race, but Fin Staghorn shut me off with a look and a shake of his head as he glanced at his boss.

A few blocks away we swung up onto a cable car and continued toward the Palace Hotel where we were staying. I had never been in San Francisco before, but Staghorn and Carlyle were familiar with the city and how to find their way around. The older man seemed deep in thought and had little to say as the open-air car rattled and clanged its way up and down the hills until we arrived near our hotel.

"Meet me in the lobby in ten minutes," Carlyle said to us as he put the key into his door on the hotel's third floor. "I've got to get out of this stiff collar."

A half hour later, Staghorn, Asa Carlyle, Wiley Jenkins, and I were in a saloon about a block from the hotel ordering lunch. If Wiley and I had been alone, we would have been elbowing our way to the free lunch of boiled eggs, smoked sausages, and cheese on the bar and washing it down with five-cent mugs of beer. But being the guests of Asa Carlyle, we were seated at a table near the front window, where plenty of light streamed in on the red checkered tablecloth while a waiter took our order. Asa Carlyle may not have been a rich man by the standards of Caleb Hale or William Rust, but he was certainly far wealthier than the rest of us. A disappointed forty-niner, he had worked and saved and invested until some fifteen years ago he had been able to purchase his first lumber mill—a small, run-down operation on Puget Sound. There had been several ups and downs since then, Fin Staghorn had told me, but he had made money and been able to expand, buying out his partner only two years ago.

The firm of Rust and Barrett, on the other hand, owned and operated several mills on Puget Sound as well as a shipyard. They were heavily invested in timberland, mill machinery, and payroll.

After the waiter had gone, Asa Carlyle leaned forward on his elbows and looked across the table at us. "Gentlemen, I don't know if you realize how grave my situation is. As Hale mentioned, the industry is in a severe slump and has been for several months. It's a periodic thing in the lumber business. The market is presently glutted, but at the rate people are migrating to California— and if the new railroads get their fares in line, there will be a lot more people coming—this state is going to need a lot of lumber for building new towns. So I'm sure the market will recover eventually. But right now there are just too many mills cutting and shipping too much timber. And that means hard times for small-mill owners. My operation is not as small as several others on the sound, but I'm not nearly as large as Rust and Barrett either. During this slump, Rust and Barrett have been gradually building up long-haul trade with Australia and Hawaii so they won't have to be so dependent on the coastal trade. In the past when these domestic slumps occurred, most of the companies, large and small, formed a cartel to hold lumber off the market to keep prices from falling too far. The cartel, with Rust and Barrett at its head, paid several of the small mills to stay closed down. They tried to convince me to do the same, but I resisted. Rode out that last dry spell by cutting production and lowering wages of my mill hands. But this time it looks like a long slump, and I may not survive."

"Why not shut down for a time and take the money for it?" I inquired.

"For two reasons. The payment is only a pittance. And while I'm cooling my heels, Rust and Barrett is consolidating its grip on the market for the future. I can't stay in business indefinitely by holding up everything for months at a time. That's why this contract is so important to me. Caleb Hale's contracting company has jobs and connections everywhere. They're supplying ties for railroads, building towns, constructing wharfage for the harbor authority here in San Francisco. So it's not likely their demand for lumber will decrease. That's why securing this contract is so critical to me. Winning will mean cutting and shipping all the timber I can in the next five years and maybe expanding; losing will mean selling out. It's as simple as that. And with all the years and effort I've put into this business, I'm damned if I'm going to lie down and die without a fight!"

7

He banged his fist on the table to emphasize his point, and several men at nearby tables looked curiously in our direction.

"We'll see to it that the Carlyle Mill Company will win that race, sir," Staghorn said.

I wondered how he could be so sure. It would take more than sailing skill—it would take a lot of luck as well.

"You're Matt Tierney," Asa Carlyle stated, changing the subject and fixing me with a penetrating gaze. The gray eyes seemed to be looking into my soul. Fin Staghorn had made a hurried introduction just prior to our morning meeting.

"A reporter?" He arched his eyebrows.

"Not for about two years, since I covered General Buck's campaign in 1876," I replied. "I've done only a little writing since then." I felt strangely self-conscious under his scrutiny, as if I needed to apologize for my lack of a steady job.

"And you're Wiley Jenkins?" Carlyle said, switching his attention to my brown-haired companion. "Fin tells me you're here to lend us a hand. Either of you had any experience as a mill hand or sailor or shipwright? That's about all I'm in the market for right now."

"A few years ago I spent some time as a bucker in an Oregon lumber camp," Fin answered. "Hardest physical labor I've ever done."

I shook my head. "Small-craft sailing on Lake Michigan and a couple of transatlantic trips as a passenger on a Black Ball packet ship are the limit of my experience."

"Fin speaks highly of you two. Says you're very resourceful, regardless of the situation. I read the newspaper accounts of your saving that Rumanian prince last year. Amazing story. The three of you are lucky to be alive. But if you don't mind working for mostly bunk and grub, we can probably use your help doing something. Welcome aboard." He reached across and shook hands with each of us.

Carlyle suddenly stared hard at something over my shoulder. I looked around curiously.

"Bill Rust," Carlyle explained in a low voice. "Of all

the saloons in this city, wonder how he happened to pick this one?"

"Looking for you, maybe?" Fin suggested.

Rust, accompanied by two middle-aged mustachioed men in business suits, went by our table. Rust looked directly at Asa Carlyle but gave no sign of greeting.

"Friendly cuss," Wiley remarked.

"Those two with him are likely company partners or executives," Carlyle mused. "Probably doesn't want to appear too familiar with the enemy in front of them." He chuckled dryly. "I doubt if they'll be thrilled with the idea of this race."

They were shown to a vacant table next to ours—the only empty window table left in the crowded saloon. The waiter removed a Reserved sign as he seated them. From where I was sitting, I could observe the three men in animated conversation. But their words were lost in the general hum of noise and occasional bursts of laughter in the room. Rust studiously avoided looking in our direction.

"Here you are, gentlemen. The best oyster stew in the city," the tall waiter interrupted, placing the tray on the edge of our table and setting the steaming bowls in front of us with thick slices of fresh bread. "Made from Olympia oysters. Olys are the best in the world!"

After the first mouthful, I was inclined to agree with him.

"Well, if it isn't Mr. Rust! How ya doing?"

I glanced up at the booming voice. A big rawboned man with short brown hair and wearing a collarless white shirt stood by the next table with his hand thrust out.

William Rust's face registered surprise, confusion, then irritation within the space of a few seconds. He hesitated, clearly resenting the interruption, as his normally pale face began to color. He ignored the outstretched hand.

"You're . . . uh . . . Mr. . . ?"

"Boggs. Alonzo Boggs. Manager of your Spruce Point mill." It didn't seem to faze him that Rust didn't recognize him. He withdrew his hand and plunged ahead like some thick-skinned politician running for public office.

9

"Oh yes," Rust replied unenthusiastically. "This is Mr. Donald Barrett, and Mr. Wilbur Aston from our San Francisco office." The two older men nodded without changing expression.

When Boggs showed no sign of leaving after a moment or two of awkward silence, Rust said, "What brings you here?"

"Well, hell, Mr. Rust, you ought to know. Begging your pardon, sir," he suddenly added, apparently remembering his subordinate status. "You closed the mill I manage. Me and a few of the boys thought we'd come down and see what was doin' in the city and wash some o' the sawdust outta our throats. Might have to look around for another job while I'm here," he added significantly.

I was so fascinated by this scene that I caught myself staring with a spoon halfway to my mouth.

Rust squirmed slightly in his chair and slid around to face the blustery Boggs. "As you know, that shutdown was just a temporary measure until business improves."

"That's all well and good, Mr. Rust, but it ain't puttin' any beans in my belly when I'm laid off. When do we reopen?" he asked bluntly.

"Mr. . . . uh . . . Boggs. I'm having an important meeting with these gentlemen just now. Why don't you come to see me later and we'll discuss it." He turned back to his companions as if to dismiss the man. But Boggs was not taking the hint.

"Where you staying so we can get together?"

"Well . . . why don't I just meet you at the bar in about an hour?" An obvious delaying tactic to get rid of the man.

"Suits me. Nice to meet you gents." With a casual wave of a huge hand, he ambled away.

Rust looked more uncomfortable than ever as he resumed his sotto voce conversation with Barrett and Aston.

I looked around to see Boggs rejoin two men who were holding down one end of the bar and making the most of the free lunch.

Asa Carlyle, while appearing to be absorbed in his

food, had also apparently heard most of what had just transpired.

"Just another example of what I was talking about." He smiled, looking at me. "The Rust and Barrett giant isn't exactly dying, but he's feeling mighty poorly."

CHAPTER 2

WE didn't linger in San Francisco. There was much to be done before the race, so we checked out of our hotel the next morning. The quickest way up the coast was by sea, and one of the Carlyle company's five ships happened to be in port discharging a cargo of lumber. It would be sailing in ballast on the early evening tide. Mr. Carlyle had alerted his captain that we would be returning with him that afternoon.

Wiley and I took advantage of the few hours we had left to have Fin give us a short tour of the city—a city that hummed with the noise of traffic of all kinds, including pedestrians and the unique cable cars. Wiley and I were both impressed. Everyone seemed to be in a hurry to get somewhere else. In the general hustle and bustle, we came upon a small knot of men surrounding a policeman on Market Street who had just broken up a fight between a Chinaman and a Mexican. The Chinaman had suffered a stab wound and was bleeding profusely from the side of his neck. As we passed by, both of them were being hustled into a paddy wagon.

The growing city was cleaner than I expected it to be. Most of the buildings were four or five stories in height and the streets were cobblestones. The whole place seemed to anchor down the series of sandhills that made up this peninsula.

About two o'clock we stopped to eat. The crisp sea breeze and all our walking had made me ravenous. As a result, the three of us spread ourselves to a good feed. Mr. Carlyle had left earlier to take care of some unspecified business, with instructions for us to meet him back at the Palace Hotel at 3:30 P.M. We were to pick up our luggage and take a carriage to the waterfront.

So promptly at 4:00 we were standing in front of the hotel with our dunnage at our feet. Asa Carlyle stepped out and hailed a driver who was leaning against his carriage nearby, smoking his pipe and waiting for a fare. The driver sprang to his high seat, but before he could even get his horse in motion, another hack came clattering around him, cutting perilously close, the driver pulling his horse to a sliding stop so close that Asa Carlyle jumped back to keep from getting knocked down.

The driver hopped down and jerked the door of his carriage open.

"Step right in, gents. Where can I take you?"

Carlyle gave him a hard look then picked up his leather valise and put his foot on the lower step.

"To the waterfront. Pier Six."

We followed him into the coach and the driver slammed the door. The carriage started with a jerk as the driver cracked his whip.

"Damned drivers!" muttered Mr. Carlyle. "Trying to cut each other out. I hate cities. Be glad to get back to my mill and the woods."

I thought to myself that this was a strange attitude for a man whose business existence depended on competition. Carlyle settled himself to read a newspaper as the coach slowed to a snail's pace when the horse began pulling a hill. I leaned into a corner and closed my eyes, letting the gentle motion of the coach lull me into a doze. But it seemed only a couple of minutes later that I was suddenly jerked alert by being flung out of my corner as the coach slid around a corner. I collided with Wiley, who was clinging to a strap on the side of the coach.

"Driver! Driver! Stop this thing!" Asa Carlyle had his head out the side window, shouting.

The high-wheeled coach bounced and clattered over the rough cobblestones without slowing. Carlyle pulled his head back inside.

"Crazy driver. I'm not in that big a hurry. He's going to get us all killed. This isn't even the direct way to the waterfront. Probably trying to get more fare out of us."

Carlyle shouted up at the driver again, but if he heard, he gave no indication, and we were continuously being bounced around as the coach careened up one street and down another. From what little I could see out the window, we seemed to be in the Chinese quarter of the city. Oriental writing appeared on shop windows, and a few Chinese faces on the street flashed by as the coach sped on. Brick tenement buildings were jammed together in long rows. The coach made one more lurching turn and skidded to a stop as the driver locked the brakes on the rear wheels.

Brick walls hemmed us in only a few feet on each side as we stumbled out to find out what was going on.

The coach had pulled into a narrow alley, and my stomach recoiled at the sight that greeted us.

Approaching silently, and sealing off any retreat to the street, was a group of six burly Chinese. They were all dressed in a mixture of Oriental and Western garb. Three wore close-fitting caps and loose-sleeved silk tops with long queues down their backs. Two had ordinary felt hats. They were all short and blocky with impassive features. But what drew my attention immediately were the short, curved swords they carried.

"What the hell is this?" Carlyle yelled. But the driver just gave him a snaggle-toothed grin. Infuriated, Carlyle leaped for the driver on the box. But he caught a boot in the face instead and was thrown back. A laugh echoed back as the driver whipped the lathered horse and the coach lunged forward. We sprang back against the bricks to keep from being run down by the high wheels. And before we could react, the coach was gaining speed and was out of reach.

The coach careened wildly to the end of the alley and turned into the next street, leaving overturned trash barrels in its wake.

The six Chinese were spreading out and edging around us. I had no idea why they were after us, but I didn't want to stay around to find out. And they didn't appear to be the type to do much talking. None of the four of us

14

was wearing a gun. My Colt and Winchester were packed in my luggage, still in the vanished coach. I hadn't anticipated needing a gun in the city. What a mistake that was! I had expected to have to keep up my guard last year in Apache country but here? Even my derringer was gone—lost with a bad poker hand three months ago.

The four of us exchanged quick glances as the six grim-faced Chinese shuffled toward us, knives at the ready. I motioned with my head toward the far end of the alley. The nearest Oriental saw our intention and leaped to get between us and the open-ended alley just as we bolted. I was in the lead, and I heard the whisper of the steel blade at the same time I saw it blur toward me. I felt it touch me below the waist, but there was no pain. I had twisted back just in time. My three companions sped by me and were sprinting down the alley with the Chinese in pursuit. The man who had swung at me was stalking me like a good cow horse who has cut a calf from the herd. I feinted right and left, and my assailant countered my moves easily in the narrow alley. I had no weapon, and there was nowhere for me to go. Then I realized that the rest of the Chinese were pursuing my friends down the alley. I spun and sprinted for the open end of the alley where we had entered. But another knife-wielding Chinaman had appeared from somewhere. I was cut off. And this time they didn't hesitate. They meant to finish me in a hurry. In desperation, I whipped off my wool jacket and tangled the arm and blade of a gut thrust by my first assailant. Before the other man could jump me from behind, I instinctively threw my back against the brick wall and felt myself fall off-balance as one shoulder tilted into a recessed doorway. I rolled back into the shadows and kicked at the wooden door behind me. It gave slightly but didn't open. A round slant-eyed face was suddenly in front of me, and a slight grin appeared as the curved sword came slicing. The restricted space hindered his swing, and the blade whanged off the edge of the arched brick alcove.

Panic lent me strength. I threw all my weight at the door behind me. It gave with a splintering sound. I half fell through the broken panels just in time to avoid the deadly thrust of the short sword as it sliced my sleeve and cut my arm. I lost my balance and suddenly felt myself rolling and tumbling down a flight of stairs in the blackness. I sprawled to a stop on a landing, got to my feet, and felt my way to the bottom by means of a handrail. There I encountered another door. It was unlocked, and I was through it in a flash, slamming it against any pursuit. The subterranean room I faced was dimly lighted by a few candles that barely punched some holes of light in the murky air that was thick with a strange-smelling smoke. Several Chinese faces looked up impassively at me from a card game. I felt trapped. There had to be another way out. And then I spotted it—a bamboo curtain shielding a doorway opposite me. Wherever it led was the way I was going. I had to get out! Before anyone had time to react to my presence, I was across the room and through the curtain. A wasted Oriental figure lay on his side on a mat with a slender white pipe to his mouth. Apparently he was in some dreamworld of the opium smoker and never knew I was there. Across this cubicle was another door. On the other side of it one stairway led up and another down. I leaped up the stairs two at a time. Another landing and a turn, another flight, and I burst out a door into the welcome fresh air of the street. I had no idea where I was, but fear put wings to my feet. I didn't see the men who had attacked us, but I was determined to put a lot of distance between us. I sprinted away, zigzagging down streets in the general direction of the bay.

My lungs and legs gave out about the same time, and I finally staggered to a stop and leaned against a lamppost, my knees trembling and the breath whistling in and out of burning lungs. I guessed I had run a good mile and a half. There was no sign of my assailants. But neither was there any sign of my friends.

As my heart gradually steadied down, I noticed the lengthening shadows. I pulled out my watch. It was 4:40. I didn't know what time the tide turned and felt I was in danger of missing the ship. But where were the others? Had they been caught and cut to pieces by the pursuing Chinese? Had the captain been ordered to wait for his boss, regardless, or would he sail on the ebb tide? Should I go find the ship and bring back help, or should I return and try to find Carlyle, Staghorn, and Jenkins myself? Even if I could find the alley again, I was in no shape to do anything without a weapon. And whatever had happened was probably over by now.

It was then I felt the cool breezes and looked down to see that the first swipe of the razor-sharp blade had neatly sliced the front of my pants just below my belt. He had clearly meant to disembowel me but instead had left only a gaping slash in the material instead of in me, exposing a good portion of my long underwear. My coat was gone, and there was blood oozing through my left shirt-sleeve from a stinging cut on my forearm. I knew I looked beat-up and ridiculous. But I had to do something! Yet I couldn't get my mind focused enough to decide what. I started walking quickly on legs that were already beginning to stiffen from my long run. A chilling breeze was drying the sweat on my overheated body.

I rounded the corner of a building into a street with some vehicular traffic and almost ran into a blue-uniformed policeman.

"Careful, there, laddie," the burly officer said, putting out a hand to fend me off as I staggered back.

"My, but you're a sight!" he said in a thick Irish brogue, eyeing my torn, bloody appearance. "Been sippin' a wee bit o'the devil's brew and doin' a little fightin', have ye?"

"No!" I protested. "But I'm sure glad to see you. I haven't had a drink. I was attacked by some Chinese back there—somewhere," I blurted out.

The cop eyed me dubiously. "Attacked you? Why?"

"I don't know. My three friends . . . I don't know what happened to them."

"Settle down, lad. Tell me what happened." He took me by the arm and guided me back out of the pedestrian traffic. I poured out my story as quickly as I could, leaving out nothing. When I finished, I had his full attention, but he didn't seem overly excited.

"I'm afraid it's not a real unusual tale. Well-dressed strangers, likely traveling with money. The hack driver probably in cahoots with a gang o'cutthroat Chinese to relieve you of your money and yer belongin's. Doubt if

17

they'd a'kilt ye into the bargain, though. Would bring a swarm of police to the Chinese quarter if white men were reported murdered there."

"If they didn't mean to kill us, it was the best acting job I've ever seen," I retorted.

"Fear will make a man sometimes imagine more than is actually takin' place," he replied soothingly.

"Does this look like my imagination?" I demanded, pulling back my bloody left sleeve to reveal the superficial six-inch cut on my forearm. "If I hadn't been falling backward, that blade would've been in me!"

"All right, lad, I believe you. But the first thing we need to do is get you to your ship and . . ."

"No! We've got to go looking for my friends. They may be lying in that alley hurt or dead."

"Can you show me where it is?"

"I . . . I can try. Truth is, I turned a lot of directions while I was running."

But I led him back the way I had come, deep into Chinatown. We walked well over a mile before I judged I was somewhere near the spot. At each corner, I surveyed the cross street, trying to recognize anything familiar—a shopwindow, a cornice on a building, trying to remember which angle the sun was at during the attack. But the buildings and the alleyways all had a maddening sameness to them. I led the patient policeman through block after block, staring at passersby in the vain hope of recognizing one of my assailants.

Finally, as the shadows of dusk were gathering in the corners of the streets and lights began showing in some of the upstairs windows, I had to admit I was hopelessly lost.

"That's all right' m'lad," the cop said, with forced cheerfulness. "If they don't turn up by mornin', I'll ask the sergeant to send a couple o'men with a paddy wagon to do a thorough search. But I'm afraid there's a good chance your friends may never be found. It's a sad fact that people disappear in this city every blessed day. I'm afraid the most o'them wind up in the bay. San Franciscans are a strange lot. They have a way o'settlin' their own differences without regard to the law. And that's especially true of our heathen brethren here in this quarter o'the city.''

My heart sank into my boots at the words of this kindly man. As I followed his broad back down the sidewalk, the truth hit me like a dash of cold water. It was very likely they had been caught, killed, and robbed, their bodies secreted in some subbasement of these rats-nest tenement buildings. I had escaped only by the luckiest of chances. It was too much to hope that they had done the same.

When we arrived back at the streetlighted spot where I had first encountered him, the policeman directed me toward the waterfront and Pier Six.

"If your ship is already gone, do ye have any money, lad, or a place to stay the night?"

It was the first time I had thought of it. I reached for my billfold in a rear pocket. It was still there. Without looking, I knew it contained only twenty dollars. I nodded. "Thanks. I'll make it. I've got a little money."

As I turned to go, he called after me, "Wouldn't hurt t'pour a little whiskey on that cut."

I could hear the twinkle in his voice as he added, "And I'd be for gettin' some new trousers. There's a sailors' mission that could provide ye with some if you'd like. . . ."

I waved an acknowledgment and left him.

A spidery trace of rigging showed faintly against the night sky as I approached the murky waterfront. A few widely spaced gaslights were being slowly smothered in the cottony tendrils of incoming fog. A large painted numeral identified Pier Six, and I held my breath as I looked for a ship. A hull bulked near in the darkness. I could barely make out J. W. BRANDON emblazoned across her broad stern. It hadn't sailed! The gangway was down, and I went aboard.

"Who's there?" a voice came from the darkness as I stepped down on deck.

I quickly identified myself.

"By God, you made it!"

A man came up and gripped me by the shoulders. "C'mon below. The old man will be glad to see *you*!"

I followed a short, broad-shouldered man in a rough

19

wool jacket and cap through a door under the raised quarterdeck into the afterpart of the ship. How was it this man was expecting me? He was a total stranger. Had he mistaken me for someone else? An overhead oil lamp threw yellow light over the varnished wood of the short passageway, illuminating a door at the end.

He stopped and rapped.

"Come in."

The man threw the door back. There, in the light of the main cabin, stood Wiley Jenkins, Fin Staghorn, and Asa Carlyle!

CHAPTER 3

MY sudden relief was so great my knees turned rubbery and I collapsed into the nearest chair. Before I could even open my mouth, the three of them were all talking at once, plying me with questions. Someone shoved a drink into my hand.

My own curiosity was not satisfied until I had poured out my own story.

"And that's about it," I concluded, sipping at the small tumbler of brandy. "What about you? How did all of you get away?"

"We outran those short-legged devils to the end of the alley," Carlyle replied. "Then we turned the corner and I remembered I had a single-shot derringer in my vest pocket. Always carry it out of habit. When we got around the corner, I got to it. The thinner one had almost caught up by then. I whipped around and put a forty-four slug in his belly from about ten feet."

"That put a tuck in the others just long enough for us to get clear of there," Wiley continued. "Don't think I've ever run so fast or so far before we finally saw a hack to hail."

"This time one of us sat with the driver just to make sure," Staghorn finished.

"Why weren't those Chinamen carrying guns?" I wondered aloud.

"Every Oriental I ever dealt with preferred a blade to

a bullet," Carlyle mused. "And their ancestors are the ones who invented gunpowder. Strange."

"I didn't see any gun belts," Staghorn added.

"We had the hack circle around, looking for you," Asa said. "Borrowed the driver's gun. But there was no sign of you or those slimy dogs who attacked us. They had even dragged off the one I shot. So we came back to the ship. We had just decided if you hadn't shown up in another half hour, we were going looking for you again."

"The hack driver who brought us back to the ship claimed he didn't recognize the other driver we described to him."

"Very likely a phony. Could have been anyone."

"Thank God we're all safe," Carlyle said. "We may never find out why it happened. I don't know of any enemies I have who hate me enough to want to kill me—*and* all my friends to boot."

"Could have been plain robbery. The policeman told me there was a lot of this going on in the city," I said.

"Reckon there'll be any repercussions about the man you shot?" Wiley asked Carlyle.

The older man shrugged. "Who knows? I doubt it, though. Thieves and murderers don't usually go to the authorities when one of their number is hurt or killed."

We fell silent for a few moments, each of us lost in his own reflections.

The release of tension and the brandy were making me very relaxed and tired.

"I guess we're mighty lucky all we lost was our luggage," I finally said to the faces in the lamplight around the small table. "Even if I did lose a Winchester, my gun belt, and all my spare clothes."

"I always carry a money belt on my person when I travel. I still have that. I like to deal in cash, and that's where I feel it's safest," Carlyle said, patting his midsection.

There was a short rap at the door, and a grizzled head was thrust inside. It was the man who had greeted me when I came aboard.

"Cook's got some hot soup and corned beef ready, sir."

"Thank you, Mr. Rowland," Carlyle replied. "Have

22

it brought back here. I'm sure we'll all do justice to it after this day."

"Mate or captain?" I asked Staghorn quietly as the door closed.

"Mate. Lonnie Rowland. Joshua Gibbs is captain. He's ashore just now."

Fin Staghorn motioned with his head. "C'mon and let's get that arm cleaned up and get you into some clothes."

I followed him out of the main cabin across a side passage into a small room. I stripped off my bloody shirt, and he poured some water from a tin pitcher over my arm and blotted it dry with a towel that hung near the head of his bunk. He took the brandy from my hand. "This will probably do as much good on you as in you." He grinned, dribbling the last of it down the length of the cut. I caught my breath at the sudden sting of it.

"There. I don't think rigor mortis will set in right away. Cut's not deep enough to bandage. Probably heal better if you just keep your shirt-sleeve down over it to keep it clean."

He pulled a seabag from under his bunk and rummaged in it. "We're close to the same size. Here, try these." He threw me a pair of cotton pants, a flannel shirt, and a dark blue pullover sweater.

While I dressed, he briefed me on the ship. She was a big, three-masted schooner, 160 feet long with a port cut into her stern under the cabin to load lumber. Big as she was, she could be handled by six seamen, a mate, a donkey engine man, a cook, and a captain.

"The hands bunk up forward in the fo'c'sle, and the captain, mate, boatswain, and cook back aft here. On long sea passages she carries a second mate but not on these short coastwise runs. There are several separate rooms located on either side of the main part of the cabin where we were sitting. The captain's cabin is at the stern on the starboard side and, of course, is the largest and most comfortably furnished. There's a pantry back aft here where some delicacies are kept, but mostly the food is prepared in the galley up in the fo'c'sle and carried back here for the afterguard. There's also a bathroom on the starboard side that's supplied with wa-

23

ter from a tank on top of the house. It's kept filled by water from overside every day. A stairway leads up from the passageway on either side to the quarterdeck overhead. Only one door leads directly onto the main deck, and that's the one you came in by. In rough weather it can be sealed to keep heavy seas out, especially when she's deep-laden. The *J. W. Brandon*'s big as a lot of full-rigged ships." He gave me an appraising look. "Those clothes fit like they were made for you." He grinned. "Keep 'em if you like. They've seen better days. With four extra of us aboard, we'll be doublin' up the berthing arrangements going back. You'll be bunkin' next door with Wiley. Mr. Carlyle and I'll be sharin' this room."

I nodded. "Fine with me." Just then the sight of a bunk anywhere was welcome.

"Let's go get some o'that corned beef."

When I awoke the next morning the ship was underway. I could feel the easy motion as she slipped along and could just hear the swishing gurgle of the water past her planked hull.

I started up. Daylight was flooding through the closed port. What time was it? I had fully intended to be awake to watch this big schooner get under way. But as I struggled into my borrowed clothes, I noticed Wiley was already up and gone from the upper berth.

I came up on to the quarterdeck by way of the port companionway. The *J. W. Brandon* was slipping through the sea with all sails set to a gentle breeze. The morning sun had already burned off most of the fog, revealing wide patches of blue sky. Looking forward, I could see the long sweep of main deck was uncluttered. The deck was broken only by the main cargo hatches, and these were secured. The ship was immense, and the tall masts appeared to rake the clouds as I glanced aloft at the triangular topsails.

"Well . . . Thought you were going to sleep all day." Fin Staghorn greeted me as he came bounding up the stairs from the main deck. "Too bad you missed breakfast. No breakfast in bed on this vessel. What do you think of her?" He swept his arm at the ship.

"Big. And beautiful."

"Yeah. She's got some nice lines for a cargo carrier. Mr. Carlyle bought her used about five years ago. She's about ten years old. Built in Maine and sailed around the horn. She handles pretty well, especially when loaded. Pretty high freeboard now. Just enough ballast down below to give some stability."

I took a deep lungful of the fresh sea air. "Is there a harbor pilot aboard?" I asked.

"Naw. We're just going across the bay to anchor for now. Need to be ready to catch the run of the tide this afternoon so we can slip out the Golden Gate." He turned his back to the sailor at the wheel a few feet from us. "Frankly," he continued in a lower voice, "the boss can't afford wharfage fees nor a pilot or steam tug either. Couldn't catch the ebb tide early this morning because it was pitch dark and foggy, and Carlyle didn't want to risk the ship in unfamiliar waters of a landlocked harbor."

"So that's the way of it," I murmured.

"Carlyle wasn't exaggerating when he said that this race would make him or break him—and the rest of us along with him."

"Not wasting too much on salaries for these few sailors," I noted.

"That's the advantage of a schooner rig," Fin answered. "These fore-and-aft sails can be handled from deck level by a crew about a fourth the size of a square rigger. Maneuver better in tight quarters and go to windward better, too. Need to send men aloft only to handle the topsails."

"Too bad there's not a paying cargo you could haul back, instead of sailing back in ballast."

"Sure is. We've got a few stores aboard but mostly ballast."

"How did you happen to wind up working for Carlyle?" I asked as we descended the ladder at the break of the poop and strolled along the port side. "Your letter asking us to meet you here didn't go into much detail. I thought you were going to help your parents run their wheat farm in Dakota."

"That was my plan when I last saw you, but it didn't work out. That plague of grasshoppers last summer wiped

25

out my Dad's crop and left him with no cash to pay off his creditors. He had to sell the place to settle up his debts."

"I'm sorry to hear that."

"Farming in the Dakota Territory is tough, all right. But my folks love that life. Dad took a job as a carpenter and handyman, and they rented a house in town. He still has hopes of homesteading another tract when he gets enough cash put aside to get started. But I think Mom is secretly hoping he'll give up that idea. She says it's too hard on him. I could tell he'd aged since I last saw him six years ago. Anyway, since they didn't need me to help there, I decided to come West and look around, since I'd heard you talk so much about this part of the country. And the sea drew me back just like you predicted it would. Guess it's in my Scandinavian and English blood."

"Yes, but working on a coasting schooner for a lumber company?" I asked. "I thought you were a blue-water sailor. All that experience with deep-water vessels, long voyages, and the like."

"That was just the problem. I love the ocean, but those long voyages when we were at sea for months at a time got mighty tiresome. This way, I can have some of both—the sea and the land."

"This kind of seamanship is a lot different from what you're used to."

"No doubt about that. The big danger is being too close to the land all the time. Coastwise piloting is a skill all its own. Especially along this coast, where there are a lot of fogs, rocks, strong currents, tides, and bars. I've been at it only a few months, but I've learned a lot already. I've been serving as mate on one of the other Carlyle ships for the past few months."

"Glad your letter caught up with us. I don't know what we can do to help, but Wiley and I were spending some time in the California gold fields anyway, so we weren't that far away. Frankly"—I grinned—"we weren't having much luck, so I was ready for a change of scenery when your letter came."

"Well, regardless of what happens, it's good to have both of you here. I didn't know about this race when I wrote, but I feel better about things already just knowing you two are here to back our play."

His words warmed me. A bond of friendship had been forged among the three of us last year by several weeks of shared danger and intrigue during a river journey up from New Orleans to the Dakota Territory—a trip we very nearly didn't survive.

We paused to lean on the rail. A fresh westerly breeze was beginning to kick up a chop on the bay and I could feel the big schooner heeling slightly to starboard with the wind pressure.

"I would imagine a man, even a young man such as yourself, would find no problem getting a berth as able seaman out here. If you keep at it, you'll probably have your own command before long."

He looked serious. "I doubt it. There are some real old hands who have most of the captain's berths secured. Unless some of them leave . . ." He shrugged. "Commanding a ship is a lot of responsibility. These owners aren't going to turn over a ship and a cargo worth hundreds of thousands of dollars to someone without lots of experience. Can't say I blame them."

"What about the captain of the *Brandon*?"

"Joshua Gibbs? Oh, he's got plenty of experience all right. He's in his late fifties, and he's been at sea ever since he was a boy. To hear him tell it, there isn't much he hasn't been through at sea."

"You sound a little dubious."

Fin glanced back and I followed his gaze. A stocky figure was strolling the quarterdeck. As I looked, he said something to the man at the wheel and then strode to the weather rail and gazed off to windward toward the Golden Gate, hands clasped behind his back.

"Well . . ." He ran a hand through his shaggy blond hair. "I hate to say anything. It'll sound like jealousy. I haven't really made up my mind about him yet. When you serve at sea with men, you see them at their best and at their worst. You get to know them. Phonies don't last long. Captain Gibbs . . . I've made a few trips with him. And there's something about him that doesn't quite ring true. It may be just his personality, but I get the feeling that he's bluffed his way through life to get

27

where he is now. He has Asa Carlyle's ear. He'll likely be the one to command whatever ship Carlyle decides to enter in this race.''

As we crossed the Bay toward the northwest, the wind increased.

"Seems strange being a passenger on one of these ships," Fin remarked as the Sausalito shore drew closer. "I keep feeling I ought to be doing something." He glanced up at the huge spread of the fore, main, and mizzen sails behind us. "If I were the mate, I'd slack off the sheets some, since we're sailing on a reach."

The ship was making good time, driving powerfully toward the shore. But I could also see as I looked back at the track of our wake that the big hull, riding so high and light, was making a lot of leeway, crabbing sideways through the water. As we neared the shore, the remainder of the small crew emerged from the forecastle and took up their places near the bases of the three masts.

I waited, but still the ship drove on. The low hills of the shore were rushing toward us now at an alarming rate. The man at the wheel stood calmly, awaiting an order from Captain Gibbs, who was pacing back and forth behind him, seemingly uninterested.

The wind was nearly over our port quarter now, pushing us faster, and I knew the captain had made a blunder in his calculations. Nothing short of a miracle could stop this hundreds of tons of deadweight from hurtling toward disaster. The details of the shoreline, a rickety dock, were becoming clear. I could see a two-horse carriage pacing along the shore road, could almost see the expressions on the faces of the passengers. I forgot Fin Staghorn was standing near me and instinctively looked around for the position of the lifeboats and braced myself for the collision when the big schooner would ram the shore.

Just then Captain Gibbs's voice came to me on the wind. "Hard up your helm!"

The helmsman spun the wheel to port, and the *J. W. Brandon* spun on her heel and came up into the wind, her big sails thrashing. She lost way so quickly I thought surely we had run on a mudbank.

Orders were passed quickly by the mate Mr. Rowland

and the halyards were let go and the three giant spreads of canvas collapsed. At almost the same time, one anchor was let go and the headsails were hauled down and the topsails clewed up. In only a matter of minutes, the schooner was at rest, her stern swinging about a hundred yards offshore.

"That was nicely done," Fin commented, still leaning on the rail, surveying the operation.

"I thought we were on the beach," I said.

"That's something you have to get used to on these big schooners. They're big and rough-planked. There's a lot of wetted surface and a lot of resistance. When the driving force of the sails is lost, they stop. This is even truer when they're deep-loaded."

"A yacht would have kept running a long ways. Guess I have a lot to learn about these vessels."

"You get on to it pretty quickly. The theory is the same for any sailing vessel. The only differences are how they're rigged and how they handle. And speaking of handling," he continued as we started aft along the deck, "I've discovered a strange thing about these schooners. When they're loaded, it takes a good breeze to move them."

"I shouldn't wonder."

"No, what I mean is that if the wind is below fifteen miles an hour, she won't move at all. But as soon as the wind picks up above fifteen—about the speed at which whitecaps appear—she'll take off like a racehorse. I've driven one of these vessels ten to thirteen knots through the water. You have to be careful, though. They're so incredibly stiff you could blow out all your sails before she'd heel ten degrees."

"Not much like sailing a thirty-foot sloop on Lake Michigan," I commented as I watched the seamen put the stops on the sails for the few hours we would have to wait here.

CHAPTER 4

AT four-thirty that afternoon the anchor was winched up by means of the steam donkey engine and we slipped out through the Golden Gate, three miles distant. The ebb was running strong, but, luckily, we had just enough land breeze to give her steerageway under inner jib, foresail, and mizzen. By the time the sun was touching the sea, we were well clear of the land and sailing north by northwest up the coast on the starboard tack with all lower sail set.

I was still amazed that so small a crew could handle a vessel of this size and said so as we of the afterguard squeezed in around the table in the ward room for our evening meal.

"The crew is divided at sea, so we really have only three seamen to the watch," Asa Carlyle said. "If it weren't for that donkey engine, there's no way they could hoist the weight of those big gaff-rigged sails. Even both watches together couldn't do it without help in any kind of wind. That little steam engine saves us a lot of money and effort. The halyards are rigged so they can be run around a steam-driven winch."

"Ah . . . here it comes," Fin Staghorn interrupted, "a traditional meal at sea—thick pea soup, bread, and salt pork. Hot tea to wash it down. And nobody can bake bread like Mullins." The cook grinned under his black mustache as he set the food in front of us.

Joshua Gibbs sat at the head of the oblong table and

was silent for the most part throughout the meal. Whether this was in deference to his boss the owner's being aboard, or whether reticence was a natural part of his personality, I didn't know. I studied him unobtrusively but could tell little about him. His hair was mostly white and his round face ruddy, whether from years of exposure to the elements or long acquaintance with John Barleycorn, I wasn't quite sure. I suspected it was some of both. He was rather short, with massive shoulders and arms and an even more massive girth. He seemed alert and interested in the conversations going on around him, his eyes darting from face to face, but food was obviously foremost on his mind, as he shoveled it in at least twice as much as any of the rest of us at table. The cook even surprised us with a rum cake he had baked earlier in the day before we set sail.

"Just by way of celebratin', sir, your safe escape from those cutthroats," he said to Mr. Carlyle as he bowed under our applause and ducked out the door. Asa Carlyle was apparently well liked by his employees. I had noticed during the day that all the crew members spoke courteously to him as they went about their business on deck. And he had returned their greetings by calling each man by name, a practice that surely earned him even greater loyalty. It was evident that Carlyle, in spite of his money and position, had not forgotten his beginnings.

The mate Mr. Rowland was on deck during the meal, but the boatswain was eating with us. Bob Billings, I heard him called. He was a lanky individual of indeterminate age, with a seamed and weathered face, and sported tattoos—a dragon on one hairy forearm, an anchor on the other. Next to Rowland the mate, Billings was one of the best sailors in Carlyle's employ, Staghorn later told me. "Steady as they come. And nothing fazes him. He'd spit in Neptune's eye," was the way Staghorn described him to me and Wiley as we adjourned to our rooms after supper.

"I'm sure gonna enjoy havin' all night in with no watches to stand," Staghorn said, stretching and yawning. "I oughta have the bosun come wake me when the midwatch comes on just so I can have the pleasure of

31

rolling over and going back to sleep." He laughed as he went into his cabin and shut the door.

The next morning found us bowling along with a fresh breeze. The wind had backed around to the southeast during the night and was coming over our starboard quarter, and all three of our big lower sails were winged out to port to take full advantage of it. Topsails had been set on each of the topmasts above the long gaffs, and the inner, outer, and flying jibs had all been set.

"She can cross a yard on her foremast," Fin said, coming up behind me on the quarterdeck. "A big square sail makes a lot of difference in a following wind on those long passages to Hawaii. I think she was originally designed as a barkentine."

I swept my eyes around at the horizon. We were out of sight of land. Since the coastline bent to the north-west, I guessed we were just giving the ship plenty of sea room to manuever.

"That's right," Fin assured me when I mentioned this. "Captain Gibbs is nothing if not cautious. A good sailor, but he takes no chances. Maybe that's the reason he's still practicing his profession."

"Or maybe caution comes with age?" I suggested.

"Can't say, since I've known him less than a year. But he always gives her plenty of offing, just in case. We're also picking up some north-flowing ocean currents. If we keep this fair wind *and* the current, we'll make a good fast run home."

Wiley Jenkins came on deck, stretching. "Can't seem to get enough sleep since I came aboard this ship. Must be the sea air."

I took a deep breath. "It just invigorates me. I want to learn the ropes on one of these schooners."

"I'm glad to hear you say that," Fin Staghorn said, squinting at me in the sunshine. "I had a feeling when I wrote you that you two could do something to help Carlyle get this contract. I wasn't sure just what at the time, but now I know, since I found out everything will be decided by this one race."

"How's that?"

"I'm going to make expert sailors out of you two in the next few weeks if you're willing."

"Why? I'm sure Carlyle is going to put his best seamen aboard his ship for that race. And that sure leaves out Wiley and me."

"Maybe not. I'm almost sure I'll be first mate, and my judgment about a crew will carry a lot of weight with Carlyle."

"But why would you want us? You need some experienced seamen who can hand, reef, and steer one of these big lumber carriers."

"You'll be experts by the time I get through with you if not greatly experienced. And I want at least two men such as yourselves, intelligent as well as determined—two men I know I can trust with my life in any emergency."

"Thanks for the confidence and the compliment," Wiley said, shaking his head slowly. "But I feel more at home on the quarterdeck of a stallion than I do here. I'm just a southern boy from Kentucky who went wandering West in the early seventies. I've turned my hand to most jobs at one time or another, from grading roadbed for the Union Pacific to mule packing for the Third Cavalry. But I've never been to sea. My steamboat trips on the Mississippi and Missouri last year were the longest I've ever taken on the water."

"Don't worry. If you're willing to learn, I'll teach you," Fin replied. "Besides, you won't have the responsibility of command."

"I wasn't worried about the responsibility." Wiley grinned.

"How about taking a turn at the wheel while we're running off the wind?" Fin asked.

"Sure."

"Let me duck below to make sure it's okay with the captain, since I'm just a passenger this trip myself."

He disappeared belowdecks.

"No problem," he said as he reappeared a few minutes later. Although his words were cheerful, the heartiness sounded a little forced to me, but I didn't question him as he had me relieve the man at the wheel. The sailor took advantage of this unexpected break by going into the lee of the charthouse to pack and light his pipe.

It took only a few minutes for me to get the feel of the big schooner. Fin gave me some instructions on steering by points of the compass that swung in a binnacle directly in front of the big brass-studded wheel. I held her north by northwest and gloried in the feeling of the schooner as she climbed the blue rollers and surged down the other side, a smother of white foam spreading from her bluff bows. My old instincts and experience as a small-boat sailor came back quickly. It was a thrill for me to control this huge contrivance of wood and metal and canvas that men had created to harness the wind. The fate of some dozen souls rested in my hands as I automatically checked the roll and surge and the tendency of the high-riding vessel to yaw before the following wind.

I steered for an hour or better before turning the wheel back over to the young seaman and joined Wiley as Fin began the task of literally showing us the ropes. His instructions and repetitious drilling continued almost uninterrupted throughout the day and on into the evening as the fair southeast wind continued.

All the next day and night and the day following, we rode the same course with the fair wind. Late in the afternoon of our third day out, the wind gradually decreased and finally died away altogether, leaving the schooner rolling sickeningly in big swells.

"The only thing worse than too much wind for a sailing ship is no wind at all," Staghorn growled as the *J. W. Brandon* rolled in the oily swell left over from some storm to the south. I saw what he meant as the gear slatted and banged, the booms jerking at their tackle with every roll. The mate allowed this to go on for almost an hour, the hollow thunder of the sails booming in our ears and grating on our nerves. When he finally decided the wind was not going to return right away, he ordered all hands to strip the vessel of her sails, excepting a deep-reefed and hard-sheeted foresail in case some breath of wind appeared. Wiley and I got our first practical experience handling sail with the crew. And happy they were to have two more hands aboard, inexperienced though we were.

The ship continued to roll in the dead calm, rolled until her bell clanged and the sea reached nearly to her scuppers in the waist.

"Well, there goes hopes of a fast run home," Carlyle remarked as we sat at supper, trying to hold on to our tin plates. Wiley had taken to his bunk with a bad case of seasickness. At the first smell of food, his pasty gray color had turned almost green. Actually, after several hours of this incessant heaving motion, my own stomach wasn't in the best of shape, either.

After a brief supper, I felt I had to get up on deck for some fresh air to settle my own queasiness. As I came out into the blackness, by way of the door on to the main deck, I paused just below the break of the poop to let my eyes get used to the darkness. I heard footsteps above me as the door of the charthouse opened and closed.

"The glass is falling, Mr. Rowland," came the voice of Captain Gibbs. "Keep a sharp lookout. I'm going to turn in early. Call me if you need me."

"Aye, sir."

The footsteps started aft.

"Oh . . . and Mr. Rowland . . ."

"Sir?"

"Don't hesitate to crack on some sail if we get a breeze. We need to make some time."

"Aye. Due north, sir?"

"I've given the helmsman the course. North by north-west if the wind is anything but dead ahead from that direction."

"Aye, sir . . ." There was a pause. "Captain, we've been steering that course for the last sixty hours or so. We must be more than a hundred miles offshore by now. Shouldn't we be making a more direct run for Juan de Fuca Strait if we can?"

"You have your orders, Mr. Rowland." There was a slight edge of irritation to Joshua Gibbs's voice. The heavy footsteps moved away.

I stood still, well back in the shadows out of the moon-light, bracing my feet against the roll of the ship. For some reason that I couldn't explain, I didn't want to be noticed. I suppose I felt embarrassed to have overheard this conversation where there was obviously an honest difference of opinion between two professionals.

The mate came down the port side ladder and went

forward along the deck without seeing me. He apparently had the eight-to-midnight watch with half the crew—four seamen. The boatswain Mr. Billings had the midwatch from twelve to four with the other half of the crew. The cook, of course, stood no watches and had most of the night in his bunk. He was available only to be called on as an extra hand in case of an emergency. Even if Wiley hadn't been seasick, he and I were still too green to be placed on four-on, four-off watches with the rest of the crew. The donkey-engine man was more of an engineer than a sailor, but he also lent a hand when needed and bunked forward with the crew.

I walked to the starboard rail and looked over. The pale moonlight showed only the faintest traces of white where the water was disturbed alongside the ship's sides as she rolled. Now and then a brief flash of phosphorescence showed in the water. The night air was pleasant. The wind today had been rather cool, even in the bright sunshine, since the air had been blowing over the cold ocean currents. I wondered idly if there was an extra pair of oilskins aboard that I might be able to use should the need arise. I reached for my pipe but then realized it had been in my jacket pocket—the jacket I had lost fending off a knife-thrust in the alley in San Francisco. I turned, leaned my back against the rail, and glanced aloft. The tall spars arched back and forth across the starry sky, the faint tracery of stays and shrouds visible in the moonlight. A peaceful, beautiful sight. The stuff poems are made of. It was good to be free of the land and all its problems, if even for a little while. The stout hull of wooden planks that buoyed us up from the bottom of the sea held about a dozen or so of us human beings in our own little world apart from the rest of mankind.

The rolling was gradually subsiding as the calm continued. The gentle motion would probably rock me to sleep. As I started aft, I noticed some of the stars being blotted out by traces of cloud coming up from the southwest on some unfelt wind high aloft. I yawned mightily.

A rush of feet on the deck over my head brought me out of a sound sleep. And lucky it did, since I was on

36

the verge of falling out of my bunk. The ship was heeled down hard to starboard, and as I eased myself over the bunk board and down to the slanted deck, I could hear the muffled shouts of orders topside. I had no idea what time it was, since it was still black as pitch. The sound of water rushing alongside the hull told me we had picked up a wind from somewhere. And what a wind it was!

I pulled myself erect and checked the top bunk. Wiley was still there, wedged in and dead to the world. I pulled on my clothes in the dark. The schooner was being buffeted violently. As I sat down on the deck to grope for my shoes, I could feel the *clump* of a big sea hitting her. I yanked the wool turtleneck sweater over my head and rushed out the cabin door, almost colliding with Fin Staghorn coming out of his cabin. In the dim light of the smoky coal-oil overhead lamp, I could see he had donned the top half of a suit of oilskins and a sou'wester he had found somewhere.

"C'mon!" he yelled. "They'll need all of us topside to shorten down. Feels like she almost had a knockdown. Pitched me right outa my bunk."

"I followed him through the empty ward room, down the short passageway and out into the dark chaos of noise that was the main deck. No sooner had the door slammed behind us than I had to grab for an iron handrail on the bulkhead to keep from being swept away as another blast of wind hurled the schooner sharply starboard. The force of the wind and flying water took my breath, and I had to turn my face aside from the stinging blast. My heart jumped into my throat as the deck tilted down. For a few panic-stricken seconds, I thought we were going over.

"Ease her! Ease her!" the mate was shouting above the roar of wind and sea. "Bring her head up!"

"She won't answer. The helm's hard up!" the man at the wheel yelled.

"Slack the fore- and mainsheets. Get a move on, or we've lost it. Slash 'em if you have to!"

The men jumped to it. I could see even the elderly cook, hatless and coatless, tailing on to a line, trying to keep his feet on the slanting deck. The three lower sails had been sheeted in hard, and the ship had been caught

37

by a sudden blast of wind hitting her from the port beam that was laying her down. While the crew struggled to right the vessel, she was rushing ahead through the water.

Slowly, very slowly it seemed, the wind pressure was eased as the sheets were slacked off and the fore and main booms swung out, nearly dragging their ends in the sea. The ship began to answer her rudder, and the bow began to come up into the wind as it righted itself. In a minute or two the vessel no longer lay so dangerously in the trough of the sea.

"Clew up those topsails!" Rowland yelled above the thunder of flogging canvas. "Douse those headsails!"

Several figures sprang to the weather rigging.

"Let's go!" Fin yelled close to my ear. "We can help get the jibs in."

We staggered and fought our way forward along the pitching, slippery deck.

Just as we reached the forecastle, the flying jib blew out with a roar, shreds of the sail disappearing into the murk to leeward.

"That's one we won't have to bother with!" Fin yelled as we joined one other man who was inching his way out on to the bowsprit. We hung over the bowsprit from the weather side and slid our feet along in a footrope of wire cable strung two or three feet underneath. Since the ship's head had come up into the wind, the bow was plunging in and out of the giant waves, throwing us high into the air one second and wetting us to the waist in a wave crest the next. Hanging over the boom and looking down, I suddenly realized that dawn must be breaking, since I could barely make out the sea, gray-green and angry, plunging up and down in the sickening space beneath my feet. I almost wished it were still too dark to see anything. After an eternity, we reached the outer jib and got hold of the downhaul. The canvas jerked us like an unbroken horse, flogging and booming, trying to yank us off our precarious perch to certain death. With Fin and the other sailor doing most of the work, we finally got the jib under control and brought it down and stopped it to the bowsprit. Then we worked our way back to the inner jib and started the same process with it. The wind pressed us against the boom to hold us in place, as we had to let go with both hands to work the sail. Suddenly the ship leaped up and to starboard at the same time. I felt myself pitch over backward. Then Fin had me in a vise grip by the back of my sodden sweater and thrust me back against the boom, where I clung, my legs growing weak in the swaying footrope.

"Hang on!" he shouted in my ear. He motioned for me to start working my way back in toward the ship. I saw that the other seaman had the sail under control.

The fast, efficient crew, with all hands working for their lives, fisted down the fore- and mainsails as well as the topsails. The schooner was plunging off more or less upright again, on the port tack under only the mizzen. This was no passing squall, I realized as dawn came up out of a gray and foam-streaked sea. My teeth chattering with fear and cold, I clung to a stanchion and gazed with awe at what the early light revealed. Long rollers came up under our port bow and foamed off toward North America, their crests a good quarter mile apart and the troughs between nearly as deep as the ship was tall. I wiped the stinging salt water from my eyes and looked again. If I ever got ashore alive, I wasn't sure I ever wanted to venture on to the sea again. The young crewmen working on deck looked just as white-faced and scared as I felt. But they were experienced and jumped quickly to the commands of the mate.

Two men were at the wheel, and Captain Gibbs was pacing the quarterdeck as Fin and I lent our hands to get the mizzen sail down, while three other sailors bent a smaller storm jib of heavy canvas on to one of the headstays. When all this was done, Captain Gibbs gave the order to run her off before it with only the storm jib until the gale should moderate in order to ease the pounding the ship was taking. The rain still stung the flesh like thrown gravel, and the wind still howled and the seas were just as high and dangerous, but the schooner rode easier and drier and it was with relief that all hands except the four-to-eight watch went below for some food and dry clothes.

CHAPTER 5

IF I thought we were out of danger, the look on Staghorn's face at breakfast should have told me otherwise. I was smiling and happy to be alive—and was I *hungry*! The cook somehow managed to put together something akin to french toast and hot coffee. The man was a wonder. He was by far the oldest man aboard. He had been helping the crew on deck. Yet he had retired to his galley and produced this meal on very short notice.

After a second cup of coffee, I began to feel warm and almost human again. Wiley Jenkins had appeared from our cabin, looking wan but at least on his feet. He sipped at some black coffee and nibbled on a piece of dry toast but said little. He looked as if he wished the world would come to an end and relieve him of his misery.

"What happened last night?" I asked Fin. "When I turned in, we were still rolling in that calm under bare poles."

"I was asleep, too, but Rasmussen told me it began to breeze up gently and the boatswain, who was in charge of the midwatch, ordered up steam in the donkey engine to winch up the big sails. The breeze continued moderate, and we were making good way, so the topsails and all jibs were hoisted. Then, just before the change of the watch, a gale-force wind hit the ship—caught her plugging along on the port tack with all sails sheeted flat. Knocked her right over. Blew out the foretopsail and sprung the topmast. Lucky we didn't lose the ship."

"Lucky is right. But we're out of danger now."

"For the time, maybe. If this gale blows itself out soon. If it doesn't, we'll probably have to heave-to under deep-reefed fore and mizzen."

"Why? We're making good time running under the storm jib. It's blowing us northeast, the way we want to go, isn't it?"

"Yes, but somewhere over that horizon is a lee shore. And with a high-riding ship and a gale like this blowing, we don't want to get too close."

Fin spoke quietly to me under the buzz of conversation at the table with his head turned away from Captain Joshua Gibbs, who sat a few feet away.

"Well, we're still headed for Puget Sound, and that's what counts," I said, draining my coffee cup and listening with satisfaction to the rushing water outside as the ship lifted and surged along in the following seas.

All day we ran off before it. I spent the first two hours after breakfast in my bunk—not because I was tired or seasick, but just to give Staghorn a chance to take my clothes on deck and hang them in the rigging to blow dry. When he brought them back, I shook a little salt out of them and got dressed. The only thing that remained a little uncomfortable was my damp shoes. Fin even rooted around somewhere in a locker and came up with two ratty jackets for me and Wiley Jenkins. They were ripped and threadbare and ill-fitting, but they were jackets, nevertheless, something to put between me and the heavy chilling wind outside.

Wiley managed to keep his light breakfast down but only by immediately retiring to lie flat on his back in his upper berth and propping the port open slightly to admit some fresh air.

"I'm okay if I can lie flat and fix my eyes on something that doesn't appear to be moving," he said as he stretched out on the bunk above me while I waited in bed for my clothes to dry. "The problem is, I can't find anything that doesn't look like it's moving, except the horizon. The clouds are even moving too fast to look steady." He groaned wearily.

About midmorning I ventured back on deck. It was a

41

wild sight. We were still running before the gale under storm jib only, and the following seas were mountainous, although the rain had stopped. Long windblown streaks of foam paralleled each other up the slopes of the watery hills. Two men had been set at the wheel, one on either side to hold her on course. I tried to guess what that course was, but the sun was blotted out by the solid overcast and the black lower-scudding clouds. The first chance I got without being obvious, I sidled up behind the two helmsmen and got a look in the binnacle. The surging of the ship made the compass card rotate slightly back and forth, but our course held fairly steady on northeast. The gale was coming at us, then, out of the southwest.

Mr. Rowland had the deck and was pacing up and down, now glancing aloft at the storm wrack, now at the sea, now at the helmsmen. The ship was making good time, but he was clearly nervous about something. He appeared so engrossed in his thoughts that I didn't speak to him but rather stayed well back out of the way. Then I went forward to where a seaman was standing lookout in the bows.

"Benjamin Haskins," the seaman said, shaking my hand as I introduced myself to him. "You a friend of Mr. Staghorn's, then?"

I admitted to that fact.

"A good man and a good sailor," Haskins opined. "He's young, but he'll make a good captain someday."

"What do you make of this?" I nodded at the wild sea.

He shifted his position on the bitt he was sitting on. "Great! Like riding a fast express train. I've been at this coasting trade only about two years, but we don't often get to take advantage of one of these sou'westers. We'll be home soon, I'd judge."

We talked a few more minutes before I got up and wandered back along the opposite side of the ship. Haskins was an experienced seaman, and had not evidenced the slightest uneasiness about riding out the gale this way. The ship was riding higher and drier with very little strain on her rigging. But I still couldn't get Fin Staghorn's words out of my mind. ". . . there is a lee shore somewhere over the horizon, so we don't want to get too close." I instinctively looked toward the forward horizon but saw nothing beyond the crest of the rising and falling seas. The heavy overcast would prevent any solar or lunar sightings to fix our position. And dead reckoning would be mostly guesswork.

I hunted up Fin Staghorn, and he agreed to continue my nautical education. With only an interruption for lunch, his instructions continued until midafternoon, forcing me to find and memorize the position and function of every bit of running rigging on the ship—sheets, downhauls, fairleads, halyards—everything. Then he tested me, giving me quick orders, and I had to immediately jump to the right line and tell him what the order meant. Sometimes I drew a blank, and he would patiently explain what he meant or take me to the proper line and point out where it ran and what it was for. With a rig as relatively simple as a schooner having such a myriad of lines and ropes for everything conceivable, I shuddered at what a full-rigged ship must look like.

Finally the maze of lines and blocks began to come into focus in my mind and make sense.

"Not bad," Fin commented when I had laid my hand on the correct line at the pinrail by the shrouds.

"Now if you can do that in pitch darkness when it's freezing cold and the deck is awash, you'll be on your way to being a seaman. Once you learn the ship, then you can learn seamanship—what types of situations call for what actions. You already have a good basic grounding in sailing on Lake Michigan, so you shouldn't have any trouble. It's the same theory—just more of it."

We knocked off, and I went back to my cabin, where I found Wiley sleeping. I stretched out in my lower bunk, and before I realized it, I had dozed off myself. When I awoke, I pulled out my watch. I had been asleep about an hour. It was 4:20 by my watch, which hadn't been set to any local time in a week. Wiley was up and gone. I went out into the passageway. Through the open door to the ward room, I saw Fin Staghorn and Asa Carlyle deep in earnest conversation at the table. They were talking in low voices, so I didn't feel I should interrupt. I went up the port stairway on to the quarter-

43

deck. Wiley was standing by the weather rail, huddled down in his ragged jacket, his face still looking pale under the leaden sky of late afternoon. The ship still surged along, rolling from side to side as she took the combers under her counter and lifted for a few seconds before the wave passed forward, allowing the ship to slide back into the trough before the next wave.

The sea was an awesome sight and struck a chord of primal fear deep within me. It was implacable and impersonal. A shout for mercy would not be heard or heeded by those marching mountains of water that flung our heavy ship along like a chip of wood.

"Don't worry." I smiled at Wiley. "This won't last much longer."

"I guess I'll be considerably lighter by the time we dock, though. By the way, when are we due to get in?"

"Wish I knew," I answered, looking forward again at the ragged sea. "Soon as I get a chance, I'm going to pump Asa Carlyle or Fin Staghorn for some information."

"Don't see much of Captain Gibbs."

"I haven't either. Think he spends most of his time in his cabin. Don't know what he does, unless he's reading or sleeping."

"Maybe he catnaps during the day so he can be fresh if he's needed during the night," Wiley guessed.

"Possibly. Seems to leave the running of the ship pretty much to the mate and the boatswain."

Just then Asa Carlyle and Fin Staghorn emerged onto the quarterdeck, and without so much as a glance in our direction or to the two men at the wheel, they went into the charthouse. I walked behind the helmsmen and casually glanced through one of the ports into the charthouse. The two men were leaning over the table, and Fin had a pair of dividers in his hand, measuring off something on a large chart spread before them. In the quick glance I got, it wasn't so much their actions that gave me pause but the looks on their faces. Never had I seen the two of them look so grim or serious. But I resolved to put everything out of my mind and leave the running of the ship to the experts. I would look forward to our landfall.

Even though it was early summer, the low-flying storm wrack was bringing on an early dusk by six-thirty. Supper was a somber affair, with the lanky form of Billings the boatswain, Carlyle, Staghorn, Jenkins, and myself sharing the table. The captain was apparently taking his meal in his cabin. Everyone was silent, engrossed in his own thoughts. The boatswain excused himself as soon as he finished and disappeared. Even the gregarious cook Mullins came and went with hardly a word of greeting.

"What's going on with this ship?" I asked Staghorn after the cook had left with the dishes. "Anything we should know about?"

"No. Nothing for you to be concerned about," replied Fin rather abruptly.

Even though we were good friends, his response left me no openings for further questioning. It was evident he didn't want to say anything more as he got up from the table and started out the door.

For lack of anything better to do, Wiley and I retired to our cabin. I wasn't sleepy and there was nothing to read, so we lay on our bunks and talked. An hour or more passed.

Suddenly there was a pounding rush of feet on deck overhead, and I could hear muffled shouts.

"What now?" I jumped from my bunk, fully dressed except for shoes and jacket. Wiley, somewhat recovered from his seasickness, was right behind me. I pulled on my shoes and jacket and went up to the port side companionway to the quarterdeck. In the dark I couldn't tell if the seas were still running as high, but the wind was still roaring through the rigging and two men were still at the wheel.

"Make sure those halyards are running clear to the winches!" Billings shouted. "Foresail and mizzen! Jump to it if you want to save your hides!"

Both watches were on deck, and the sailors were scrambling to their positions.

"What's going on?" I asked the nearest man at the wheel. He didn't reply for a minute as he leaned out and stared ahead into the blackness.

"Lookout spotted land dead ahead!" he finally yelled into the wind over his shoulder.

My stomach contracted, and my knees suddenly went

weak. I had to stagger over and hang on to the weather rail. As the stern of the *J. W. Brandon* was flung skyward on a following crest, I strained my eyes forward but could see nothing beyond the dim white triangle that was the storm jib.

"What are they going to do?" Wiley shouted at me above the roar of the wind.

"I don't know. Looks like they're trying to make sail."

Apparently steam had been kept up in the boiler of the donkey engine, because it was only a matter of minutes before the wooden hoops began to slide up the mizzenmast. The following wind caught the sail immediately before it was up and slammed it hard to starboard against its restraining tackle. As the fore and mizzen sails continued to inch upward, the wind caught the spread of canvas and the ship seemed to leap forward even faster. The two men at the wheel had to struggle even harder to keep the ship from broaching.

Both the boatswain Billings and the mate Rowland were on deck, but at first I saw nothing of the captain. Then I spotted him in black oilskins, emerging from the starboard companionway onto the quarterdeck. He watched the operation while steadying himself against the wild movement of the ship but gave no apparent orders to the mates. I wondered if it were he who had given the initial order to hoist sail. With the force of the wind, I half expected to see something in the rigging carry away. But both fore and mizzen were somehow winched up successfully. The ship was wallowing fearfully as it rushed ahead in a smother of foam. The masts had no backstays, and I wondered how much longer they could stand the strain.

I had been so interested in watching the ship that I had forgotten to look ahead. But the next time the schooner's stern was flung skyward on a crest, I stared into the darkness and my heart nearly stopped as I could just make out what looked to be a white surf spouting high against the unseen rocks of a coastline.

I glanced over at Captain Gibbs. Asa Carlyle was standing next to him, as was Fin Staghorn, all hatless. Carlyle was saying something to the captain that I couldn't hear. Then the captain stepped away from him and gave some command to the men at the wheel. The men spun the wheel to port, and the ship, making a good twelve to fourteen knots, answered swiftly, turning on her heel. She came across the combers and continued to turn, her bow coming up into the huge seas. The sailors worked madly to take in the slack of the sheets as the sails thundered like giant flags in the wind. We had turned the ship's head about 150 degrees and were now catching the big waves on our port bow.

I now understood the maneuver. They were trying to set enough sail to give the ship the driving power to claw off the lee shore back out to sea. But, even in ballast, the ship rode high and lighter than normal. Wiley and I grabbed the weather mizzen shrouds to keep from being flung across the deck as the schooner lay over perilously to starboard.

"No, Mr. Carlyle, she won't stand it!" I heard Captain Gibbs yell behind me.

"Give her the mainsail, Captain. It's our only hope. She's making leeway faster than she's going ahead."

"I tell you, it'll take the sticks out of her, or we'll turn turtle!" Joshua Gibbs shot back.

"Damn it! I'm the owner of this vessel, and I'm giving you a direct order to set the mainsail!"

Joshua Gibbs hesitated, holding on to the iron handrail around the charthouse, staring at the wildly plunging ship. "Maybe double-reefed," he finally said in a voice so low I could hardly catch his words.

"Damn the reef!" shouted Carlyle. "Give her the full main." He turned to Staghorn. "Pass the word to Rowland to get that main set—fast!"

The word was passed and I had never seen the sailors work with such speed. The donkey engine did it, for no human arms could have raised that big sail against that power of wind.

But no sooner was it in place than even I knew it had been a mistake. The ship was driving ahead all right, but she was also sliding leeward toward destruction nearly as fast. The overhead clouds shredded just long enough for me to see the thundering surf in the pale moonlight only a few hundred yards away. There was a break in

47

the boulder-strewn coast where some sort of inlet appeared and then a lower shoreline where the rollers blasted themselves to foam on a sand or gravel beach. Then the clouds passed over the moon again and the scene was darkened.

Carlyle saw the same thing the rest of us saw. If we continued as we were going, the ship either would be knocked flat or would be driven relentlessly ashore where we would all meet our doom in a pounding, ice-cold surf and splintered timbers. A bigger-than-usual wave hit our port bow, and the high-riding ship heeled down until the sea foamed over her lee rail to her hatch coamings. I vaguely saw the dark forms of three sailors who had lost their grips slide down the canting deck into the cold flood in the scuppers. The ship shuddered and freed herself from the tons of boarding water as she righted. But the wind against that huge spread of canvas threw her right back over and down.

"Get ready to douse all sails, Captain," Carlyle ordered.

"What?" Gibbs was incredulous.

Asa Carlyle made an impatient gesture and motioned to Fin Staghorn. "Pass the word to the mate to drop all sails!"

Fin passed the word.

"Stand by your anchors," Asa said as this was being done.

This order was passed forward also.

Anchoring? On a lee shore? Even I knew better than this. Had the man panicked and gone mad? Even though he was the owner, he had just committed an act of mutiny and taken over command. And now he was giving an order that was certain death.

CHAPTER 6

THE operation went off without a hitch. The anchors were let go off either side of the bow. And before they had time even to hit bottom, all three big lower sails collapsed on the booms with their heavy wooden gaffs. For a few terrifying seconds, the ship rolled broadside in the trough of the sea. Then her anchors caught and brought her bow up again, and the limber cable whined off the winches as the scope was paid out quickly. Each anchor was attached to 30 feet of heavy chain that in turn was connected to 200 fathoms of cable. Nearly all of this was allowed to run out, and, when the winches were secured, our stern was so close to the beach I could hear the thunder of the surf, even with the wind blowing the sound away from me.

No sooner had the ship stopped moving backward than the main deck forward of the mainmast became unlivable with bursting seas. The schooner leaped and jerked at her restraining cables like a wild horse trying to shake off two lariats. With every jerk, I expected the tons of deadweight to snap the thin-looking cables and send us crashing into the pounding surf. Every plunge half buried the forward part of the ship, and the only dry part of the deck was the raised quarterdeck where I stood.

Captain Gibbs, Staghorn, Asa Carlyle, Wiley Jenkins and I were there, I'm sure almost holding our collective breath for the next few minutes as we waited to see if the anchors would hold. The captain gazed intently toward the shore in the brief periods of moonlight that shone through the breaking clouds. I felt sure he was trying to get a fix on some point of land as a reference in order to tell if our anchors were dragging.

The sailors, including the men at the wheel, had been dismissed to seek the relative safety of the forecastle, as the mate and the boatswain came aft to join us.

"That long scope of cable gives her more spring and flexibility," Fin yelled close to my ear. "Room to jump and buck without breaking the cables—I hope!"

The captain and Carlyle had some hurried words alone near the rail, and then the captain went below, followed by the rest of us. The main cabin was quiet and calm by comparison to the wind and sea topside. It was also warm and dry. Except for the pitching motion of the room, it was almost as if we had stepped into a room ashore.

As if by unspoken agreement, we all gathered around the table in the ward room, pulling off our oilskins and coats. Captain Gibbs was the only person absent. I assumed he had gone to his cabin.

"Gentlemen," Asa Carlyle said, when he had gotten our attention, "what most of you just witnessed on deck was, by the law of the sea, an act of mutiny, pure and simple. I admit it. I assumed command from Captain Gibbs in an emergency. But I did it for one purpose only—to save this ship—my ship—and everybody on it, including me. I want that clearly understood. A captain at sea is the sole authority in charge of his vessel, even outranking the owner, his employer. If anyone, including Captain Gibbs, wants to bring charges against me later, so be it. Right now, I have more important things on my mind. All of you had better pray that those anchor cables hold or that the seas moderate or both. This is a trick I learned from an old captain I sailed with many years ago on the East Coast. We were caught in the tail end of a hurricane off Cape Hatteras, and he let go the hooks off a lee shore. Said he had never seen anchors drag *up* a bank. It saved our vessel and our lives. And I'm banking on that happening here."

I didn't know what had happened to Joshua Gibbs,

50

but it was evident that a mistake in judgment or a hesitancy to take decisive action in an emergency forced Carlyle to relieve him of command for the time being. I didn't know how many of the crew were aware of this, since most of them were working up forward and the orders were relayed through Billings and the mate. But the two men at the wheel saw what happened and would probably relay it to the rest, thus undermining the captain's authority for the rest of this trip and maybe for the rest of his working life.

But it was done, and there was nothing to do now but hope that his decisions had been the right ones.

It was decided that only one man would be needed on watch to give the alarm if our anchors began to drag, so Billings the boatswain and Mr. Rowland the mate arranged to split the watches between them and let the crew have all night in.

The schooner was taking a fearful pounding, and Carlyle sent the boatswain into the lower hold with a lamp to check for damage below the waterline. While he was gone, Carlyle directed that someone go forward with a small cask of brandy—enough for each of the crew to have a small dram in appreciation for their efforts in saving the ship. I volunteered to take it and bring back some cold food for us.

I strapped the one-gallon wooden keg to my belt in order to have both hands free. But even so, it was a hazardous trip. No lifelines had been strung on deck, but the motion of the ship was fore-and-aft plunging instead of the side to side motion, which probably saved me from going over the side. As it was, I was washed off my feet only once and swept up against the main hatch cover, bruising my knee. But I made a rush and reached the lee side of the forecastle house just in time to avoid another sea sweeping the deck. I was out of breath, limping and shivering from my soaking in the ice-cold water. But I left the brandy with a grateful crew and brought back some bread, cheese, pickles, and cold leftover tea from the cook. Getting back aft without spilling the tea or soaking the food was some trick, but I timed my rushes between bursting seas and made it.

The boatswain had come back from the hold to report

51

that a few of the portside planks had started and water was about two feet deep in the lower hold. Carlyle pondered this information and decided to leave the pumping until later. But he instructed the man on watch to take a sounding on the water level every hour.

Wiley and I returned to our cabin after eating our cold food. Since my only set of clothes was soaked again, I pulled a blanket off my bunk, wrapped myself in it, and lay down on the deck beside my bunk.

"Why don't you just undress, get into bed, and warm up?" Wiley inquired, snuggling into his blankets.

"If we survive this, I want to have a dry bunk for later; if we don't, I want to die fully dressed," I replied, wrenching off my sodden shoes.

I didn't sleep much that night as I lay on the hard deck listening to the ship creaking and groaning and working in all her joints and timbers. I knew this was normal, but I still had the uneasy feeling during the long night hours that the vessel was coming apart. I wondered how many feet of water were in the bilge. But along toward daylight I finally fell into an exhausted doze.

When I opened my eyes, I was distinctly aware of two things—a sore throat and the easier motion of the ship. Daylight—sunlight—shone through the porthole. I got up stiffly and went up on the quarterdeck. Mr. Rowland was on watch.

"Good morning, Mr. Tierney." He greeted me, squinting into the bright morning sunlight.

"Good morning. Looks like we're going to live to sail another day. Our anchor cables held."

He nodded. "And most important, the storm has passed on, and the sea is calmer."

Although a fair surf was still running, the ocean was a mill pond compared to the day before.

Even though my clothes were still damp and I shivered in the light wind, I took a deep breath of the fresh air and breathed a sigh of relief and satisfaction.

"We've got another foot of water in the hold, but Mr. Carlyle said to leave it be. Says it gives us a little more ballast. I knew he was a seaman in his younger days, but

I never knew how good he really was until now. He sure enough saved us." He nodded his head.

Some of the sailors were working on deck, cleaning up the raffle of broken lines and tackle and splintered wood. Then I saw that several sections of the bulwarks in the eyes of the ship had been torn away by the savage, pounding seas. One of the lifeboats was also missing.

"Where are we?" I asked Rowland.

He shrugged. "That's what Mr. Carlyle and Captain Gibbs are trying to figure out now." He gestured toward the charthouse, and I saw these two men poring over a chart, every few seconds lifting their heads to scan and point toward the shoreline less than a quarter mile behind our stern. There seemed to be some disagreement between them. I found out at breakfast that they both agreed we were on the coast of Vancouver Island, but just *where* was the disagreement. But all doubt was dispelled when a sun sight was taken at noon and our position worked out to be at Nootka Island, just to the north of Nootka Sound. I was amazed as Fin and Wiley and I examined the charts. We were far to the north of where I thought we could be. But the storm combined with the north-flowing current had driven us much farther to the north than I ever imagined was possible.

In appearance, at least, Captain Gibbs was back in command. He decided to make sail and duck into Nootka Sound, since we had a chart for that inlet, to get temporary shelter to pump and to make temporary repairs to the ship before making sail south to Puget Sound. Just after lunch, steam was gotten up in the donkey engine to hoist our anchors. But after several futile tries, the captain realized that with the scope of cable that was out plus the fact that the anchors were buried so deep, the donkey engine couldn't raise them. After Captain Gibbs's consulting Mr. Carlyle, the cables were slipped and left behind with two large pieces of wood to float the cable ends in the hope they could be retrieved later.

The crew hoisted only the mainsail when it was discovered that the whiplashing the ship had endured had loosened the shrouds and sprung the foremast.

As a precaution against just such an eventuality as

this, the captain's cabin of the *J. W. Brandon* contained a volume of detailed sailing instructions for the west coast of Vancouver Island, where so many vessels had previously met their doom.

By some stroke of Providence, we had come to anchor off a long sandy beach about a mile west-northwest of Maquinna Point of Nootka Island. Two or three miles farther west and we would have struck an underwater ledge of rock known as Bajo Reef. But in spite of constant preparation for the unexpected, a seafarer's life is still controlled by forces largely beyond his control. Hence, most sailors seem to be very superstitious, very religious, or very optimistic. Carlyle was the latter.

With a light sea breeze, the ship was sailed west by south about three miles around the tip of Maquinna Point into the calm waters of aptly named Friendly Cove inside Nootka Sound. Nootka Island's sand beaches rose gradually inland to a forested height of more than two thousand feet. It presented a beautiful, fertile, and deserted appearance.

Since we had left our anchors, the mainsail was dropped and the ship drifted to a stop in a spot where soundings showed about eight fathoms of water. The pumps were manned and the bilges cleared of water in about three hours. Some twisted cotton caulking was forced into most of the larger leaks between planks in the hold while the standing rigging was tightened and the ship generally made as seaworthy as we could get her.

While this was going on, I looked up Fin Staghorn and pressed him for information about what had actually taken place and where we stood.

"I think it's best for me and Wiley to lie low and keep our mouths shut, seeing as we're Carlyle's newest employees," I said.

"I tell you what," the stocky blond said, "that was a mighty near thing. In my several years of deepwater sailing, I've never come any closer to losing a ship than we just did. I'm convinced Carlyle took the right action in anchoring the ship. But that necessity probably could have been prevented if we had hove to several miles offshore instead of running with the gale. It was the captain's judgment that the storm was too strong to hoist enough sail to allow us to heave to. I don't know. The ship was being overpowered by the wind all right. Gibbs was in command, and it was his decision. Maybe he didn't realize we were closing with the shore so fast. But it's his job to know at least our approximate position.'' He shrugged and looked around the deck to be sure we were out of earshot. ''As to whether Carlyle had the right to usurp Cap'n Gibbs's authority, I don't know. Cap'n Gibbs is a longtime employee, and Asa Carlyle had faith in him. That faith may have been shaken some now.''

The cook Mullins had his galley in good order again. With a steady deck under his feet and a bright sun shining overhead, he soon had some smoke issuing from the galley stovepipe, and about an hour later, he served up a good hot meal of beef, boiled potatoes, and cabbage.

While this was going on, the ship was drifting quietly. The light northwest wind we'd had that morning was cut off by the high-rising timbered slopes of Nootka Island. So the schooner was left to fend for herself, with only an occasional sounding being taken to be sure we didn't go aground on some unmarked shoal. The incoming tide was pushing us gradually back into Friendly Cove. Normally the captain would be worried about wrecking his powerless ship on one of the several rocky islets that projected from the water in the middle of the cove, Fin told me. But we were moving so gently and gradually that this was no concern. The cove was about 200 yards wide and about 400 long, with a couple of small extensions bending back out of sight at its upper reaches. The shore on the west side of us was rocky and about 60 feet high, topped with virgin timber that looked to be spruce and pine and cedar.

''The tide is just about slack now. It's due to turn within the hour,'' Staghorn told me and Wiley Jenkins as we stood near the rail after supper enjoying the cooler air and the fresh smell of the trees. ''I imagine Cap'n Gibbs and Mr. Carlyle will both want to slip back out to sea with the tide. If we hadn't lost our anchors, they'd probably just snug down here for the night. But as it is, the only thing they could do would be put a line or two ashore in a small boat and tie off to a tree. And this shoreline may be too rocky and shallow to allow us to lie close up to the bank. No, he'll probably take her back to sea tonight. We should have some decent moonlight. But even so it'll be tricky with just the ebb tide to carry us. Maybe a little land breeze will spring up just after sundown and give us a push."

He had hardly finished speaking when Mr. Billings the boatswain passed the word to get underway, and the sea watches were set.

"Set the fore and mizzen!" Mr. Billings hollered when his watch reported on deck.

"I thought the foremast was sprung," I remarked to Fin.

"It is, but the wind is negligible, so there won't be enough strain on it to worry about. It's a good maneuvering sail."

As the sun dropped over the wooded hill to the west, I could just barely feel a movement of air against my cheek. The heavy, baggy sails showed no signs of feeling it, though.

One of the sailors packed and lighted his pipe, and I savored the aromatic smoke as it blended with the resinous smell of the evergreens.

"Indians!"

I thought one of the crewmen was trying to make a joke to break up the serenity of the evening. But when I looked back behind the ship, I saw two long, dugout canoes with high prows, like Viking ships, gliding smoothly toward us. I counted the bare torsos of eight burly paddlers on each side of the giant boats.

"What's this?" Wiley asked, sounding as stunned as I was to see this apparition come gliding out of the shadows of the forested cove.

"Probably a band of Nootkas wanting to trade," Fin said. "According to the chart, there's a village up at the head of this cove. I've never seen it."

The ornately carved canoes quickly overtook us, since the schooner was making very little headway.

The seaman lounging at the wheel deserted his station and rushed to the rail to look. Out of old habit, I reached for my Colt before I realized it had been lost in San Francisco.

"Are you sure they want to trade?" I asked Staghorn as the big seagoing canoes both came along the starboard side.

"Let's hope so," he replied, not looking as sure of himself now.

The paddlers backed water, and the big thirty-foot canoes slowed to a stop alongside. They did not appear to be armed, I noted with relief. Blankets were thrown loosely over something in the bottom, maybe skins or something else to be offered in trade.

A stout breech-clouted warrior stood up in the stern of the second canoe and said something I didn't understand, at the same time signaling that he wanted to come aboard.

"Captain," he finally said.

Joshua Gibbs had been summoned, and he was leaning over the rail on the quarterdeck. "What do you want?" he shouted down to them.

"Come aboard. Trade," the man, who reminded me of a personification of Buddha, managed to articulate in English.

"No . . . No . . . Nothing to trade. Go. We sail!" Gibbs yelled, waving them off with an impatient gesture. The man, whom I took to be some sort of chief, stood with folded arms and gave no sign that he understood what was being said. Instead, he repeated, "We come aboard. We trade."

The word had spread and the off-watch was on deck now, all hands lining the starboard rail to get what was probably their first glimpse of Nootka Indians. The men in the canoes appeared to be short, with broad, deep chests and mostly round, flat, Asiatic-appearing faces. About half of them sported mustaches or beards—not as thick or heavy as most white men's whiskers, to be sure, but certainly more facial hair than I had ever seen on Indians before.

There was a hurried conference on the quarterdeck aft between Captain Gibbs and Asa Carlyle.

"These Nootkas have been tremendous whalers for generations, I hear," Fin Staghorn said to us. "They harpoon the gray whale from those canoes, about like the whalers of Nantucket do from their whaleboats.

These people have had contact with the white man for at least a hundred years, since Captain Cook stopped here in 1778. There has been some sharp dealing, some hurt pride, some misunderstandings, and some ferocious battles and massacres—some of them right around here. I've never been to this place before, but I've read up on the Indians and the history of the whole northwest area and Vancouver Island when I came out here a few months back.''

"I hope history isn't about to repeat itself," Wiley commented, eyeing the rope ladder that was being let down over the side of the ship for the Buddhalike figure to come aboard. Except for breechclout, the Indian wore only a wide conical-shaped woven hat, like an inverted basket, making him look even more Oriental.

"Nothing to worry about," Fin said. "Like a lot of the other tribes, the Nootkas have been decimated by white man's diseases and whiskey. They're still a proud people, but they've fallen prey to white civilization just like all the others.''

The sailors were yelling down to the men in the canoes, gesturing, and trying to get the Indians to show them what was under the blankets. But the impassive paddlers paid little attention. Finally Rowland the mate gave them a sharp order to keep still as the chief and two of his aides came over the side. The nakedness of the aides was draped with capes of some kind of animal skins that appeared, from this distance, to be beaver. They both wore their black hair long and had thin, drooping mustaches.

Except for the man who stood at the wheel, none of the crew, including the mate and the boatswain, thought of approaching the quarterdeck where some sort of dialogue was going on among the three Indians and Captain Gibbs and Asa Carlyle. For a man of short, ample proportions, the chief carried himself with a great deal of dignity. The conversation was punctuated with a lot of gesturing. At one point, the two aides swept off their fur capes and spread them on the deck in front of Carlyle and the captain and stepped back grandly nude that our men might observe the beautiful pelts they had thrown down. More emphatic gesturing took place. Finally the chief was brought forward to the main cargo hatch in the waist of the ship, and with the help of several of the crew, the hatch was opened so the chief could descend a ladder into the hold.

"Apparently doesn't believe we're not carrying anything of value," Fin commented quietly to us while this inspection was taking place.

"Why doesn't he just throw them off so we can get outta here?" the impatient Wiley demanded. "We've got a good three miles to go to get out to sea, and the sun's already down."

"A certain amount of protocol has to be observed. You've dealt with enough Indians to know that most of them are very formal, ritualistic people."

"Huh! Most of the southwestern and northern plains tribes I've dealt with give you a lot more respect if you shoot first and worry about the niceties later."

The inspection tour over, the chief and his aides, who had donned their fur robes again, climbed over the side, down the rope ladder into their canoes. The paddlers shoved away from the sides of the schooner and, at a verbal command from their leader, brought the ornate vessels about and started back up the cove.

The captain called Rowland and Billings aft, and Fin Staghorn, Wiley, and I went, too.

"What did they want, Cap'n?" the grizzled mate asked.

"Cartridges and whiskey," Joshua Gibbs replied shortly.

"That's all? Nothing else?" the boatswain said.

"That's it. Near as I could make out, they had all the blankets and manufactured goods they needed. They wanted to trade fresh fish and venison."

"Probably want to get drunk and celebrate last month's whale hunt," Carlyle added. "He didn't believe we had no cargo until I let him go down into the hold. Couldn't imagine why we were sailing around up here with an empty ship. Told him we had all the food we needed and didn't need to trade for any more."

"Well, I sent that old scutter packin'. Takes a lot of nerve to call me a liar to my face," Captain Gibbs said, his face coloring slightly.

"Nonetheless, you didn't need to be quite so insulting," Asa Carlyle chided him.

Instead of replying, the captain turned to the helmsman nearby. "Keep her in midchannel until I give you the word." Then he turned to Billings. "Hoist the main and start your sheets. We need to take advantage of this light land breeze while it lasts. Have a man keep a sharp lookout from the bow. These are unfamiliar waters with lots of rocks. And we're losing the light fast."

"Aye, sir," the boatswain replied, turning to carry out his orders.

But before he had taken two steps, a flaming arrow came arching over the side and hit the foresail. The heavy canvas gave, and the arrow didn't penetrate. But it fell, blazing, down into the sagging foot of the sail. Before anyone who saw it could react, a horrible scream came from overside and a blazing torch was heaved on to the deck. Then a burst of rifle fire drowned all other sounds, and echoes of the explosions slammed back from the rocky hillside.

CHAPTER 7

WE all instinctively hit the deck.

"Where's it coming from?" someone yelled.

"Those war canoes. They've slipped up on our port side this time!"

I could hear feet scrambling on deck. Then another fusillade of shots and I could see splinters struck off the mizzen boom over my head.

"Damn! They've shot Stacey!" I heard someone yell from up forward. John Stacey had been the lookout in the bow of the ship. I regretted having neither my Colt nor my Winchester.

I had no idea if there were any weapons at all aboard the schooner. I scuttled on my hands and feet to the rail and started to ease my head up for a look during a slight lull in the firing, but thought better of it as the shooting picked up again. The volume of shots indicated repeating arms.

The man at the wheel was flat on his stomach, holding the wheel by the bottom spokes. The captain and the mate were both crouching on deck.

"Get that fire out!" Captain Gibbs bellowed. It was a long minute or two before three sailors came running with buckets. Securing lines to the handles, they dropped them overside. But before they could get them filled, flames leaped up the canvas foresail, enveloping it quickly. The blaze lighted up the entire ship, and the rifle fire began again as the attackers tried to pick off the figures running about the decks. The bullets thudded into the masts and whined off the wire rigging. The light breeze fanned the fire, blowing flaming pieces of sail on to the deck, while the crouching sailors were kept busy wetting down the deck and putting out the blazing bits. The torch had been pitched back over the side.

A rifle exploded nearby, and I saw Billings lying on deck in the waist, firing through the hole in the base of the rail that formed one of the portside scuppers. The boatswain must have found the only gun aboard, since no one else seemed to have produced a weapon. With the volume of fire coming from the canoes, I dared not lift my head above the rail. From their low position, the Nootkas could not get a good line of fire at anyone on deck, especially the closer they approached the high-sided schooner. The boatswain was still banging away with the Winchester through the scuppers, with what effect I couldn't tell.

As the blazing remnants of the foresail burned away and fell to the deck or blew over the side, I realized how dark it had become while all this had been happening.

"Watch it! She's comin' down!"

The sailors sprang out of range as the halyards of the burning sail began to part and the big gaff swayed dangerously. Even as I glanced aloft, the last support gave way and the wooden gaff came crashing down the mast in a shower of blazing pieces of canvas.

The helmsman was now sitting on the deck, holding the wheel near the bottom, but his view forward was blocked by the charthouse.

I wasn't aware of where the breeze was pushing us until a warning shout came from forward.

"Port your helm!" Captain Gibbs yelled, springing to the wheel himself with a speed that belied his bulk. He spun the wheel over, and as the schooner slowly answered, I could just make out the thicker darkness of the rocky bluff looming up close under the starboard bow. I heard a thumping and bumping noise, and my stomach tightened. We must have wandered too close to the rocky shore.

As the schooner glided back into midchannel, the banging noise continued with a steady rhythm. The ship was not hitting the rocks! I arrived at the starboard rail with Wiley just as Captain Gibbs got there.

The other canoe was alongside the ship, and I had time for a quick glimpse of one Indian holding a long spike against the hull at the waterline while another burly Indian swung a heavy maul against it. Several of the other murky forms raised their rifles as soon as they saw our heads.

"Damned heathens are trying to scuttle us!" Captain Gibbs roared as he leaped back. His words were almost lost in the blast of rifle fire. Splinters flew from the wooden rail.

"They created a diversion on one side so they could hammer a hole into us on the other!" Wiley said as we crawled back out of range. How I longed for a sudden, strong wind just now!

"Billings! Get over here!" Captain Gibbs yelled. And then to us, "Two can play that game. I just wish I still had my old Dragoon Colt. I'd put a few holes in that damn canoe—and in them, too!"

The boatswain came running across the deck.

"You got plenty of shells for that Winchester?"

He nodded.

"Then get up on that poop and see if you can get off a few quick shots at the canoe right below us. And hurry!"

Billings thumbed three or four more cartridges into the loading gate before bending his lanky frame and bounding up the stairs into the darkness.

"Too bad there isn't time to have cooky boil up some water to pour on'em," the captain growled.

"Or sink their canoe with one of our lost anchors," Wiley added.

Billings pumped six or seven shots over the side as fast as he could work the lever. I heard a yell and a splash as the firing stopped. There was a single answering shot, and Billings flopped over on his back without a sound, his rifle clattering to the deck beside him.

Wiley, Captain Gibbs, and I rushed to his side, and in the dim, flickering light of the still-burning sail, I could see a dark stain spreading on the deck behind his head. Wiley felt for a pulse, and then we saw where the bullet had penetrated his throat.

63

"Dead. Looks like a lucky shot went right through here. Probably severed his spine," Wiley said, withdrawing his hand and wiping it on his pants.

"Damn!" Captain Gibbs breathed. He straightened up, still looking down at the dead man. "Call Mr. Rowland up here," he said to no one in particular. Wiley moved to obey. The shooting and the banging on the ship's side had stopped. The schooner glided quietly in the darkness and the sailors gradually came out from cover to peer over the sides.

From where I stood, I could see the faint outlines of the big war canoes dropping astern. They had apparently given up their strange, abortive attack.

The land breeze picked up slightly, and we nosed out of Friendly Cove into Nootka Sound. The long, lingering twilight and the rising moon showed a scarred *J. W. Brandon* the way safely back to sea.

When we had cleared the land, a proper course was set. The breeze was light from the southeast, coming over our port bow. Mr. Rowland went below to check for damage and found that the Indians had managed to pound a small hole in the hull before being driven off. Water was spurting in, but the hole was quickly plugged with a small piece of wood and sealed with tar.

While the watch on deck cleared up the wreck of the foresail and putting things in order, the bodies of boatswain Billings and Johnny Stacey, the lookout who had been killed, were carried aft and laid on the cabin table. Two of the sailors off watch took charge of washing and dressing them in clean clothes from their seabags.

Two other sailors had been slightly wounded in the attack and were tended in the forecastle by Wiley, who had some rudimentary medical knowledge.

As the night progressed, I found myself sleepless and pacing. After all that had happened, I could not close my eyes. The two dead men had been covered with a piece of canvas and left on the cabin table. The men, solemnfaced, came aft through the cabin singly and in pairs as the watches changed to stand silently, gazing at the still faces of the men who had so lately been their shipmates. Then they would fold the canvas carefully back in place and go out without a word.

Some time during the small hours of the midwatch, Staghorn came into the main cabin and stood at my elbow as I watched a young sailor paying his last respects. The overhead coal-oil lamp was turned low and swung slightly with the movement of the ship. The small skylight had been propped open to admit some fresh air that was being deflected downward by the mizzen sail above.

Fin was silent until the sailor replaced his cap and left.

"Bad business," he said to me in a low voice, as if to preserve the funeral hush.

"Yeah. What do you reckon caused that attack?"

He shrugged. "Mr. Carlyle thinks it was the crude way Captain Gibbs talked to that Nootka chief. They're haughty people; they have tremendous pride. And they'd do 'most anything to keep from losing face in front of their tribesmen. I don't know whether they thought they could disable or sink this ship, but I'd guess the attack was revenge . . . and maybe a little plunder if they succeeded."

"Do you think it was Gibbs's fault?"

"I don't know. We probably will never know for sure. The important thing is, Asa Carlyle believes it. Captain Gibbs is from the old school. He believes in dealing with Indians as ignorant savages not to be taken seriously. As you've probably noticed, there's not much of the diplomat in him."

"It was a pretty costly diplomatic failure."

He nodded. "I guess that's probably true of most sea captains, especially the older ones. They get used to their absolute authority. They may be fair, but they are used to being obeyed without question. And they are usually pretty blunt about it."

"What will this do to Joshua Gibbs's career?"

"Carlyle will probably get rid of him. When two men of strong will clash, it's always the boss who wins."

"That will take him out of the running for captain of the vessel that enters the race," I remarked.

"I think he lost his chance for that before we ever saw those Nootkas."

"Does Asa have another skipper for the job?"

65

"He has two others—younger men in their late thirties he might use," Fin said slowly, running a hand through his shaggy blond hair. "Remains to be seen, though. Carlyle's a hard man to figure sometimes. I've known him only eight months. Other men who've worked for him several years say the same."

"Well, that's not our worry."

We stood silently for a few moments.

"We'll probably have a burial at sea tomorrow," Fin said finally.

"What rotten luck!"

"There will probably be some repercussions for those Indians from the Canadian government when we report this." He stretched and yawned. "Think I'll turn in. I'm dog-tired."

Our run down to Puget Sound was uneventful, except for the burial of Stacey and Billings. About midafternoon of the day following our escape, the jibs were backed over and the schooner hove to while all hands gathered at the starboard rail for a scripture reading and short eulogy by Captain Gibbs. Then the bodies, sewn into spare canvas and weighted at the feet, were slid overside and disappeared with a splash. That's all there was to it. As the schooner got under way again, I had an empty sensation in the pit of my stomach. Even though I had not known Stacey at all and Billings only slightly, it was difficult to adjust my mind to the fact of their deaths. Human life hung by a tenuous thread that was easily snapped. Despite my recent close call in San Francisco, I had gradually gotten the notion that nothing disastrous could befall me, that I was somehow immune. These sudden deaths had shaken that assumption.

When we reached Cape Flattery at the mouth of Puget Sound, the wind was light and Carlyle engaged a steam tug to keep from wasting any more time. Even with a tow, we were nearly twenty-four hours reaching Port Gamble where Carlyle's mill was located. We had been reported overdue during the bad storm that had hit the coast and were feared lost, along with several other area ships. The families of the sailors were overjoyed to see the *J. W. Brandon* tie up at the company pier. Billings was a bachelor, so his belongings were sent on to his aged mother in Vermont. Stacey's young widow was shocked and grieved to the point of having to be temporarily sedated.

These things, however, I found out later. My first concern on arriving at Port Gamble was to get my feet on solid ground again. I felt as if I'd been aboard that ship for months.

While we were still staggering around, trying to get our land legs back, Carlyle directed Staghorn to show Wiley and me to our temporary quarters in the bunkhouse where several of the single millhands and sailors, including Fin Staghorn, were housed. The long bunkhouse was plenty spacious and had lots of empty bunks to accommodate many more men than were presently occupying it. But it was built of very rough-cut planks, many of which had warped out of shape, leaving gaps for the wind and rain to blow in. Rags and moss had been stuffed into the largest cracks by some enterprising occupants earlier. At least the bunks were warm and reasonably soft and the roof didn't leak.

We docked late on a misty afternoon and it was the next day before Wiley and I felt up to examining our new surroundings.

The mill was much larger than I had pictured it. Although presently running at only a fraction of capacity, the buildings and grounds, including Carlyle's cream-colored two-story frame house, covered several acres of cleared land that began at the water's edge by the company wharf and a small shipyard, and sloped gradually up toward a solid wall of timber about a mile away.

Carlyle's holdings included several square miles of prime timberland adjoining the mill property. Whether he owned all this outright, I didn't know. When business was slow, Fin told us, Carlyle usually bought the timber he needed. But when business was good, he hired and put to work his own logging crew on his land. They cut and hauled out by ox teams commercial-grade timber that grew within a half mile of the water. But by nearly anyone's standards, Asa Carlyle was a wealthy man—cash-poor and overextended perhaps but well-to-do nonetheless.

Port Gamble was a small community—really a company town, I discovered, with a small school, store, houses, and even a telegraph that connected this rather isolated spot with San Francisco. Victoria, British Columbia, to the north reigned as the fashion and cultural center of the sound. Olympia was the territorial capital, and steamers made regular rounds from there to Seattle to all the major sawmill towns of Port Townsend, Port Ludlow, and Port Gamble.

Standing at the top of the long incline near the line of woods, one could look out over the picturesque setting at the big home, the mill, bunkhouse, and outbuldings, the shipyard, the stacks of sawed lumber near the wharf. The green of the trees and grass was broken by browns and yellows of lumber and buildings and stumps. The blue sky arching over the green hills and blue water that bordered the mill town created a setting that no artist could do justice to. From a distance came the faint chuffing of the steam engine, punctuated by agonized whine from the big head rig as the logs were fed into the circular saw.

Rust and Barrett had tried to buy out Carlyle at least twice in the past when the market was stronger, but he had refused to sell. Port Gamble was an ideal spot for a mill—deep, sheltered water for loading ships, thick stands of big timber close at hand, and a level spot for the mill and other buildings. Rust and Barrett would have increased their wealth considerably. As it was, Rust and Barrett's main mill and headquarters were at Port Townsend, miles to the north. They also maintained business offices in San Francisco.

Even though the employees at the Carlyle Company were paid from $1.15 to $3.27 per day depending on their jobs, Wiley and I had agreed to work for only bed and board. Consequently, we felt more freedom to come and go as we chose, to become familiar with the operation of the mill and layout of Port Gamble. Our expenses, such as they were, were already provided for by money we had set aside. Wiley had access to what remained of a small inheritance from his father, and I had some income from my feature articles. We both had some gold left from a generous reward given us by

Prince Ferdinand Zarahoff for helping save his life last year. And our shares of a small placer claim in the Black Hills were still supplying a trickle of gold.

We parted with some of this money to reoutfit ourselves at the Carlyle company store, replacing our lost clothes—from underwear to shirts to sturdy canvas pants, boots, and an extra pair of heavy work shoes, jacket, even a toothbrush and a broadcloth suit each.

Wiley had enough money to see us through for a few weeks. As soon as I could get to a bank in Seattle, I could draw a draft on my bank in Chicago for some money of my own.

It was in the dining hall of the mill on the third day that we met ''Taps'' O'Neal.

CHAPTER 8

JOSEPH Taps O'Neal was one of those characters who occasionally appears on the frontier—a man so out of his element that he hardly seems credible. He was employed as a rigger in the Carlyle shipyard.

Due to the cutback in the number of employees at the mill, we were the only ones at one end of a long wooden table in the mess hall. He introduced himself.

"You boys new here?" he inquired of Wiley and me as he buttered a piece of bread.

We glanced at each other, and I finally answered. "You might say that. We're friends of Fin Staghorn. Mr. Carlyle just put us on temporarily."

"Doing what? I thought he was cutting back and letting hands go," he asked bluntly.

"Oh, a little of this and little of that," Wiley replied noncommittally.

"We're just getting room and board—no pay," I added quickly as if to justify our being here. "So you're a rigger?" I said, steering the subject away from us. "What do you do?"

"Mostly just help with repairs on any of the company's four ships—replacing worn or broken shrouds, stays, fairleads, gaffs, blocks—anything to do with the standing or running rigging."

"Been at it long?" I asked, digging into my steaming potatoes and gravy. "Somehow I can't picture you doing that kind of work."

O'Neal was slightly over six feet in height and weighed about one-ninety. He had thick slightly wavy dark hair and a ready smile. But his hands, when I shook with him, even though rough and callused, seemed too long and slender to belong to a manual laborer. He had a healthy-looking tan from being outdoors, but his cultured speech and his hands made me suspicious.

"I've been a rigger about a year," he replied around a mouthful of food.

"How did you get into that trade?"

"I needed a job," he answered. "I've had experience rigging high-wire equipment in a couple of circuses, and I've done some work in the theater—props, special effects, curtains, scenery—that sort of thing."

"Where'd you acquire that nickname?"

"Taps?"

"Yeah."

"I started out in the theater onstage as a tap dancer in variety shows and musical revues."

"I thought there was more to you than just being a laborer," I said.

He laughed. "Performing is still my first love, but I couldn't keep steady employment that way, so I got into other areas of show business—behind the scenes. That eventually led into what I'm doing now. That, and the fact that I'm pretty familiar with various kinds of ships and boats."

"Where are you from?"

"Eastern shore of Maryland. That's how I happened to be familiar with boats. Did a lot of working as a crewman on various fishing and oystering boats—bugeyes, skipjacks, and pungeys—on the Chesapeake while I was growing up."

"Quite a background," I commented.

O'Neal was very open and gregarious. He was the type of person I instinctively trusted. After a few minutes' conversation, I found myself telling him all about myself—how I had been brought to this country by my parents on an immigrant ship from Ireland when I was only eight years old and had grown up in Chicago, had served briefly in the last few months of the War Between the States, later worked as a reporter for the *Chicago Times*

71

Herald. My assignment as a war correspondent in General Buck's campaign against the Sioux had introduced me to the West and led me to leave my newspaper job. It was on this campaign that I met Wiley Jenkins, black sheep from a well-to-do Kentucky family whom I had come to like and trust. We had shared several adventures since.

That afternoon Wiley and I took a closer look at the shipyard where one of the Carlyle ships was in dry dock having its hull cleaned, patched, and repainted. Another, smaller ship was taking shape in the shipyard, its frames standing gauntly like the ribs of a giant skeleton.

O'Neal was working on the rigging of the *J. W. Brandon* that was still in the water, tied up alongside a small pier nearby.

Asa Carlyle was pacing up and down among the workmen and the odd pieces of lumber, piles of shavings, tools and clamps, coils of rope, and reels of cable. He seemed deeply engrossed in thought and didn't see us. He had pencil and pad in his hands and stopped now and then to make some notation. After a time he walked off and headed back toward his house without a word to anyone. He obviously had something on his mind, since he was usually very friendly with his workmen.

We watched the workmen for a while before wandering back toward the bunkhouse. I was beginning to feel a little useless. Wiley and I had not been assigned any duties, not even any menial tasks such as cleaning up. Staghorn had been immediately sent out on another ship that had just finished loading when we limped in on the *J. W. Brandon*. The mate of the outbound ship had come down with chills and fever, and Fin was needed to replace him. The run in the company's largest ship, a barkentine, was down to San Francisco again. Wiley and I, left to our own devices, were beginning to feel like extra baggage.

"How about a little run down to Seattle?" Wiley asked as we sauntered toward the sawmill. "The steamer stops here tomorrow."

"Good idea. I hear it's a real up-and-coming town."

We spent the rest of the day walking the streets of Port Gamble. We went through the mill again but were

72

unable to talk to the mill hands because of the noise and the fact that they couldn't take their attention off their jobs without risking losing a hand in the machinery.

We notified Carlyle late that afternoon about our intentions to go down to Seattle.

"When Staghorn gets back in a few days, I want him and the two of you and maybe a few others to meet with me about that race."

"Right, sir. Anything you want us to be doing in the meantime? After all, you are feeding and housing us."

He paused thoughtfully. "Have you made yourselves familiar with my operation here?"

"Sure have."

"I can't think of anything just now. Go ahead to Seattle and enjoy yourselves. I'll see you in a few days." He waved a dismissal.

When we saw Taps O'Neal the next morning at breakfast and he discovered we were planning a trip to Seattle, he told us of a touring company of Shakespearean players from San Francisco who were performing *Julius Caesar*.

"It's been years since I've seen a good Shakespeare play," Wiley said. "Let's go see it. It would bring back memories of home and my earlier years. And it would be a touch of civilization I haven't had since we were in New Orleans over a year ago."

O'Neal poured himself a second cup of coffee and fell silent at the table while Wiley and I enthusiastically discussed our plans.

Finally, as the steam whistle sounded and the tall rigger rose to go to work, he said slowly, "How would you like a little company on your trip?"

We looked at him curiously.

"I know Seattle and I know the theater. What about it?"

We nodded in unison. "Sure."

"Today is Friday," O'Neal went on hurriedly. "I have Sunday off anyway. I'll talk to the foreman. My work is pretty well caught up now. Just waiting for some cable I need. He'll probably let me off until the first part of the week." He started out the door and then turned back. "Will you be at the bunkhouse?"

73

"Yes."

"I'll meet you there in about an hour if I can get away." Then he was gone.

"Like a kid at Christmas," I remarked.

"I haven't been that excited about anything in a long time," Wiley said.

"Maybe that's the price of getting older and having more experiences," I mused. "Nothing to look forward to with any real anticipation."

"I'm not quite thirty-one. Hope I'm not at that point yet. From a few things O'Neal said, he has to be in his late thirties, although he doesn't really look it."

"Maybe it's just that we haven't been tied to a steady job for a few years. We've forgotten how thrilling it is to get a few days off."

Wiley laughed. "You're right. We've been damned lucky. Just enough money to provide some leisure and an interesting life. What more could a man ask for?"

The steamer docked at nine-thirty, debarked a few passengers, and took some aboard, including Wiley and me and Taps O'Neal. The rigger was with us, bag in hand.

The gangway was up, and we were away within the hour. It was a clear, sunny day and we enjoyed the beautiful scenery all the way to Seattle.

We lounged in deck chairs while O'Neal did most of the talking. He asked us about the voyage back from San Francisco.

"From the looks of the *J. W. Brandon*, that must have been quite a storm. I've never seen a foremast sprung like that. The topmast was nearly gone."

"With your experience as a sailor, you probably would have handled it better than we did," I commented.

"Wish I had been there!" His eyes glistened at the thought. "And then that attack by the Nootkas to top it off! The adventure of a lifetime!"

"If that's what you have a hankering for, there are plenty of Apaches in the Arizona Territory who would be glad to oblige you," Wiley drawled.

O'Neal laughed. "No, thanks. I need to live near the sea. And also somewhere close to a city that has a theater. I'm a frustrated actor, I suppose."

"I thought you were a dancer."

"I am. But I enjoy playing dramatic roles, too. Not as good at that, though."

"Why are you working as a rigger, then?"

"I'm hoping to live frugally enough to be able to put some money aside and go into business for myself someday before I get too old. I'd like to open a theater of my own."

"Not to get personal, but I don't know how you'll do that on a workman's wages."

"I'm beginning to see that myself—especially when I blow a week's pay going to Seattle or Victoria every month or so."

"You aren't blowing your pay getting drunk and raising hell and gambling, are you?" Wiley inquired, a hint of a smile at the corners of his eyes.

"Nope. That may be what a lot of lumberjacks and mill hands are looking for, but you don't have to go all the way to Victoria or Seattle for that. There are plenty of places in Port Townsend for that—or Port Gamble, for that matter. No, I go for what I'm going for now—to attend the theater."

"Is this the type of thing you go to see?" Wiley asked, holding up a flyer we had picked up when we came aboard. "Here're a few of the coming attractions at Yesler's Hall in Seattle—'Haverly's Minstrels—July 1, 2, 5; John Maguire—Monologue of Dramatic Sketches and Oddities—September 7; Merits and Workings of the Phonograph—Demonstration—September 11, 12; Cleave Vaudeville Company—October 14.' Sounds like a real interesting lineup," he finished, making a wry face.

"That's what most of the frontier towns get—variety or minstrel shows. In fact, there's a man calling himself Professor Hermann, a self-styled world-renowned prestidigitateur who's been touring all over the West. Claims to have appeared before Queen Victoria, the emperor of Russia, three U.S. presidents." He laughed. "Bills himself as the world's greatest living magician—'eclipsing in his marvelous feats of legerdemain the great Hindu jugglers,' to quote a handbill I saw recently."

"Is that the only kind of entertainment the people around here want?" Wiley asked.

"Most of the men in this region are not your well-educated, discriminating theatergoers. They prefer something a little earthier than Shakespeare. Although . . . they'd probably love some of those earthy lines in Shakespeare if they were in modern English." He laughed. "The Comique, the theater where *Julius Caesar* is being performed, was built just two years ago, in 1876. It's one of the best box houses in the Washington Territory."

"Box house?"

"It has twenty-four boxes in the balcony that are curtained off. It usually runs variety shows, but they're trying to organize a permanent company, I hear. The theaters are starting to work themselves free of saloon entertainment. Of course, some of these box houses don't have the best of reputations. The girls work the boxes between acts, selling drinks and whatever else the customers are interested in or can pay for. But I've been to this Comique several times. And so far, at least, it's been a first-class theater. They mix variety shows with plays. And they don't stand for any of the rougher element in there—no spitting on the floor, walking on the seats with caulked boots, throwing things, fighting, shouting drunken obscenities at the performers. They keep a couple of bouncers for that sort of thing. After a few rows, most of the lumberjacks got the idea that they were going to have to behave themselves if they wanted to see a show at the Comique."

Seattle turned out to be a fast-growing town with building going on everywhere. The boom, we found out, would have been much more frantic and rapid if the Grant administration's financial panic of the midseventies had not halted indefinitely the work on the Northern Pacific Railroad. A short spur had been completed from Kalama to Tacoma in 1873. But there remained a big gap between there and Bismarck, Dakota Territory, and nobody knew for sure when the building would resume. In the meantime the people of the Washington Territory looked westward and southward to the sea and California to market their wares of lumber and fish. And the immigration and the building went on at a somewhat slower pace than it might have had the region been connected to the east by rail. The roads in this perpetually wet climate could hardly be called passable thoroughfares. The mud was unbelievable. Road building and road maintenance was a joke among the residents in these parts. All eyes turned to the sea for cheaper and easier travel. One or two men on horseback might do reasonably well, but coach or wagon travel was difficult, to say the least.

But all of this was only in the backs of our minds as we made our way through the unpaved streets that were still slightly muddy from the last rain. It seemed to me that some type of corduroy or cobblestone paving would have to eventually be used, at least in the towns.

The Comique turned out to be just as O'Neal had described it—a big, two-story wooden structure. We paid extra for one of the curtained boxes in the balcony on the left side, near enough to the stage to see and hear the actors very well. The chairs were upholstered in dark red velvet, and the entire theater was reasonably new and well-maintained. The house lights—gas jets set in ornate wrought-iron sconces along the walls—illuminated the flowered, rose-tinted wallpaper and the gold-and-red curtains draping the boxes.

The seats below were filled, for the most part, with a well-behaved, decently dressed clientele. Apparently, Shakespeare didn't appeal to the rougher element of the city.

Promptly at 8:00 P.M. the house lights went down and the curtain went up. The valves feeding the gas battens of the footlights and stagelights were turned up from somewhere offstage.

The scenery had been kept to a minimum, although the costuming was authentic-looking and ornate. It had been so long since I had been witness to a Shakespearean play that it took until a few minutes into the opening scene to accustom my ears to the archaic English. But I gradually became engrossed in the story, even though many of the expressions and figures of speech still went past me. In the second scene when Calpurnia, Caesar's wife, came onstage in a crowd scene, I heard Wiley catch his breath slightly and lean forward in his seat. The actress was of medium height, had a good figure under the flowing Roman gown and blond hair whose

77

sheen caught and reflected the light. She had a classic face—finely chiseled chin and features that probably were beautiful even without the stage makeup. Her voice in the single line she had to speak was clear, and her movements were graceful and natural. A stunning vision of loveliness.

I glanced sideways at Wiley. In matters of the heart, he was defenseless. I could see he was smitten at first glance. His concentration was even greater shortly after, when Calpurnia tried to warn Caesar of her prophetic dreams and premonitions of his murder.

As the play progressed and Caesar was stabbed to death by Brutus and fellow conspirators, the problem of the unfamiliar English faded and I became more engrossed in the familiar story. And by the time the players reached the scene of Mark Antony's eulogy at Caesar's funeral, I was hanging on every word.

". . . I thrice presented him a kingly crown,/Which he did thrice refuse. Was this ambition?/Yet Brutus says he was ambitious;/And sure, he is an honorable man. . . . My heart is in the coffin there with Caesar,/And I must pause till it come back to me."

The speech rolled on. "Marvelous! Marvelous!" Taps O'Neal murmured as the actor, in the guise of Mark Antony, finished speaking the lines that so stirred up the crowd to demand the reading of Caesar's will that turned them against Brutus. I silently nodded my head in agreement. Even to my inexpert observation, the man had a marvelous talent. The other actors and the two actresses were good, but this man spoke the words of the immortal English bard as if they were rolling off human lips for the first time. He was creating a lively art.

So the play proceeded until finally Brutus fell on his sword, the final lines were spoken, and the curtain dropped to uproarious applause from the audience. After two curtain calls, and more applause, the curtain was let down for the final time and the house lights were turned up.

"I've got to meet that girl," Wiley said as we made our way out of the box and downstairs through the milling crowd in the lobby.

"What girl?"

"The one who played Calpurnia."

"She didn't have a very large part, but she gave a nice performance," Taps said.

"I don't think it's her performance Wiley is interested in," I said.

"She's the most beautiful girl I've ever laid eyes on. I've just got to meet her," Wiley insisted. "I think I'll go by the stage door."

O'Neal and I looked at each other. "You think that's really a good idea?"

"She's probably married," Taps added.

Wiley's face dropped slightly at this, but he bounced right back. "Won't hurt to find out. Besides, a lovely creature like that doesn't come along every day—and one with talent, too."

I heaved an exaggerated sigh. "I guess we'll have to let him go," I said to Taps. "He never seems to tire of having his hopes dashed and his heart broken."

O'Neal laughed as we started around the front of the theater in search of the stage door at the rear. "I guess we'd better find out this angel's name," he said, pulling a playbill from his inside coat pocket.

"It's Darcy Olivia McLeod. I already looked," Wiley said.

"Fairly mundane name for so ethereal a creature," Taps commented, with a wink at me.

"Okay, okay, make all the fun you want to, but nothing ventured, nothing gained," Wiley shot back.

We came around the back of the theater, and there was the lighted stage door. But there were already five men standing there, hats in hands, and three of them held small bunches of flowers.

"Looks like you'll have to get in line," I said under my breath.

"Maybe they're here to see the girl who played Portia," Wiley returned without much conviction in his voice. Remembering the nondescript brunette who had played the part, I just smiled.

We stopped about twenty feet from the group and conferred.

"Are you sure you really want to wait?" I asked.

Wiley nodded but without the enthusiasm he had displayed before.

"It may be a while," I continued. "And you're bucking quite a line here."

"Well, I think I'll stick for about thirty minutes. If she's not out by then, or if I can't get a word with her, I'm ready to go."

But it was hardly five minutes later when the stage door opened a crack and a homely middle-aged woman thrust her head out.

"Miss McLeod is not seeing anyone tonight. She has an urgent engagement and must leave immediately."

There was a murmur of disappointment from the group of five who had crowded up around the door.

"If you would like to leave your names with these flowers, I'll take them to her." The set of her jaw and the bulk of her body blocking the entrance allowed no argument.

The rivals looked suspiciously at each other, then two of them pulled out pencils and began to scribble notes on the cards attached to their bouquets. We stood back in the shadows, taking no part in this.

The woman collected the flowers and slammed the door abruptly.

"So much for that," Taps said as the five suitors put their hats back on and dispersed.

"Let's go eat. I'm starved," I said, taking Wiley by the arm. He was looking forlornly at the closed door with the hissing gas jet set in its iron bracket above it.

Just then the door opened and Darcy McLeod came out, her blond hair nearly hidden in the hood of a blue traveling cape she was wearing. She was escorted by the actor who had played Marc Antony. He shut the door quickly behind him, pulled a hat down over his face, and taking Miss McLeod's arm, guided her away into the darkness. Although it had not been evident onstage, the actor walked with a decided limp.

They had not seen us, but Wiley started forward to say something to her. But before he had taken more than two steps, another man moved out of the shadows from the corner of the building and started after the couple. The quick glimpse I got of him as he passed through the edge of light showed a man of medium height wearing a tan canvas jacket, brown corduroy pants tucked into high, brown riding boots. The hat kept his face obscured, and then he was gone into the darkness.

Instinctively, I put a restraining hand on Wiley's arm and motioned for Taps and Wiley to keep silent. The figure did not attempt to catch up to the pair but only walked quietly behind them in the shadows as they approached the front of the Comique Theater and hailed a hack.

"Come on." I led the way, striding swiftly toward the street where some of the theater patrons were still standing and talking in small groups by the light streaming from the lobby's open doors.

As the door of the carriage closed, the driver set his horse in motion. I had lost sight of the other man in the crowd but then sighted him again as he stepped up into the high coach, saying something to the driver and pointing in the direction of the disappearing hack ahead of him. He slammed the door and the hack was off.

"Let's go!" I said, dodging through the people on the boardwalk and looking quickly around for a cab.

"Where are you going in such a hurry?" Taps wanted to know.

"If I can find an empty hack quick enough, we're going to follow those two coaches."

CHAPTER 9

AND find one I did. The one-horse hacks had been lined up out front to handle the crowds, and I grabbed the door handle of one just ahead of a well-dressed man in muttonchop burnsides who was raising his arm to hail the driver.

"Where to?" the short driver asked, preparing to climb on to the box.

"See that hack turning the corner up ahead? Just keep it in sight."

I'm sure Taps and Wiley had no idea what I was doing, but they sprang in beside me and the coach lurched forward, throwing them back into their seats before the door was even shut.

"What's all this cloak and dagger business?" O'Neal wanted to know, straightening his tweed jacket.

I couldn't give him an explanation because I didn't really know myself. "Just a hunch. Did you see that man following those two?"

"Sure, but so what? Probably just a disappointed suitor, trying to get an opportunity to talk to her or get her autograph."

"Maybe, but it didn't look like that to me."

"What's it to us?" O'Neal asked.

"Maybe nothing. But if he means to do them some harm, I think we should make it our business. Besides"—I grinned—"what else did you have to do tonight?"

A slow smile crossed O'Neal's face as he looked from

me to Wiley and back. "You two are crazy, but this is more fun than working."

He was still grinning as the coach slid around a corner and piled all of us to one side. I thought of the last time I had been bounced around in a hack. But this time we were in control of the situation. After a block or two, the coach slowed, and I thrust my head out the window. I could see another hack about fifty yards ahead of us.

We probably traveled just over a mile by my estimation before we came to a stop. A few seconds later the driver opened the side door.

"Here we are."

"Where?"

"Those two coaches. They've stopped just ahead of us."

Curiosity was straining at the driver's features as his eyes darted back and forth between us and our quarry, but we ignored the unspoken question as we paid our fare.

We pretended to stand in a group and talk for a few seconds as the two hacks ahead of us pulled away. Miss McLeod and her actor-escort entered the lobby of the Fisk Hotel. The corduroy-clad figure busied himself looking in a shopwindow until the couple was inside, then he, too, entered the hotel. After a short delay, the three of us also followed. The lobby was brightly lighted by an overhead coal-oil chandelier, and our feet fell quietly on a large Oriental rug. The well-groomed clerk behind the registration desk stood ready to sign us in, but we made an abrupt left turn through the open double doors into the dining room that led off the lobby, following our quarry into the darkened interior, where we could hear a low hum of voices over the tinkling of silverware and dishes.

The dining room was heavy with dark wood but brightened by the white linen tablecloths and individual candles on the small circular tables.

"You won't believe it, but this is where I was going to suggest we come to eat. Best place I've found in Seattle," O'Neal said as I led the way to a table without waiting to be seated. I selected a table as near as possible to the man we were following, who in turn was seated near Darcy McLeod and her companion by a window on the far side of the room. I tried not to look in their direction but realized as we sat down that we were still out of earshot of any conversation from the actress's table. None of the other patrons in the place seemed to recognize or care who the Shakespearean performers were.

Over my menu I studied the lone man who sat nearby. He had removed his hat before giving his order to the waiter. He was clean-shaven with a rather round face and reddish-blond hair that was thinning on top, bushy and slightly graying around the ears. The face was bland—altogether as forgettable and undistinguished-looking a man as I had ever seen.

My attention was distracted by the waiter who arrived to take our order.

"The chateaubriand is superb!" O'Neal said.

"A specialty of the house," the tall waiter agreed, scribbling on his pad. "And you, sir?"

"A little rich for my blood," Wiley said. "I'll take the beefsteak and potatoes, medium-rare."

I ordered the same, and the waiter withdrew after taking our order for drinks.

Another waiter had taken the order from Miss McLeod and her escort. A minute later he returned with their drinks—what appeared to be a large brandy for the actor and a glass of wine for the actress.

O'Neal and Wiley noticed my eyeing the sandy-haired man nearby.

"Figured out what's going on yet?" Wiley asked.

"I haven't the foggiest notion," I admitted. "If he weren't keeping such a close eye on them, I might say I'd made a mistake and the whole thing was coincidence. But he's tailing them, all right."

"Some personal grudge against the actor, maybe?" O'Neal suggested.

I shrugged. "Who knows? What's that actor's name, anyway?"

"David St. George, so the program says," O'Neal replied. "Can't say as I've ever heard of him, but he's a superb actor. And I keep getting the strangest feeling that I've seen him before on the stage."

"Maybe David St. George is a stage name," Wiley said.

"Could be."

"More than just a possibility," Taps agreed. "When I lived back in Maryland, I took in all the plays I could and knew just about every good actor or actress by sight and name if not personally. 'Course, I've been out here the past few years and out of touch, but that name just rings no bells at all. I would at least have heard of an actor with the talent that man has." He glanced over at the couple who were engrossed in conversation. "Maybe if I let it simmer in the back of my head, I'll eventually remember where I've seen him before."

Except for the slight limp, there was nothing particularly distinctive about the actor listed in the playbill as David St. George. He was of medium height—maybe five feet, nine inches or so, was clean-shaven, had a straight nose, dark eyebrows, and dark hair that minus the stage makeup was showing some tiny streaks of gray. His face was rather lean, and not even the glow of the candle about two feet in front of him could entirely erase the dark shadows under his eyes. His gestures and movements, even offstage, seemed somewhat exaggerated and theatrical, perhaps from the force of long habit. He displayed a rakish air, as if he were continuously performing some swashbuckling role. All in all, he gave the appearance of a well-used actor of about forty.

The waiter brought our drinks—bourbon and water for Wiley and beer for O'Neal and myself. The stranger at the next table was nursing a beer and openly watching David St. George and Darcy McLeod.

"Well, I don't know what's going on, but as long as we're here on my hunch that they were in danger, Wiley might have a chance to meet the young lady. She's a beauty, all right."

Our conversation flagged. When I finally laid down my napkin and slid my chair back with a contented sigh, I had a craving for a pipeful of good tobacco. But my pipe was gone with the rest of my luggage in San Francisco, and I hadn't thought to buy another one. Must make a mental note to do that.

It was only then I noticed that the sandy-haired man

85

had eaten nothing. He was still sipping his beer and staring at the couple. Whatever he was up to, he made no secret of the fact that they were the entire focus of his attention. I couldn't tell if he was watching both of them, just the actor, or just the woman.

One other thing I noticed as I leaned back in my chair, crossed my legs, and engaged in a desultory conversation with Wiley and Taps was the fact that David St. George was very much aware of the scrutiny he was receiving. He was also well into his third or fourth large brandy.

"About ready to go?" Wiley asked, signaling the passing waiter for our check.

"Not just yet," I said quietly, motioning for him to stay seated. He glanced back over his shoulder and then settled back into his chair. O'Neal also saw what I was watching.

David St. George was glaring back at the sandy-haired man, obviously irritated. He drained his brandy glass and signaled for another. The actress put her hand on his arm and said something to him, but the sneer that came to his lips was obvious even from where I sat. He threw another hard look at the stranger. The stranger was still calmly watching St. George as if he were the most interesting curiosity he had ever seen. And the actor was growing more agitated by the second.

Suddenly the actor jumped out of his chair and in two or three short steps was standing in front of the sandy-haired man.

"Mister, if you want to look at me, here I am! Take a close look!"

Several people at neighboring tables looked around at the actor. His clear voice had penetrated the buzz of conversation, and a sudden silence fell.

The sandy-haired man just looked up at him and smiled, saying nothing.

"What do you want, anyway? Am I some kind of freak or something? You've been hounding me ever since we got to town. Every night this week I've seen you following me. Is there something you want? If not, you'd better disappear because if I see you following us

86

or harrassing us anymore, I'll have to take some stronger action to put a stop to it.''

The stranger gave him a mocking smile. "As far as I know, there's no law against looking at someone. And you are a public figure in show business. What's the matter, got a guilty conscience?'' He tipped up his beer glass to his mouth.

While the glass was still tilted up, David St. George slapped it out of the other's hand, smashing the glass and spraying beer several feet across the carpet, even hitting our tablecloth.

The stranger jumped to his feet, but the actor did not follow up with any blows. Instead, he stood stock still, balling his fists at his sides, his pale complexion suffusing a deeper red in the candlelight, either from anger or the brandy he had consumed.

Several of the patrons had begun to move out of the way, anticipating a fight, and the headwaiter was approaching, weaving among the tables from the back of the room.

But there was to be no fight this night. The stranger backed away, wiping his sleeve across his face to dry the beer.

"Why don't you shoot me?'' he said in a low voice, so low that I had to strain to hear him. "I'm sure you have a pocket gun hidden on you somewhere. After all, you specialize in derringers, don't you? Here, let me turn my back to make it easier for you."

He picked up his hat and turned abruptly away. David St. George's eyes bulged from his head, and I saw the muscles in his jaw working. He opened and closed his fists at his sides and I'm sure would have throttled the stranger. But the lone man strode out the door of the dining room just as the headwaiter arrived.

The big man, who probably was really a bouncer in evening clothes, took St. George by the arm. "I'm sorry, sir, but I'm going to have to ask you to leave."

The actor muttered something under his breath and turned back to his table. Darcy McLeod was still sitting there, thin-lipped and pale. David St. George pulled out some greenbacks from an inside billfold, laid them on the table and took the blond actress by the arm, threw her cloak to her and started to escort her out, to the stares and mutterings of the diners.

"Miss McLeod! Miss McLeod!" I jumped up and intercepted her as she passed our table. David St. George gave me a black look. "Who the hell are you?"

I ignored him. "Miss McLeod, may I have your autograph?" I thrust a menu at her.

She hesitated, glancing at the clouded face of her escort. "Maybe another time . . ."

"My friend here has been dying to meet you." I hurried on, paying no attention to her reluctance and the angry David St. George. I pulled Wiley forward.

After a tense moment she relaxed suddenly and smiled. "Certainly." Then to the actor, "David, I'll be along in a minute."

He glared at me briefly then limped on out of the dining room.

She took the menu I had snatched off an adjoining table and the pencil I had pulled from my pocket.

"I'm Matt Tierney, and this is Wiley Jenkins."

"Joseph O'Neal, Miss McLeod," Taps added, crowding up with us. "My compliments on an excellent performance."

"Oh, you were at the theater tonight?" she asked, arching her brows up at us, pencil poised.

"Yes, and it was great," Wiley answered.

"Thank you." She smiled. "It wasn't a large part, but I enjoy Shakespeare very much." She finished signing the menu after asking our names again. As she handed it back, she looked at the handsome Wiley, giving him a smile that would have melted an iceberg.

"Thank you, gentlemen," she said. "Perhaps I'll have the pleasure of seeing you at the Comique again. *Julius Caesar* will be playing for another week before our company of players leaves for Tacoma. If you don't mind seeing the same play again, perhaps I'll see you again before we leave." She favored us with a final smile, but I noted that it was subtly directed at Wiley Jenkins in particular. She started to put on the cape she had draped over her arm, and Wiley moved quickly to help her. She was about five feet, five inches tall. As she shook her head to clear her shoulder-length blond hair from the hood of the cape, she brushed Wiley's face with it.

Then she was gone to catch up with David St. George, leaving a delicious hint of fragrance behind. By the time we paid our bill and walked outside, they were nowhere in sight. I guessed they were probably staying in this very hotel and had gone upstairs.

"Well, you were right," Taps said as we walked outside into the cool, moist night air. "We could very well have had a shooting in there. Sure would like to know what that was all about. Sounded like a personal grudge of some kind. Did you hear what he said to St. George right at the end?"

"Yes. Sounded like he was trying to goad him into a fight."

"Well, at least we were there to intervene if they had started some gunplay."

"Maybe we could have kept them from killing each other or some innocent bystander," Taps said. "You're right. This is more interesting than working."

Wiley wasn't listening, and I could tell from the look on his face that his mind was on the lovely Darcy Olivia McLeod.

"C'mon," I said to Taps. "Let's get this moonstruck kid to a hotel room and into bed."

CHAPTER 10

"GENTLEMEN, I called you here to lay out exactly what I plan to do in regard to this upcoming race," Asa Carlyle said with no preliminaries as we sat in the spacious parlor of his large house six days later.

Rays of the morning sun were slanting through the picture window and warming the room. Fin Staghorn, who had returned the night before from San Francisco, shared the horsehair sofa with Wiley Jenkins. I sat in a comfortable overstuffed chair to one side. I guessed Carlyle had called us to his house in order to have some privacy and comfort rather than meeting in the small cluttered office near the mill that was occupied by Cyrus Johnson, his company manager.

Carlyle paced back and forth in front of us, now and then pausing to lean on the round marble-topped table in the middle of the room that contained a dusty Bible and an ornate coal-oil lamp. As Carlyle paused to collect his thoughts before proceeding, I was painfully conscious of the absence of Captain Joshua Gibbs.

"Rust and Barrett have more resources than I do and will probably spare no expense to win this contract." He stopped again and stared out the window down toward his mill. But he probably saw only some vision in his mind's eye.

"It's a well-known fact that a vessel with a longer waterline will almost always beat a vessel with a shorter waterline. In other words, everything else being equal, a big ship will beat a small one. Knowing that, I plan to construct a small ship to enter this race." He held up his hand as Fin started to say something. "Let me finish. It's not as crazy as it sounds. There are several reasons for it. First of all, it's economical. As you know, Fin, the ships I own are all getting some age on them, and all but one were bought used. They are in relatively good condition, but I don't feel they are suitable for a race like this. The money I would have to spend dry-docking and reconditioning them would be better spent on a new vessel. I have neither the time nor the money to commission the building of a new barkentine or three-masted schooner. Even before this race was proposed, I had designed and was planning to build a smaller ship—a two-masted schooner, and incorporate a few ideas of my own that I believe will make a better coasting schooner. In fact, it's already taking shape on the ways, as you have seen." He stopped his pacing and pointed in the general direction of the waterfront and his shipyard. "It's been over fifteen months in the building already."

"How do I plan to win with a schooner that will measure less than one hundred feet on deck? First of all, I want a vessel that is more maneuverable than a larger ship, so she can be handled easier in small harbors. She will have a long portion of her keel that is straight—no curve to it. This is for safety and strength. I've seen too many lumber ships break their backs and founder when they've grounded on bars with a load aboard. A straight keel will give her something to rest on—more rigidity. She'll have more deadrise so she can sail upwind with little or no ballast when empty. Her beam will be adequate but not extreme, and she'll have a clean clipper bow. For this race only she'll have taller-than-normal topmasts in order to make up in sail area something of what we'll be giving up in length. With her fore and main, bigger-than-usual topsails, jibs, and various staysails, she'll be overcanvased. But"—and here he turned and pointed a finger at all of us for emphasis—"here are the three things I'm really counting on to win this race. First of all, have you ever taken a good look at the sails on one of these big lumber schooners? Even when new, they set like baggy old grain sacks. They don't make

91

maximum use of the wind. Apparently, no one has ever given them much thought. But I'm taking a lesson from the yachtsmen. I'm having a new set of sails made to my special order by a sailmaker in Maine. He's promised to have them here by the time my vessel is done. They're costing me over six thousand dollars, but with the proper curvature, strength, double-sewn flat panels, they'll be worth it. These sails will be the best drivers made today by the best sailmakers in the world.

"Secondly, seasoned softwood is lighter than the same number of board feet of green lumber. It so happens that I have more than a full load of spruce and douglas fir and pine that has been air-dried for over a year—an order that was placed then canceled before it could be loaded for delivery. We'll still have plenty of weight onboard when loaded, but she won't be near as heavy as she would be with green lumber—and she won't be near as heavy as their larger ship. The race rules concern themselves only with board feet—not with weight. I'm confident that Rust and Barrett will be so overconfident in their own superiority with a big ship that they'll never bother about such a small detail as weight. They'll just figure to overpower us, especially when they find out how small our ship will be.

"Now third and last—Fin, you will be in command of this schooner for the race."

So there it was. I think Staghorn had an inkling it was coming, since none of the other Carlyle company captains was present, although I understood one of them was at sea just now. Still, the look of delighted surprise on Fin's face seemed at least partially genuine.

"That's not going to make Joshua Gibbs and the other skippers too happy," Fin finally said.

"Don't worry about that. Gibbs and I had a long talk, and he has decided to retire from the sea and take up some occupation on the beach—maybe get into the ship chandlery business.

"But if you have any misgivings about this, now's the time to spit them out."

"Well, I'm flattered, but I don't have my master's papers."

Carlyle waved his hand as if batting away an irritating

fly. "Doesn't matter. You're in my employ, and this is for just one trip. You've had a lot of deepwater experience before the mast in square riggers and only a few months as mate on my coasting schooners, but I think you can do the job. You've got a good head on your shoulders, and the men trust your judgment. Besides, over the years I've seen the sea take its toll on men. If they stay with it to middle age or past, they tend to get conservative and careful. Just human nature, I reckon. But rather than being safe, conservatism can be downright dangerous. The sea must be challenged with bold decisions all the time. No"—he shook his head—"the sea is a young man's occupation. Besides, younger men—youths, really—make the best crewmen because they don't gripe so much. They can stand the discomforts of cold and wet and lack of sleep and hours on end of sail handling better than older men. To them, it's still adventure—not work."

He was pacing back and forth again, raking the fingers of one hand through his slightly graying hair.

"One thing more I didn't mention about the design of this new ship. She'll have only one deck; no 'tween decks. And she'll load from one main cargo hatch on the deck—no stern loading ports to weaken the hull. She'll be small, but she'll be stout. If we win this contract and I stay in the lumber business, I plan to use her to get in and out of small ports up and down the coast—a schooner that should be able to get over most shoals and bars. If we don't win"—he shrugged—"maybe I'll just sell everything off and keep this new ship. Maybe go do some interisland trading in the South Seas."

He paused and stood facing us, chewing on his lower lip, his brow knitting. "Anything I've left out?"

Silence for a few seconds, then Fin spoke up.

"Have they set the date for the race yet?"

"Not yet."

"When will the ship be ready to launch? We'll need to run some trials first to get the feel of the vessel, both empty and loaded."

"It'll be a few weeks yet at least. But I'm putting every available man on it. Even hiring back a few of the mill hands I laid off. They can free up the shipwrights from some of the menial and unskilled work. I've got them working every possible hour of daylight, taking advantage of this fair weather. Just to give you an idea, we're shooting for about the last week of August or the first of September. I'll work that out with Caleb Hale and the Rust and Barrett people. In the meantime, you will pick your own crew. You won't need a donkey engine man because all the sails on this new ship can be handled by hand, even by a small crew. No steam. The men will still need to go aloft to handle the topsails, except to clew up. But except for that, this ship should be much easier to handle than the *J. W. Brandon*, for example. Every vessel has its own feel, even those that are built as alike as human hands can make them. But if we're lucky, this schooner will be a sailor's dream. A sailor's dream . . ." As his voice trailed off and he stood staring out the window, I caught a mental image of the sleek copper-bottomed schooner slicing the waves under a cloud of white sails. I was only about two weeks past my wrenching experiences on the *Brandon*, but already my vow to stay ashore was fading. I thought of this new yachtlike schooner as more fun than terrifying. I was catching race fever. I wanted as bad as Carlyle to topple the Rust and Barrett giant.

As we started toward the door, I happened to glance through the door into the adjacent dining room.

"Beautiful wall hanging," I remarked, indicating the square light brown plaid. "The Carlyle tartan?"

"Alas, no, lad," he replied, shaking his head. "The Carlyles have never merited a tartan. That's the Burns tartan. My grandfather was a Burns. A good, lowland commoner's name but elevated to a much higher status by the famous poet Robert Burns. My grandfather Leland Burns was a cousin of his. As much as I love the freedom of my mother country, the United States, there are old world traditions that I miss, even though I never experienced them myself. Ah, well"—he sighed—"maybe the name Carlyle will someday mean something."

"It means something now," Fin Staghorn said, his hand on the door handle. "And before we're through, a lot more people are going to know it."

"You know the old man pretty well," I remarked to

Fin as the three of us walked down toward the mill. "He did just about what you predicted he'd do. You even looked surprised when he selected you to captain the race ship."

"I was. I was pretty confident I'd be a member of the crew, hopefully even the mate. But I had no idea I'd be in command. As I told you before, he's got at least two other qualified experienced captains he could have selected. After what happened during that storm, I figured Joshua Gibbs was out of the running."

We automatically gravitated to the skeletal beginnings of the new, unnamed ship that was scheduled to carry the destiny of the Carlyle company. She was being planked up. Workmen swarmed over her as we watched.

"I hope they don't get in too much of a hurry and do a sloppy job," Fin said aloud.

"No need to worry about that," a muscular, graying man nearby said, overhearing the remark. Swinging a maul in one massive fist, he walked over to us, wiping a shirt-sleeve across his perspiring brow. "I'm in charge of this crew. The men know what this ship means. Their jobs are riding on it. Besides, these fitters and joiners are professionals. They take pride in their work. We may be working fast, but we're not cutting any corners."

Fin Staghorn smiled and nodded with satisfaction. The lines of the sleek vessel were starting to become obvious now as the steam-bent planking went on. She was going to be a beauty.

Taps O'Neal was nowhere to be seen. His part of the job had not yet begun. It would be some time yet before the masts were stepped and the riggers put to work.

As we walked away, Wiley mentioned something about O'Neal.

"Ah, so you've met him," Fin said. "An interesting fella. Did he tell you he's not only a rigger but a damn good sailor as well? He's been sailing on the Chesapeake since he was old enough to walk. In fact, he doesn't know it yet, but he's one of the crew members I'm going to select for the race."

"Did you know about his theatrical background?" Wiley asked.

"He mentioned something about it but never went into much detail."

Since Fin had gotten into port late the night before, we had not had an opportunity to brief him on our sojourn to the theater in Seattle. Wiley filled him in about our trip the weekend before.

"The theatrical company has moved on to Tacoma today for a run of about ten days," he concluded. "But if there's such a thing as love at first sight, it happened to me the first time I saw Darcy McLeod walk out on that stage."

"Infatuation at first sight, you mean." I grinned. "Happens every time you see a pretty face."

He ignored me. "And the more I see of the lady, the better I like her. And I believe the feeling may be mutual. At least she prefers me to all those perfumed hounds drooling at the stage door after every performance." He smiled. "I've got quite a few of the lines of *Julius Caesar* memorized, since I saw the play three times this week."

"She looked like she was enjoying the company of that actor who played Mark Antony—David St. George," I said.

"Did she know the man following St. George?" Fin wanted to know.

"I questioned her about that," Wiley said. "She let on that she didn't know who the man was or what he wanted. But she did say he had been shadowing the actor since they had made a run of *Richard III* in San Francisco a few weeks back."

"Strange. And the man hasn't made any overt move—just follows St. George around?"

"That's all. Stares at him. Tries to get the actor riled by playing on his nerves."

"I've heard of gunfighters—hired killers—who use that tactic to goad a man into drawing so the victim can be gunned down. Then the killer can plead self-defense and get off," I mused. "Maybe someone has targeted this David St. George for assassination."

Wiley shrugged. "Don't know. Darcy said the actor has been trying to date her for several months, but she isn't really interested in him, even though they work together every day. He kept insisting and got pretty pushy about it, so to keep peace in the acting company, she accepted a few dates with him for dinner after the show. One of those dates was when we saw them last weekend.''

"That's her story," I replied. "No woman wants to let on that she's interested in someone else if she's out with you. She's probably got men friends in every city where the troupe has played. She draws men like hollyhocks draw bumblebees.''

I noticed the slightly pained expression on Wiley's face and hastened to add, ''Of course, she took to you right off.''

"There's more to her than meets the eye," Wiley started to say. But I had heard this same story about other girls he had lost his head over in the past, so my mind drifted away as he rattled on about her other qualities. He had stayed in Seattle last weekend when Taps O'Neal and I had returned on the ferry the next day to Port Gamble. He had finally torn himself away from Darcy Olivia McLeod and returned on Wednesday. I couldn't help but wonder if she knew more about this business of David St. George, and his tormentor. If the man had been a hired killer, he'd had a perfect opportunity to dispatch his quarry when the actor had knocked the drink out of his hand that night at the Fisk Hotel dining room. But then I remembered that neither man had obviously been carrying a weapon. Even if the man in corduroy had been carrying a pocket pistol or a sleeve derringer, not even hired killers gunned down unarmed men in public no matter the provocation. But maybe the episode we witnessed was just one more step on the carefully planned road to get the actor to respond with some deadly weapon. I wondered if knowing the identities of both these men would give me a clue.

"Did Miss McLeod give any hint that David St. George was not that actor's real name?'' I asked, interrupting Wiley in midsentence. He stopped, suddenly aware that I hadn't been listening to him.

"You didn't happen to ask her if it was a stage name?''

"Well . . . no, not exactly. She only indicated she knew him as David St. George. They've been working

97

together for about ten months. He joined the cast in New York City before they started their western tour."

"Did you see that fellow trailing him after that night at the hotel?"

"Oh, yes. I saw him in the theater every night I was there. David St. George tried to duck him after the performance, but I saw him tailing him as the actor left. Darcy said she wasn't romantically interested in St. George, but she felt sorry for him. She said that man was making the actor a nervous wreck. She said it got so he couldn't remember his lines for looking out in the audience to see if he could spot the man. In fact, the last night I was there, she got so irritated at the distraction he was causing she told me she was going to confront this man and see if she could find out what he was up to. She hinted that she might suggest David St. George hire a bodyguard, since the law couldn't do anything to stop this man because he really had not done anything wrong."

"A war of nerves," Fin commented.

"Well, we'll probably never know the outcome of it, whatever it is," I said, concluding the discussion.

"Maybe we will," Wiley said. "I plan to meet Darcy in Tacoma this weekend after the Saturday night show. We're going to rent some horses and go riding in the hills on Sunday. I'll see if this man has followed the show down there."

"Are you going, too?" Fin asked me.

"Why not? I won't get in Wiley's way. At least not during the performance." I grinned.

"If you're going, I might join you," Staghorn said. "What's playing?"

I looked the question at Wiley.

"I'm afraid it's *Julius Caesar* again."

"Well, I guess I can stand it. More interesting than hanging around here just now."

"When we get back, I think we'd better get busy and earn our keep, even if it's just as unskilled laborers," Wiley said.

"Good idea. I'm getting excited about this race. And I'd like to have a hand in putting this schooner together."

"We'll start as soon as we get back," Wiley agreed.

CHAPTER 11

"FIRE! Fire!"

Normally I am not a heavy sleeper, but at first the shouts failed to wake me. It wasn't until the door at the end of the long bunkhouse banged open and feet pounded hollowly on the wooden floor that I was roused.

"Fire! Everybody out! Fire! Let's move it!"

The man was still yelling as he went out the door at the far end of the room, and I was already up and pulling on my pants. There were eight or nine other men asleep in the bunkhouse, and there was a lot of scuffling and confusion in the dark before someone finally located a lamp and lighted it. By that time I was stamping my feet into my boots and heading for the door. From standing watches at sea, Fin Staghorn was used to springing awake and dressing in the dark, and he was the first one outside. I was right behind him, followed by Taps O'Neal and Wiley Jenkins. As soon as we turned the corner of the building, I could smell the smoke of the fire on the predawn breeze, and then I could see the dull red glow of the fire. The upper end of the long mill was ablaze. We went toward it on the run, and the closer we got, the bigger it looked. My heart was in my throat. At the sight of the roaring, crackling flames, my mind went back for a few seconds to the searing, windblown, out-of-control inferno that had engulfed the town of Deadwood the year before while Curt Wilder and I had been pursuing two outlaws among the burning buildings. The sudden

99

memory was so vivid that I slowed and stopped, staring blankly at the wall of flames that leaped before me and reflected from my mind's eye.

Several shrill blasts of a steam whistle brought me back to myself. More men were running toward the mill from the houses that formed the small community. A bucket brigade formed and I jumped into line between two men I didn't recognize. I had lost sight of Taps, Fin, and Wiley. The nearest water was the edge of the harbor, only about fifty yards away, and bucket after bucket swung forward from hand to hand, was flung on the fire, and cycled back empty by another line. I was somewhere near the middle of the line that was passing the full buckets. After a few minutes of this, I began to sweat from the exertion and the heat of the fire. There was a hesitation, a slight break in the rhythm of swinging the buckets, and I had a chance to glance at the fire. It was bigger than when we started. Apparently it had started at the lower end of the long mill shed where stacks of sawed lumber were sheltered, and the slight breeze was fanning it toward the other end of the building that housed the steam boilers, engines, and saws. The fire was feeding on itself, the resinous wood crackling in its all-engulfing maw. As the procession of water buckets started forward again, I could see our efforts were doing little or no good. The men at the head of the line finally had to back away from the intense heat, their faces red and their hair and eyebrows singed from unexpected tongues of flame that leaped out at them.

The realization that our efforts were useless gradually spread down the line as the men slowed and stopped, gazing futilely at the blaze, empty buckets dangling by their sides. As we looked, the flames burst through the roof of the building near the midpoint, and part of the lower end of the building collapsed with a roar, throwing showers of sparks and blazing pieces of shingles a hundred feet into the air on the heated blast.

"Come on, I've got an idea!" Taps O'Neal yelled, running forward. "Let's get this end of the building soaked down. Hurry!"

The men gradually began to move. The bucket brigade

re-formed and began to pass the full buckets toward the unburned half of the mill.

"Get a move on, or the whole yard could go!" Fin Staghorn yelled as the mill hands and shipwrights were slow in getting organized.

"Matt! Wiley! Some of you men! Come with me. I've got an idea!" O'Neal yelled above the turmoil. He motioned for us to follow him as he ran around the blazing mill toward the shoreward side. When we caught up with him, he was lifting the tongue of an empty wagon that stood on a slight rise above the burning building.

"Give me a hand with this." He grunted.

"What are you doing?"

"Get this wagon in position so we can roll it down this slope into the mill."

"What good will that do?" one of the men asked, as he helped lift the tongue and swing the wagon around. "Except burn up a good wagon?"

"If we can hit that wall hard enough where the fire has weakened it, we can collapse it. Break and scatter the fuel. We can maybe interrupt the fire."

Some of the men looked their doubts at each other and hesitated.

"It's worth a try, isn't it?" Taps insisted. "Throw a few rocks in here to make a heavier battering ram. We can do it. If it hits the walls just at the edge of the fire, she'll bust through."

Some of the men still hesitated.

"Look, the wind has died down and they're soaking the roof and walls. It'll work. Isn't it worth losing a wagon to save the machinery?"

Just then I saw a figure astride the ridgepole, emptying a bucket of water on to the roof. Evidently, someone had gotten a ladder up on the opposite side. With a lack of wind, the flames were now shooting up instead of blowing toward the man on the roof.

"Go ahead and do it," a familiar voice said. I looked around and there stood a disheveled Asa Carlyle. "We've got to try something, or we'll lose it all."

Since they had the boss's blessing, the men went to it with a will. While two of the men gathered up what rocks they could find and lift, two more ran to scoop some water out of a nearby horse tank to soak the wooden wagon. Once we got the wagon in position, rear end facing the mill, Wiley and I lashed the front axle to the support rods of the footboard to keep the vehicle from veering out of line. Carlyle told one of the men to run around the building and tell those on the other side what we were doing.

When everything was ready, we lined up on both sides of the wagon and started pushing. As the heavy wagon picked up speed, we fell away from the spinning iron-shod wheels and jogged to a stop, watching the battering ram heading for the burning mill.

The wagon hit precisely where we had aimed it. The wall collapsed in a blazing shower of broken boards, and the wagon disappeared inside. A cheer went up from the men.

"Come on. We may have a chance now!" Taps yelled.

We formed a short bucket brigade from the horse tank and shortly got the remaining fire on this side of the wall under control. The slacking of the wind was a Godsend. This, combined with the wet roof and walls, retarded the spread of the flames. From the yells of the men on the other side, they were taking heart and pitching water as fast as they could handle the buckets. Several men on our side had soaked gunny sacks in the horse tank and were beating out the remaining flames that still burned the splintered edges of the broken building.

Two men were on the roof chopping with double-bitted axes.

We could see the wagon inside ablaze, and the large stacks of lumber in the lower end of the building still burned brightly along with parts of the collapsed roof and walls, but the leading edge of the fire had been fought to a standstill. It took another hour, but our combined efforts saved about a third of the mill.

An overcast dawn had crept up unnoticed during our battle, and it was full daylight when all the men and many of the women of Port Gamble were able to step back and survey the damage, slapping each other weakly on the back, speaking quiet words of congratulation. We were all red-eyed and smoke-blackened, in various stages of dress, many barefooted. I saw two of the men pouring water over their heads to wash off some of the grime. The huge piles of lumber and parts of the shedlike building still blazed, pouring a thick column of gray smoke into the sky, but it had been isolated, and the all-important steam engine and head rig had been saved. During the early part of the fire, some windblown sparks and pieces of flaming shingles had started some small blazes in the scrap wood and shavings of the shipyard, but some alert latecomer had spotted them, and they were put out quickly before they could enlarge and spread.

"Whew!" Wiley sighed, wiping his face with a soggy shirt-sleeve. He sat down weakly on the ground, gazing numbly at the scene of triumph and of wreckage. I knew his reserves of energy and adrenaline, like mine, were beginning to drain away.

"If there had been anything flammable inside the middle of that building, knocking the wall down with that wagon would never have worked," O'Neal said. "Even then it was a long shot. The dropping off of that breeze was probably the biggest single thing that saved this mill. That, and the good soaking the men were able to give the roof and walls."

"We've never had a fire here before," Asa Carlyle said slowly. "I've personally drilled into my employees the need, the desperate need, for caution around a lumber mill—especially one that has no fire-fighting equipment."

"Did you have any insurance?"

He shook his head. "Only one company would even talk to me, and their rates were out of the question."

I looked at him. His face showed the effects of sleeplessness and strain. In the gray morning light, the small lines around his mouth and forehead seemed deeper. He looked older.

His statement didn't seem to call for a reply, so I said nothing. Fin Staghorn was a few yards away sousing his head in the horse tank.

Then the mill owner seemed to shake himself and noticed the several-dozen dirty, bedraggled people standing around and beginning to drift slowly away.

"Breakfast will be served shortly in the mess hall for anyone who wants it. All you can eat—on me. Give the

103

cooks about a half hour to get it ready!" he announced loudly.

The men nodded and murmured their approval, grinning through sooty faces, and some of them began sliding toward the mess hall, while others went to clean themselves up.

Asa Carlyle looked at the stacks of lumber billowing smoke as the fire consumed them.

"You were almost looking at the funeral pyre of the Carlyle company," he mused aloud. I followed his gaze and understood what he meant. But the major part of the mill was saved; the shipyard with its new schooner abuilding was safe; the dry lumber we would be carrying was safe; the fenced-in pond near the shore, which held a good supply of huge floating logs, was undisturbed.

"I can't understand it," he continued, shaking his head as he started again toward the mess hall. "Fear of fire was one reason I haven't been having my men work on the schooner at night. I'm afraid of the open flames of torches around all that wood and piles of shavings. You can see why." He gestured at the smoldering pile behind us. "I've heard of spontaneous combustion in piles of sawdust and piles of coal. Maybe that's what happened. There was no one in that mill since quitting time yesterday."

"At least no one that we know of," Fin Staghorn said.

"What do you mean by that?"

"I could have sworn I caught a whiff or two of coal oil when we were soaking down the area around that pile of burning lumber."

"You think it was started deliberately?" Carlyle stopped and looked at Staghorn incredulously.

"I don't know. I'm just telling you what I smelled. Was there any coal oil stored in that building?"

"No. I never allow it. Cyrus Johnson, my manager, is very strict about enforcing that order. If he wasn't in San Francisco, I'd get an answer from him right now."

"After breakfast that fire may have burned down enough for us to get close and take a look around," Fin said.

Asa Carlyle was grim. "The word *arson* sticks in my throat. I don't even want to think about it."

"We may have to think about it," Staghorn said. "Someone could be trying to put you out of business."

CHAPTER 12

"I don't like this idea," I said, shifting uneasily in the shadows beyond the lights of the Palace Theater in Tacoma.

"But I promised Darcy we'd try," Wiley protested.

"Then why don't you do it?" I asked, a little irritated.

"You're better at this sort of thing." Wiley almost pleaded.

"Whatever that means!" I retorted under my breath. "We don't have any reason to accost this man. Besides, even David St. George didn't ask us to get involved in this."

"Okay, okay, so it's for a selfish motive. Darcy can't concentrate on me when she's worried about this idiot following the actor around and harassing him. Besides, when the company is on the road like this, she doesn't know anyone else she can trust."

"I'll do it for the sake of our friendship, but it's against my better judgment." I reached inside my jacket and shifted the weight of Wiley's loaded .45 that was thrust inside my belt. I still had not replaced my own weapon that had been lost in San Francisco. "Better get outa sight. They'll be coming any minute."

Wiley Jenkins slid away into the darkness to where Taps O'Neal and Fin Staghorn were waiting by a hack about fifty yards away. The theater crowd had pretty well dispersed, but a dozen or so people still lingered.

There were still too many people around. This whole thing might backfire, and I could wind up in jail.

It was probably no more than ten minutes, but it seemed like a half hour before I saw the slightly limping figure of David St. George emerge from the stage door and, cape swinging from his shoulders, start toward the street. My eyes swept the theater and the shadows of the nearby alleyway. I stepped back farther into the shadows of the big shade tree on the corner where I was waiting. I almost hoped the mysterious man would not show up to tail the actor. But it was a vain hope. I had seen the man in the theater during the performance. And from the way David St. George glanced around and kept looking over his shoulder when he came out, I knew his nerves were on edge and he was expecting his tail to be there—somewhere.

And sure enough, here came the sandy-haired man, striding after David St. George and making no move to stay out of sight. It was as if he wanted the actor to know he was there. I let him walk past me. As he started to raise a hand to signal a hack, I stepped up quickly behind him, at the same time sliding Wiley's gun from my belt, covering the action with my coat.

"Hold it right there, mister!" The cocking of the Colt coincided with the pressing of the muzzle against his side.

He froze in his tracks and slowly lowered his arm.

He had jumped slightly when I spoke in his ear, but he recovered himself quickly and, without looking around, said, "All right, whoever you are. I haven't got much. But my money's in my inside coat pocket. Take it easy. I'm not making any sudden moves."

"I don't want your money. Just move forward naturally without turning around and get into that last hack in line—the one where the three men are standing by the back wheel."

He did exactly as I ordered him, without replying.

As soon as we were all seated inside the coach, the driver pulled away and started down the street. While I kept the .45 trained on him, Wiley checked him for weapons and lifted a short-barreled .38-caliber revolver

106

from the man's shoulder holster. Except for that, he was unarmed. I made sure of that by checking him myself.

"Is this some kind of kidnapping?" he asked when I had taken his gun and handed the .45 back to Wiley. He looked from one to another of us, but in only occasional light coming in the coach windows, he apparently didn't recognize us as three of the same men who had been close witnesses to his confrontation with the actor in the Fisk Hotel about two weeks previously.

"This is not a kidnapping, and we mean you no harm," I said, softening my tone. "Provided we get some answers from you."

"Like what?"

"Why do you keep following that actor, David St. George?"

"It's none of your business."

"We are making it our business."

"Who are you men, anyway?"

"I'm asking the questions. We'll just say we're friends of David St. George and Darcy McLeod."

"I think he's a great actor, and I'm trying to convince him to give me lessons. I'm also an aspiring actor, and I want to be taught by the best."

"A lie." This from Wiley. "You can do better than that."

"Let's have it straight," I said.

"If you think I'm doing something wrong, why don't you bring in the law?" His manner was calm but cautious.

"You're causing a lot of distress to Miss McLeod," Wiley said. "Now you're going to tell us who you are and what you're up to."

"Or?"

"We're not going to kill you, if that's what you're thinking. But we can make you wish you had started talking straight to us."

I could tell from Wiley's somewhat faltering tone that he had not really thought through what we would do to this man if he absolutely refused to say anything.

I reached forward and flipped back the man's coat lapel and slid his billfold out in the same motion.

O'Neal reached into a side pocket for a match and struck it against the inside of the door, holding the flare toward me so I could read the contents. I slipped the small .38 into my left coat pocket and leaned forward to examine the contents of the billfold. There was a fifty and two twenties and a five in greenbacks, but before I could extricate some papers and cards, the match went out. Taps struck another one. I finally shuffled out a business card that announced in a flowing, ornate script, "Timothy Cooper—Custom Harness and Wagon Parts—Fairfax, Virginia." At a quick glance, most of the other papers appeared to be receipts for hotel rooms, various names and addresses written on slips of paper torn from a notebook, a stagecoach schedule, a stub of a theater ticket.

O'Neal uttered an exclamation and dropped the match as it burned his fingers. I shoved everything back into the billfold except the business card and handed the leather container back to the stranger.

"Is Timothy Cooper your real name?"

"Yes."

"A long way from your business in Virginia, aren't you?"

"I daresay you gentlemen are not natives of the Washington Territory either."

"Look, Cooper, I'm asking you one more time, what's your connection or interest in David St. George?" I said.

"Why don't you ask *him*?" he retorted.

"Because I'm asking you. And if you don't open up with some answers in a hurry, I'm going to cut your gizzard out and feed it to you." My voice was deadly earnest.

Where before he had been jaunty, almost cocky, he suddenly fell silent, and I could sense him stiffen. He had no way of knowing we weren't the most bloodthirsty bunch of cutthroats on the West Coast.

"Okay, I'll tell you," he finally said after a long pause, during which the only sounds were the hoofbeats of the horse and the soft noise of the iron-shod wheels rolling over the packed dirt street. "But first, I want two things."

"And they are?"

"First, your assurance that I won't be harmed, and, secondly, that you buy me a good meal."

"Agreed."

He let out a sigh as if even if he didn't entirely believe me, he had at least bargained for his last meal and a little time.

"Okay, start talking." By default, I had become the spokesman for our group.

"I talk a lot better over a thick steak and a glass of wine," he replied, the old self-assurance returning to his voice. Or was it bravado?

"Do you have a preference in eating places?"

"I'm a stranger here."

I nodded at Taps O'Neal. He rapped on the ceiling of the coach and the driver pulled the horse to a stop. O'Neal stuck his head out the window and instructed the driver to take us to the best restaurant he knew of.

Less than an hour later we were seated in a restaurant whose decor and prices were somewhat lower than those of the Fisk Hotel, but the food was just as good. Cooper attacked his meal as if he hadn't eaten in two days.

"Almost literally true," he said around a mouthful of meat when I made that observation.

"But you have money in your pocket," Wiley said.

"Traveling on a very slim budget. Hotels, stages, and trains don't reduce fares, so I have to cut corners where I can. Need to keep my weight down anyway."

The man did not appear to be destitute. He was wearing a gray wool suit in place of the corduroys we had first seen him in. His black boots were run-over and mud-spattered. I noted the shirt cuffs edging out of his coat sleeves were somewhat frayed, and he was wearing no vest and no watch. So possibly his story about his finances was true. His somewhat round face was freshly shaved and his sideburns trimmed. There was nothing unkempt about his appearance. But there was nothing distinctive about his appearance either. He was about five feet eight, of average build. But, I had discovered when I patted him down for weapons, he had muscles under that suit as hard as iron. Overall, he had a bland appearance, with his washed-out coloring and sandy hair.

He was fortyish in age and would easily vanish in any crowd.

Rather than interrupt him again, I let him finish his meal while the three of us ate.

When all of us had finished, Cooper pushed his chair back and accepted a slim cigar that Wiley offered him. When he got it going good and his head wreathed in fresh tobacco smoke, he began his tale.

"David St. George is not that actor's real name. I have been trying to find him for the last thirteen years. I've followed a lot of false leads and spent a lot of time and money trying to track him. But the hottest tip came only a few months ago when this touring company was in New York getting ready for their western tour. I didn't catch up with the theater company until they had reached Kansas City, but once I got a good, close look at him, I knew David St. George was my man."

"Are you a bounty hunter?" Wiley asked. The same question had just crossed my mind.

He smiled faintly as he leaned forward to knock the ash off his cigar in an ashtray. "You might say that, although my reward will be in much more than just money."

"Just who is this notorious man posing as David St. George the actor?" Taps O'Neal asked.

"He's John Wilkes Booth, the assassin of President Abraham Lincoln."

"I thought we had all this nonsense ironed out," I said angrily. "It's not too late to take you out and drop you in the sound."

"I'm telling you the God's truth!" Timothy Cooper declared in a hoarse whisper, glancing around to be sure we were out of earshot of the other tables. He needn't have worried, since we were some of the last patrons in the place.

"Okay, okay," he said, spreading his hands. "Let me start at the beginning, and maybe you'll believe me. First of all, my real name is Timothy Cooper, and during the war I was an operative in the National Detective Police—the NDP—which later became known as the United States Secret Service. When the president was shot, I was put on Booth's trail, along with all the other

110

available men in the service who were in Washington City. Without going into all the detail, I'll just tell you we never got him. I still don't know if he had any outside help, but if not there were some odd coincidences that allowed him to escape. For example, the city's whole telegraph system mysteriously failing just when it was most needed to send out the alarm. And all the roads out of Washington were immediately sealed except the one he escaped on, over the Navy Yard Bridge across the Potomac.''

"What do you mean, you never got him?" Wiley interrupted. "He was shot in a barn someplace in Virginia. They identified the body and everything.''

Cooper gave a short laugh. "That's what everyone was supposed to think. The man who was shot was a Confederate undercover agent who had been captured and imprisoned. He had just been released after agreeing to work for the War Department. His name was Captain James William Boyd, and he resembled Booth somewhat, although he was a few years older.''

"I remember hearing rumors at the time about a coverup," Taps O'Neal said. "Also read a few editorials in newspapers about it. But didn't pay much attention then. You know how some people are always trying to push the conspiracy idea and make things more complex than they really are.''

"Well, it was true," Timothy Cooper said.

"Assuming it wasn't Booth, why would the government officials want to do such a thing?" Wiley asked.

"Two reasons. First, they had to capture or kill their quarry quickly to show the American people they were in control of the situation. Apparently, this was an honest case of mistaken identity. But when Lafayette Baker, the head of the NDP, realized that the real Booth had somehow slipped through his fingers, he seized on James Boyd as a lookalike, pressured some influential people to swear it was Booth, and declared Lincoln's killer dead. Of course there were all kinds of discrepancies. Dr. Mudd testified that the man whose leg he set shaved his mustache while staying overnight at his house, and the body that was later passed off as Booth's had a mustache. Boyd had a leg wound from the war that

111

refused to heal properly and continuously gave him trouble. It was the *right* leg. Booth broke his *left* leg when he jumped to the stage from the president's box." Cooper paused to let this sink in. He leaned back in his chair and puffed on his cigar that had nearly gone out.

"What was the second reason?" I asked.

"Several high-ranking politicians in the administration were plotting to get rid of Lincoln so he could never carry out his merciful reconstruction policy after the war. They wanted to treat the South as a conquered enemy and reap the spoils of war. And several of them were making big profits by smuggling cotton out of the blockaded South and selling it for huge profits in the North. After these men failed to keep Lincoln from being reelected in 1864, they hatched a plot to have him murdered. Booth came to their attention as a possible man for the job, since it was rumored he was behind two kidnap attempts on Lincoln. After the war it was discovered that Booth had been selected by southern leaders to kidnap Lincoln. They wanted to hold him for ransom and force the release of rebel soldiers in northern prisons. With Lincoln out of the way, these radical Republicans in Congress and their dishonest friends could seize control of the government and put their own plan for the conquered South into place. Edwin Stanton, the secretary of war, was probably the worst of the lot." Cooper jerked the cigar out of his mouth and savagely spat a piece of tobacco to one side. "If the man had sported a cloven hoof and a strong smell of sulfur, he couldn't have put me more in mind of Satan. No normal human could be that devious and evil. Anyway, to make a very long story shorter, some of these men enlisted Booth, who was a southern sympathizer, to help them kidnap Lincoln. They convinced him that Lincoln had only bad things planned for the South, and by kidnapping him, he could personally help end the war sooner, as well as making himself a pile of cash."

"I remember when there were a couple of attempts to get to Lincoln a few months before he was shot," O'Neal said.

Cooper nodded. "For various reasons, the attempts failed. Anyway, Booth became more and more obsessed

112

with the idea of getting rid of Lincoln, not for profitable motives but for ideological reasons. At least that's the information I have. I have no way of knowing exactly what was in Booth's mind at the time.''

''Hell, all that was thirteen years ago,'' Wiley said. ''Why are you still chasing the man you think is Booth? Who cares? What difference does it make now? The country thinks he's dead.''

But Cooper was not to be hurried.

''When Boyd's body was passed off as Booth's, I was present as an operative on the deck of the ironclad *Montauk*. Not one of Booth's relatives was called to identify him. I got a look at Dr. May's affidavit concerning the body and heard what he said when he first looked at it. He knew it wasn't Booth, since he had removed a growth from Booth's neck some time before. His written statements have obviously been changed to make it appear that he said Boyd's body was Booth's. But there was a fifty thousand dollar reward for Booth, dead or alive, and that money was divided up among the NDP operatives who had chased Booth, even those who weren't in on the shooting of Boyd. Stanton, Lafe Baker, my boss, Senator Conness, and a lot of other business and government officials both appointed and elected wanted Booth dead so he couldn't be put on trial and tell what he knew about the plot to have Lincoln forcefully removed from office and their part in it. So when they realized that Booth had escaped and the wrong man had been shot, they went ahead with the ruse, hoping that the American people would think Booth dead and quickly forget about the whole thing after that travesty of a trial. Eight so-called conspirators who happened to have been acquainted with Booth were tried and four of them hanged. They hanged the wrong people. But anyway, the public believed it. What choice did they have? If anyone turned up later claiming to be Booth, he would never be believed. And of course, the real Booth would never do such a thing, so the real, high-level conspirators were safe.

''Well, as I said, the money was paid to the Secret Service operatives, not so much as a reward but to buy their silence about the coverup—about five thousand dollars apiece blood money."

"And you took your share, of course," Wiley said.

"No. The whole thing made me sick to my stomach. When they knew I would not close ranks with them, I was forced out of the NDP on some pretext. I eventually went into business in Fairfax. As things began to recover after the war, I did a good business in harness and wagon parts. But I never got over it. I was bitter about being let go from what I hoped would be a career in the Secret Service. I countered my dismissal by trying to expose the fact that booth had escaped, but the official story drowned my voice out completely, even though there were a number of others including newspaper editors who knew of, or strongly suspected, a coverup and said so in print. But I was determined to continue the search on my own. I knew without help it was probably a very long shot, but for the next few years I checked out every rumor of Booth. I heard he was in England, that he had gone to India, changed his name. I heard he was in Australia, was running a saloon in Kansas. Most of my leads, of course, turned out to be false. But I guess I have something of a bulldog quality about me. If I felt there was some merit to a report of a Booth sighting, I'd go and see for myself. I had some old friends in the NDP who kept their eyes and ears open for me. I think they were almost as interested as I was. Anyway, I was so obsessed with this quest for the real Booth I spent nearly all the money I had traveling around and paying informants. I would drop everything on a moment's notice, close my shop and leave town. Finally my business began to suffer and my wife eventually left me. Said I was crazy." He shrugged, grinding out the cigar butt in the ashtray. "Who knows? Maybe she was right."

He stopped speaking and we sat silent for a few moments. Cooper had drawn us all under his spell with this tale of intrigue.

"It's true, whether you want to believe it or not. You're the ones who forced me to tell you what I was doing."

"Even if this man *is* John Wilkes Booth," Taps O'Neal

said thoughtfully, "how do you plan to go about proving it? You know he won't admit to it."

"Hell, you know David St. George is not John Wilkes Booth," Wiley Jenkins snorted before Cooper could answer.

"Have you ever seen Booth?" O'Neal shot back.

"No."

"Then be quiet. I have, when I lived in Maryland. I'm not a critic, but I'd say he was the equal of his brother Edwin and just about as good as his father, Junius. He was an actor of great power and range. You remember I said how good David St. George was when I saw him a couple of weeks ago and how familiar he looked? And that limp he has? It all fits. The man could very well *be* John Wilkes Booth."

Wiley looked at him, then at Timothy Cooper, then back at me and Fin Staghorn. He opened his mouth to say something then shut it and leaned back in his chair.

"I repeat," O'Neal said, speaking to Cooper, "how do you plan to prove this man is Booth?"

"Obviously, I don't have any direct proof, or I would have confronted St. George already. No, even though I'm convinced he's my man and I have been since I saw him act and later got a good close look at him, my only hope is to make him reveal himself."

"How do you plan to do that?"

"I saw Booth act in a play once during the war before he became notorious. And I've made a long study of Booth over the years since, through fellow actors, friends, have read reviews of his plays, studied photographs, talked to bartenders who worked where he hung out. I found out a lot about him. He's moody, a brandy drinker, subject to highs and lows, very emotional. A ladies' man. I guess he has the classic artistic temperament. He knows I'm on to him. The more I can work on him psychologically, the more chance I'll have of making him break and admit to being Booth. He thinks I have some proof, and he's scared. If I keep at it, I'm sure I can make him crack."

"Who's going to believe it if he does?" I asked.

"The Lincoln assassination case is officially closed, and many of the conspirators are either dead or retired.

115

It's old news. But I think I can cause a national sensation and plan to write a book about it that will make people realize they were duped. I will justify this long quest. I'll also make myself a wealthy man and will write my name in the history books.''

"If he is Booth, he wouldn't hesitate to kill a second time to keep you quiet,'' I said.

"I don't think so. I think I know this man well enough to know he'll run and hide before he'll kill. He was young, he was dedicated to a cause, and he thought he was doing right when he shot Lincoln.''

"A desperate man will do 'most anything. He could kill you.''

"Where did you get all these so-called facts about this big plot and coverup?'' Wiley asked, still dubious about Cooper's story.

"You forget I was there and was witness to much of what I told you—a lot of which never got into the press. I was a member of the federal Secret Service, or the NDP as it was then known. I have contacts and ways of tracking down information that the average person knows nothing about.''

"I still don't quite understand how you plan to force this David St. George into admitting he is John Wilkes Booth,'' I said. "If he does break down and admit it to you just to get you to leave him alone, what good is that?''

"He'll be able to verify what I'm virtually sure of now. But most of all, he'll be able to fill in details of his escape and hiding, details of his private life, the background of the plot involving the assassination. He can furnish me with further proofs that I'll need to back up my story when it's published. Many of these people are still living, and not only will reputations be destroyed, but there could be criminal charges brought, unless the statutory limitations have run out.''

"Don't you think he'll be arrested and put on trial? At the very least, his life won't be worth anything once his identity is generally known. Lincoln was loved and revered by many, many people. And a lot of them wouldn't hesitate to make their own justice.''

"I've done a lot of thinking on this in the past few

weeks," the former operative answered. "If nothing else, I may be able to strike a bargain with him to share the profits of his infamy. Of course he'd have to go into hiding again, probably in some other country. But one way or another, I will get the story from him, if I have to threaten him with death myself. I've invested too much of my life in this to let go now."

The set of his jaw told me he was in dead earnest.

"And if we try to stop you?" Wiley asked.

"You can't do it legally, and if I read you right, you won't do it illegally. I thought at first you were a bunch of robbers or killers, but now I'm betting you're not. I've learned to read people—to pick up on small hints. And you aren't killers. You might interfere with me temporarily, but there will be other times and other places. I won't let David St. George out of my sight. I'll follow him wherever he goes. I have the patience and persistence. You don't."

His statement seemed to put a period to the conversation. There seemed nothing more to say.

CHAPTER 13

COOPER took a few swallows of water from the glass in front of him and leaned back in his chair, content to be silent and observe our reactions.

I was ready to go, but Taps, Wiley, and Fin apparently had no such thought in mind. They all had rather vacant, faraway looks on their faces. Wiley seemed intent on a broken thumbnail; Taps was contemplating the bottom of his empty beer mug. The fantastic tale we had just heard had rung the gong of their imaginations. But for all I or any of us knew, it was just that—a fantastic tale without a word of truth in it. The man sitting in front of us could just as easily be an actor. Maybe he thought if he made up a strange enough story, we would believe it had to be true and let him go. But if he were an actor, I had to admit that he was very good. His sincerity was convincing. We had no way of proving or disproving his story. We didn't even know if his name was Timothy Cooper. The business cards in his billfold could have been faked or belonged to another man. But if this man were a phony, then who was he and what did he have to gain by duping us with such a weird story? Was this some elaborate practical joke on Wiley cooked up by Darcy McLeod, perhaps? I shook my head. It was all very confusing. There were just too many possibilities and not enough concrete answers.

"You said you were there when this body of the man

shot in the burning barn was identified as Booth?" Taps finally asked, wording his question carefully.

"Yes," Cooper replied. "The scene is etched on my memory as permanently as acid on metal." His voice sounded sad, almost weary.

"And this was aboard some ship you mentioned?" O'Neal urged.

"The *Montauk*. An ironclad that was used as a prison ship. Moored at the Navy yard at Washington. Security was very tight, and I had to have a special pass signed by both the Secretary of War and the Secretary of the Navy. Everybody who came aboard did. Stanton had named a so-called Identification Commission of a dozen people, none of whom knew Booth very well at all. Most of the people who could have identified him, such as a few of his coconspirators and relatives, including his brother Edwin, were in custody and imprisoned on the *Saugus*, the ironclad moored alongside the *Montauk*. But they were not brought over to identify the body." He paused as the waiter drew near. "You think I might have a brandy—and another cigar?" he queried me in a polite tone. I nodded my assent and he placed the order with the waiter as Wiley reached inside his coat to produce another long, slim cheroot for him. Cooper drew out a match, struck it on the edge of his wooden chair, and soon had the air filled with aromatic smoke.

"Now where was I? Ah, yes. The weather was warm and muggy, and they knew they had to get this identification business over with and officially recorded in a hurry, since the body was already showing signs of deterioration. It was laid out on deck on a long narrow table. A big tarp had been rigged overhead to give some shade. General Holt, Judge Advocate General of the army, was there to record the comments of the witnesses who were paraded up, one by one to look at the body. In one fashion or another, they all said it looked like Booth."

"Who were these witnesses?" Wiley asked.

"Well, I can't remember all of them right now, but they were such people as William Moore, Secretary of War Stanton's personal secretary, some lawyer named Monroe I never heard of, but I think he was related to the captain of the *Montauk,* my chief, Lafayette Baker, and his cousin Luther Baker, Surgeon General Barnes and his assistant, and Charles Dawson, a clerk at the National Hotel where Booth sometimes stayed.''

"How were they supposed to identify a man they didn't know?'' Staghorn asked.

"Mostly by having seen him onstage or by drawings or photographs they had seen of him on Wanted posters. Charles Dawson said he recognized the body as that of the man who had registered at his hotel several times and signed the register as Booth. But the most convincing evidence was a tattoo of the initials JWB on the back of one hand near the wrist. Dawson said he recognized this tattoo as having been on Booth's hand. Of course, it was strictly coincidence, because James William Boyd also had his initials, JWB, tattooed on one of his hands.''

Wiley and I looked at each other. "A bit too coincidental, wouldn't you say?'' Wiley suggested to Cooper.

"Normally, as a detective, I would agree with you,'' Cooper replied, "but this whole episode was so bizarre from the beginning that I almost had to suspend drawing any firm conclusions as more and more of the pieces of the puzzle became known. There were all kinds of coincidences that defied explanation. For example, Boyd was traveling with a blond young man named David Herold with whom he had escaped the federal authorities. The official story at the time was that Herold was helping Booth get away. Actually, it turned out that Booth was traveling with a smuggler friend named Edwin Henson who resembled Herold.''

He paused in his narrative as the waiter brought his brandy and the drinks the rest of us had ordered. Fin placed some coins on the tray, and when the waiter had withdrawn, Cooper continued. "But getting back to the body, most of the Identification Commission knew no more about what Booth actually looked like than I did, and I wasn't a member of the commission. I was just one of the underlings of the NDP who had been ordered aboard to fill out the ranks and supposedly to provide protection for the dignitaries should it be necessary. But you're right. The government realized they needed at least one witness with better credentials if they were to carry off this hoax. So they sent a message to a Dr. John Frederick May to appear. Several months before, this doctor had removed a growth from the back of the neck of a man calling himself John Wilkes Booth. When the good doctor didn't show up right soon after he was summoned, Colonel Lafe Baker himself went to his house and escorted him back to the ship. That's how important they thought this man's testimony was."

He paused to sip the brandy.

"What did Dr. May have to say when he saw the body?" Wiley urged as Cooper took his time getting back into the story.

Cooper stared off into space for a few seconds then gave a short grunt of derisive laughter. "Well, the first thing they did was to ask him how he had known Booth and under what circumstances. He told them it had been about eighteen months to two years before that he had removed a neck tumor from a man who came to his office identifying himself as the actor Booth. But the incision had been torn open before it healed, and the man had returned to have it stitched again. Only after Dr. May had answered these questions did Surgeon General Barnes have the covering taken off the corpse's face."

"And . . . ?"

"He immediately said something to the effect that the body bore no resemblance at all to the man he had treated. Then he looked around at all the disapproving stares he was getting and took another, closer look at the body. I think he felt the pressure that was being put on him by all those high officials of government. They were in no mood for any contradictory answers. Surgeon Barnes asked him to describe the scar on Booth's neck, and Dr. May complied. Then Barnes said he had described the scar perfectly. But"—and here Timothy Cooper leaned forward and stabbed his smoking cigar at us for emphasis—"not once did Dr. May examine the back of that neck to see if the scar he had described was there. And besides, the bullet that killed Boyd had passed through his neck, severing his spine. The body had not been cleaned up, and there was dried blood caked all around the neck. Dr. May did have the body propped up

121

into a sitting position. He made some remark that this body looked much older and more freckled than the man he had treated. He said he didn't think the man he had operated on had been at all freckled. He finally admitted that the features did resemble those of Booth but added something to the effect that he had never in his years of practice seen such a change in a human as the difference in the man he had treated and the yellowing corpse before him. And he mentioned that the *right* leg was very swollen and turning black from a fracture of one of the long bones. And as I said earlier, Booth had broken his *left* leg when he leaped to the stage from the president's box.''

"How old were Booth and Boyd?''

"Booth was twenty-seven at the time and had smooth, blemish-free ivory skin that he was very proud of. Boyd was forty-three, had reddish-brown hair and skin that tended to be freckled. Also, Dr. Samuel Mudd had testified earlier that Booth shaved off his mustache the night he spent at his house. And the corpse I saw had a long, untrimmed mustache that was even curling up its nose.'' He leaned back and sipped at the brandy. "Later I was able to get a look at the notes that General Holt made of the witnesses' remarks. Some of Dr. May's statements had been inked out and other words inserted above or between them to make it appear that he had had no doubt about the corpse being that of John Wilkes Booth. And of course, it was the edited version that was released to the press and introduced at the trial.''

"Didn't Dr. May ever protest this?''

Cooper shrugged. "Not that I know of. He was probably glad to be off the hook. If he had put up a squawk about it or gone to the press with an entirely different story, he probably would have wound up on trial for perjury or been sentenced to prison on Dry Tortugas in the Gulf of Mexico like Dr. Mudd was just for treating a stranger with a broken leg.

"Oh, I forgot to mention that one of the members of the Identification Commission was a photographer named Alexander Gardner. He was told to make only one exposure of the body. One of Secretary Stanton's men named James Wardell was with him at all times to make sure he carried out orders. As soon as the plate was exposed, Wardell escorted Gardner off the *Montauk* to a nearby darkroom. I never saw the photograph but later heard through a friend in the Secret Service who knew Wardell that the plate was confiscated and wound up in Secretary Stanton's possession. Interestingly enough, photographer Gardner's assistant, who was also a member of the ID commission, was Timothy O'Sullivan—the same man who was a famous photographer during the war and has recently been making quite a reputation for himself as a photographer in the western part of the country.''

He paused again to fish another match out of his side coat pocket and relight his cigar that had gone out. Even a good cigar relighted more than once tends to lose its fine aroma, but Cooper didn't seem to mind the rank odor as he puffed it back to life. He took his time and savored the taste of the brandy. He may have been a man dedicated to a cause, but he was also a man who had obviously not lost an appreciation of fine food and drink.

I was no longer in any hurry to leave. I, too, had been drawn under his spell; I was standing with him on the hot deck of the ironclad that sultry day in April 1865 viewing the corpse of the man who might or might not have been John Wilkes Booth. I could see the hard faces of those government officials who were conducting the process of identification. I could feel the pressure on the witnesses to say the right thing.

"Even if the body was definitely not that of Booth, how does anybody know for sure he got away? After all, he hasn't shown up in thirteen years." This from Fin Staghorn. "Weren't there other people shot?"

"Oh, definitely. The rewards finally totaled about three hundred thousand dollars, and this brought out a frenzy of amateur bounty hunters. I'm glad I wasn't slim, dark-haired, and wearing a mustache at that time." He chuckled dryly. "Several innocent Booth lookalikes were shot, including a couple of civilians named Boyle and Watson. The NDP took care of disposing of their bodies. Even an NDP operative named O'Dwyer was accidentally shot by one of our own NDP detectives. Of course, this was all hushed up, and no one was prosecuted.''

"Then how do you know that one of these so-called lookalikes wasn't the real Booth?"

"Because these men were immediately identified correctly by relatives as soon as they were shot. But there were lots of other reasons to indicate that Booth really got away. I guess you remember that Booth's diary was found."

"I read about it at the time."

"Right. And this diary, of course, gave details of Booth's activities and his shooting of Lincoln as well as his movements later. But it also named names of high officials in Lincoln's cabinet, Edwin Stanton, several senators, investors, bankers, various politicians. Booth mentions several of them as plotting with him to kidnap Lincoln, mentions the arrangement of secret passwords among them, the payment to Booth of fifty thousand dollars by Jacob Thompson with instructions to give fifteen thousand dollars of that to Senator Conness, the agreement of payment of another twenty thousand dollars to be left for Booth in a sealed envelope at the home of a Senator Wade. Booth mentions meeting and talking to my boss, Lafayette Baker, chief of the NDP, Jay Cooke the financier, and others. So you can see why all these bigwigs were frantic to have Booth silenced one way or another."

"How come these men weren't arrested and tried for treason?" I interrupted.

"Ah, men with that much power and influence have ways of protecting themselves. This diary was sent by the two detectives who found it to Lafe Baker, who turned it over to Edwin Stanton. He promptly locked it up in his safe, and when he showed it to a congressional investigating committee two years later, eighteen pages had mysteriously been torn out of it. Stanton testified under oath that the pages were missing when he received the diary. Those pages haven't been seen since."

"Then how did you know what those pages contained?"

"I saw that diary before it ever got to Lafe Baker. I was coming down the Potomac on the *Jenny B* with Luther Potter and two other detectives to join the hunt for Booth when we were met at the dock at Belle Plain by Luther's brother, Andrew, and several NDP opera-

124

tives who had the diary. Several of us read it. Luther stayed aboard and took it back up the river to Washington and delivered it to Baker." He took a long sip of his brandy, leaned back, and crossed his legs.

"I believe that was one reason I was forced out of the NDP."

"Why's that?"

"I wasn't one of the inner clique in the NDP. There were the Potter brothers and Luther Baker, cousin of our chief, Lafayette Baker. There was a lot of patronage and nepotism in the early days of the Secret Service. Anyway, I was always considered something of an outsider. When they realized I knew what was in that diary, they were afraid I would say something in public about it, especially since I refused my share of the reward money. So they had to devise some pretext about me being incompetent and insubordinate to force me out of the service. That way, if I ever made public what I'd read, who would believe a disgruntled former operative who'd been fired for misconduct and obviously discredited?"

"I see what you mean."

"Where was the diary found? And how do you think Booth got away?" I asked, mainly to test his version against what I recalled reading years before by some editorial writers who were dissatisfied with the official story of Booth's shooting at the Garrett tobacco barn. But even as I formed the question, I was having trouble dredging up the particulars from the dust and cobwebs of a cluttered memory.

"The way we reconstructed it later, when Booth and Henson left Dr. Mudd's house the day after the leg was set, they headed on horseback for Zekiah Swamp, about a dozen miles away. This swamp spreads several miles along the backwaters of the Potomac River. It's damn near impenetrable, with dense undergrowth, tangled vines, waist-deep stagnant water, quicksand, snakes, mosquitoes. In short, a good place to get lost. Most folks didn't know it, but there were a few free Negroes living in Zekiah Swamp. Their log cabins were scattered around on some of the higher ground. Well, a Negro man later reported guiding two white men through the swamp to the home of a southern sympathizer Booth knew about, named Cox. They arrived at Cox's house, called Rich Hill, before daylight, and Cox hid the two men about two miles from his home in some dense growth. The next day he notified his stepbrother, Tom Jones, who lived nearby and asked him to see about getting Booth and Henson across the Potomac River into Virginia. Jones had been active during the war rowing various fugitives across the river to southern soil. Booth was apparently writing up his diary while he was lying hidden in the woods, being supplied with food and blankets by Cox and Jones.

"We later pieced together that the NDP operatives, who were crisscrossing the general area around Port Tobacco at the time, were almost constantly within a few miles of Booth and Henson.

"Jones sold Booth and Henson a small, flat-bottomed boat and showed them where to cross one dark night when the searchers were not in the immediate area. But the tidal current swept them back to the Maryland shore. Booth couldn't help row because of the inflamed condition of his leg. Henson did the rowing. They did get across the next night, Friday, exactly one week after the assassination. Jones had . . ."

"How do you know all these details?" Wiley interrupted.

"The diary and later questioning of the people who aided Booth," Cooper replied shortly. "But as I was saying, Tom Jones had told them to contact a widow on the other side named Quesenberry. They found her house, with Booth hobbling on a makeshift crutch, and she took them in for the night. An in-law of Jones's met them at the widow's and passed them on to another southern sympathizer the next day. Then, for some unknown reason, they doubled back and camped in some thick growth along Gambo Creek that flows north into the Potomac. Then, apparently, something scared them off early Sunday morning and they disappeared, leaving behind them at their campsite the diary, two empty quart brandy bottles, a billfold with over two thousand dollars Union cash, a pistol, a compass, some letters of credit on Canadian banks, and some pictures of six

126

pretty young ladies. An Indian scout with the detectives actually found the stuff.''

''They must have been in a mighty big hurry if they left all that behind.''

Cooper nodded. ''Likely drunk, too, judging from the two quart brandy bottles. Booth was prob'ly trying to dull the pain in that leg. I'd say they had a mighty big scare, in any case. Likely they heard somebody coming. No way to know—until I get the details from Booth himself—that St. George fella.'' He smiled slightly, apparently at the thought of his quarry so near. ''Or Booth, being a very melodramatic fella and wanting to keep his name in the limelight or to justify his actions, maybe left the diary on purpose to savor the big stink it would cause when it was made public.'' Then he shook his head. ''But I can't see him leavin' all that money behind and his letters of credit on those Canadian banks. Way I figure, it had to be somethin' scared 'em off in a hurry. Anyway, the trail begins to fade from there. We later talked to the Negro ferryman who remembered taking two men across the Rappahannock from Port Conway to Port Royal. It's thought that they met Booth's former Negro valet, Henry Johnson, somewhere along the way, who supplied them with horses. Weeks and even months later, after the rest of the country thought Booth dead, Lafe Baker had a few of his trusted men still scouring the eastern part of the country, trying to pick up the trail of Booth. Booth or his accomplices were supposedly seen in the railway station in Philadelphia and later in New York. But no one knows for sure.'' He shrugged, taking another long sip of his brandy.

Silence ensued for a minute or two as we all digested this part of his story. Some late customers, two well-dressed couples, came in and were seated at the far end of the restaurant.

''How did James Boyd and David Herold end up at the Garretts' farm?'' Staghorn asked.

''David Herold had been arrested early as a suspected conspirator and forced to help the NDP in their search for Booth in southern Maryland. While riding that way, the NDP encountered the freed Captain Boyd, who was allegedly on some spy mission for the government and riding toward Mexico. He was forced to come along and lend his experience as a former undercover agent. It was thought that Boyd, as a Tennessean and former Confederate, would have better luck gaining the confidence and getting information from the southern sympathizers they questioned along the way. He and Herold were to make up some story that they were trying to find Booth in order to help him. But this didn't work too well. They almost got themselves shot a time or two, so Boyd and Herold were able to escape one night while the detectives were asleep. They rode on south and came to the Garretts' farm in northern Virginia, where they stopped to ask if they could spend the night. The two of them had camped out only a few miles from Booth and Henson and crossed the Potomac within twenty-four hours of the real fugitives. A special force of twenty-five cavalrymen headed by Lieutenant Doherty and Luther Baker, Lafe's cousin, had been sent south from Washington by Lafe Baker. This force, picking up the trail of the pair, thought they were on the trail of Booth and Henson, especially since witnesses told them one of the men had a bad leg—Boyd's old leg wound that was acting up again. Anyway, after about two days straight in the saddle, this force finally caught up with the pair during the night at Garrett's farm, where Boyd and Herold were sleeping in the barn. And . . . well, you know the rest. . . ."

"What about this David Herold?" Taps asked. "Didn't he know Booth?"

"A couple of years later, Lieutenant Doherty stated that Herold, when he surrendered and came out of the barn before the fatal shooting, asked why cavalry was after them. Herold seemed amazed when Doherty told him the other man was Booth. Herold told him it was James W. Boyd. And David Herold, even though he was rather dull-witted, certainly should have known, since he was in on the Lincoln kidnap plot earlier with Booth.

"When Stanton found out the wrong man had been shot, he made sure Herold was kept in isolation until the military conspiracy trial so Herold couldn't tell anyone that the man who had been shot in the Garrett barn wasn't Booth. In fact, all the prisoners were forced to wear inch-thick padded hoods that covered their entire heads except for the mouth and nose, in addition to arm and leg irons. Stanton was making sure they were incommunicado.''

"I remember seeing drawings of those hoods in some magazines," Staghorn remarked.

"Of course, Herold was never allowed to speak in court and was then convicted and hanged with the others, permanently sealing his lips.''

"If this body was really Captain James Boyd, the spy, wouldn't some of his kin have known him?''

"Boyd's wife was dead, and his kids in Tennessee were farmed out to various relatives. He had been gone from home during most of the war, and since he had been in various prisons and was working undercover, none of his people really knew where he was—or probably even suspected that this body could have been Boyd's.''

"What happened to the body?'' Staghorn wanted to know.

"Lafe Baker had it secretly buried at night beneath the stone floor of the old army arsenal along the river below Washington City. Baker revealed the location in a book he wrote and published in 1867.''

"Is it still there?''

"No. Booth's family petitioned the government to let them have it. And finally, in 1869, the body was disinterred for reburial in the family plot in Baltimore.''

"Seems like that would have been a good time for the family to settle this identity business once and for all,'' I said.

"They took a brief look at it, I understand, but naturally, it had deteriorated considerably, and Booth's mother and brothers seemed satisfied that it was John Wilkes. At least they never publicly questioned it. Maybe they were just tired of the whole thing and wanted to get on with their lives. You can imagine the pain and embarrassment it caused the Booth family. And older brother Edwin was and is one of the most famous actors in the country.

"Anyway, now that I've finally, after all these years, got Booth in my sights, I intend to pressure him until he breaks. I've got him pegged as emotionally unstable. Maybe he inherited a streak of madness. I've heard his old man, Junius Brutus, was as crazy as a loon. But the old boy could act. And I knew Wilkes couldn't stay away from the stage indefinitely. I heard that he acted under an assumed name in London a few years ago, and I went there in 1871 trying to track him down, but couldn't. Once I break him, maybe I can somehow get the Booth family to let me exhume that body in Baltimore to add proof to my case. Wilkes always had a weakness for good-looking women, so maybe I can work on him through this Darcy McLeod he seems to have cottoned to."

"Over my dead body you will!" Wiley gritted in a low voice.

Cooper shrugged, seemingly unconcerned with the threat.

"Let's go," I said, getting up and reaching for my billfold to pay for the meal.

"Are we just going to leave him here?" Wiley asked, apparently frustrated.

"What would you suggest?" Taps O'Neal asked.

"Well, at least we know what's going on. And forewarned is forearmed," Wiley said, apparently trying to save face.

"May I have my gun back?" Cooper asked, not moving to leave the table in the nearly empty restaurant.

"Oh yes." I reached into my coat pocket and drew out the short .38. "You won't mind if I unload it. Just a precaution."

I thumbed open the loading gate and dropped the stubby cartridges one by one into my palm. Then I handed him the shells and weapon separately.

As the four of us walked out, Cooper still sat at the littered table, staring at nothing.

CHAPTER 14

GETTING involved in the problems and affairs of others is the best way I know to bring down trouble on one's own head. But keeping my life uncomplicated was not one of the things I did best. The things in a man's life he can control and the things he cannot control are usually bound up in a complicated, inseparable weave. I had thrown in my lot with Asa Carlyle in an effort to save his company by winning the upcoming race. In this effort I had braced myself for anything that might come along. So far, I reflected, the last few weeks of my life, since meeting him in San Francisco, had been about as much under my control as if I had been astraddle a log of douglas fir shooting wildly down a mile-long flume. All I could do was hang on and ride it out to the bottom.

And now another strange situation had arisen over which I had no control. I had gotten myself involved at the behest of Wiley and Darcy McLeod by temporarily abducting Timothy Cooper. It was not directly my problem, but still, a feeling of helplessness and uncertainty was tugging at the back of my mind the next morning as Wiley and I saw Fin and Taps off on the early ferry for home. Then the two of us set out to report the Cooper story to Darcy McLeod at her hotel.

I had met the girl only once and so was totally unprepared for her reaction. When Wiley had summarized our confrontation with Cooper, she threw back her head and laughed, a genuine, musical sound that filled the room.

"Is that all this is about?" she said. "Why don't we just have the sheriff or the police or whatever kind of law they have in this territory just arrest this man? He's obviously deranged." Then her smile disappeared and a slight furrow appeared between her eyebrows. "He may even be a dangerous lunatic."

I was confused and a little embarrassed. We had come here with a serious story, and she believed none of it. I began to wonder myself if we had been taken in. In the cold light of day, and without Cooper himself to enhance it with convincing details, the story did seem somewhat ridiculous.

"You don't think there's a chance his story could be true?" Wiley ventured.

She shook her head, and the sunlight streaming in through the front window shimmered on the gold of her hair. "Of course not." She laughed. "How could you even *think* such a thing?"

Wiley, obviously not wanting to contradict her but still believing Cooper's story, hung his head and didn't reply.

"I was worried about nothing," she went on. "I'd better tell David right away. He'll be relieved."

Wiley and I glanced at each other.

"You may not need to tell him."

"Why?"

"It could be he already knows."

She looked seriously at both of us. "You actually believe that David is Booth, don't you?"

"Darcy, how well do you know David St. George?"

She looked offended. "Well, I've certainly known him longer than I've known you, Wiley Jenkins. If I'm that poor a judge of people, maybe I was also mistaken about *you*."

"Miss McLeod, we're not saying he *is* John Wilkes Booth. We just want you to consider the possibility. After all, David St. George *is* an actor, and a good one," I said. "You may not really know him at all."

She acknowledged this with a nod of her head. "I plan to tell him what you found out, anyway. What can it hurt? This Cooper will eventually tell him, I'm sure. I think the man is a lunatic, and I want David to be aware

132

of what he's trying to do, especially if he can't be arrested until he does something drastic.''

"Fair enough. We'll just leave it at that for now and see what develops," Wiley said. "Now how about it if we treat you to a late breakfast?"

For the five weeks following our encounter with Timothy Cooper, I not only worked as a common laborer in the shipyard with Wiley but also worked on a one-man publicity campaign for the race by inserting carefully worded ads in the Seattle newspaper and occasionally wired a short item to one of the San Francisco papers. I even shot off a few things to my old paper *The Chicago Times-Herald* and to the *St. Louis Post-Dispatch*. Carlyle could not spare much money for this effort, so occasionally I used my own money or disguised the ad as a news item that was free on a slow news day.

Sunday September 8 had tentatively been agreed upon for the start of the race. It was getting well on past mid-July, and as yet the race had not really taken hold of the public fancy.

"I've been in touch with Rust by telegraph. Even took a trip up to Port Townsend about ten days ago to see him in person. He still seems cool to the whole idea of this race, just as he did at that meeting in San Francisco. He didn't seem interested in putting out any publicity about it. I believe that his company looks on this as really beneath their dignity, as just another business venture and the less said about it the better.''

Asa Carlyle seemed to have aged since I had met him. The stress was etching deeper lines in his forehead and his lean cheeks. I knew he was in debt, and he stood in imminent peril of losing everything he had worked for most of his adult life.

The mill had been nearly rebuilt since the fire and was back in operation. The new schooner, still nameless, was also nearing completion. There was little or nothing for Wiley and me to do now except watch as the finishing touches were put on the interior of the after cabins. The launching was probably less than a week away. The masts had been stepped, the rigging set up, but specially made sails had not yet arrived from Maine. And this was another concern of Carlyle's. He had taken to roaming his property, showing up at odd hours at the mill or the shipyard, sometimes talking to one of the workmen, sometimes silent and preoccupied. Now was one of those times. He had walked up to us while Wiley and I had been finishing our lunch out in the sunshine, sitting on a big old vine-covered stump near the shipyard.

"Rust was pretty evasive when I asked him about their preparations for this race," Carlyle was saying. "Not that there's much I can do about it, but I'd like to know more details of what we'll be up against. I want to know what ship they'll be using. That biggest barkentine of theirs can carry up to a million board feet of lumber." He paused and squinted out toward the harbor where the water sparkled in the bright noonday sun.

"Since you two don't have much to do right now, I'd like you to run up to Port Townsend and mingle with the mill hands and some of the Rust and Barrett workers during their off-hours. Port Townsend is a port of entry for the sound, and there are lots of sailors in and out of there constantly, so you won't be noticed. Find out what you can but don't be conspicuous. I'll send Fin Staghorn with you. I don't have anything else for him right now, and he's familiar with Port Townsend."

Wiley grinned. "Sounds like fun to me."

"It may sound like fun, but it's very serious to me," Asa Carlyle said, still looking grave.

"Don't worry," Wiley assured him, "we'll do a good job for you. When I said fun, I meant it will be interesting and exciting after a few weeks of doing some real work around here."

Thinking back on it a few days later, *fun* was definitely not a word I would have used to describe our sojourn in Port Townsend.

But just now I was looking forward to a change of pace and scenery. Staghorn had been to Port Townsend previously, but Wiley and I had never been closer than when we were towed past it some weeks earlier on the damaged *J. W. Brandon*. The three of us took the next steamer north. It was an all-day trip, and we didn't disembark until late afternoon, just an hour or so before the steam whistle blasted the end of the workday for the mill workers at the Rust and Barrett sawmill.

As we stepped off the ferry at the long pier of Port Townsend, I was impressed by the size and activity of the place. Even making allowances for the fact that I had probably grown used to the small, one-industry town of Port Gamble, Port Townsend looked like a burgeoning city by comparison. The lower Port Townsend that first greeted my eyes was spread out in a long, rather narrow flat strip of land at the base of a bluff.

"The mill and the local offices of the Rust and Barrett Company are located up above," Fin Staghorn said, orienting us to the layout of the place. "That's the respectable part of Port Townsend. The red-light district and every sort of dive and gambling hole you can think of is located down here."

"Sounds similar to Natchez," Wiley remarked.

"Looks fairly busy for this time of day," I said as we walked off the long pier with the dozen or so other disembarking passengers.

"There are some ships in port, but this is nothing. Things will really liven up after dark."

After a quick walking tour of the lower town, during which we were solicited by several prostitutes, Fin led us on a steep climb up the bluff to the upper town. It was a totally different community. The quiet, tree-shaded streets were lined with modest houses punctuated with church spires every few blocks. The wealth of this community was evidenced by the multistoried wooden structures with cornices and porches decorated with gingerbread, many of them surrounded by large yards and wrought-iron picket fences.

"The homes of the sea captains and the Rust and Barrett executives," Fin explained.

"Looks like there's plenty of money to be made in shipping and in lumber," Wiley observed.

"Only if you're at the top of the heap," Fin replied. "The loggers and mill hands and sailors are the ones who provide all this for the few lucky ones who were born at the top or somehow managed to claw their way up. Most of the top men in the Rust and Barrett organization were born into wealthy families who made their money in shipbuilding and lumber in New England."

"Can't say that Asa Carlyle was born with a silver spoon in his mouth," I said.

"No, just a lot of pride and determination."

"Well, it's about time he had a little luck to go along with it," Wiley remarked.

On the outskirts of the picturesque little town was the big company sawmill that was humming like a beehive. At first glance there appeared to be no economic problems here. The look of wealth and prosperity was everywhere. And farther to the southwest, beyond the mill complex, rose thick stands of giant conifers. The supply looked endless. If this had been the only millsite that Rust and Barrett owned, it would have been enough to make them a prosperous company. But they had several other sites on the sound that were capable of producing nearly as much lumber as this one. It was no wonder the marketplace could not absorb all the sawed timber that could be turned out without the company's shipping a considerable amount of it to Australia or the Sandwich Islands or cutting back on production, as the whole industry was now being forced to do.

Since it was now nearly six o'clock and we hadn't eaten since daylight, we went looking for a restaurant. By the time we found one and had finished our supper, the workday had ended for the mill hands. And as we started back down toward the lower part of town near the waterfront, many of the young loggers and mill hands were headed that way, too. As the light of the westering sun slanted across the water and the long summer evening came on, I counted seven ships lying at anchor in the harbor.

Saloon hopping was not something I enjoyed, but it was about what this assignment amounted to. We started with the watering holes we noticed most of the workmen frequenting.

"Take it easy on the drinks," I cautioned Wiley as we pushed through the batwing doors of the first saloon. "We've got a long night ahead of us and we need to stay alert."

He gave me a sour look. "How many times have I

heard that from you in the past couple of years?" he asked only half-jokingly. "Why did I team up with someone who thinks he's my guardian angel or my father?"

I shrugged and replied lightly, "Someone has to keep track of you, or you get carried away. Sometimes don't know when to quit." I noticed the blackjack and poker tables in the room as we entered. "As long as I'm lecturing, if you get into any card games, be cautious. We're here to gather information, not to lose money or get into any scrapes."

"Yes, Daddy, I'll be careful."

I knew Wiley was irritated, but I also knew he had a tendency to get a little wild unless he had someone close by to keep him in check.

We edged up to the bar and ordered beer. I could see the place was already beginning to fill up, mostly with men in work clothes.

"Might be a better idea if we split up," Fin Staghorn suggested. "We could cover a lot more territory in less time. And there are plenty of dives to cover. It will probably take some time to get into some casual conversations to see what we can find out."

Much as I disliked the idea of leaving Wiley alone, I agreed. The early evening would be no problem; it was later on that he might succumb to the alcoholic camaraderie of these men or the lure of the gambling tables.

"There are a lot of saloons down here," Fin said in a low voice to us as we leaned on the bar. "Believe it or not, this is one of the higher-class places, so you can imagine what some of the dives are like along this waterfront. Why don't we each take a different place along this street and mingle for two or three hours. We can meet at the Blue Duck on Water Street about ten-thirty and compare notes. Watch your back and don't show too much gold," he warned us as Wiley and I headed for the door.

"Don't worry. I haven't got that much gold." Wiley grinned.

I managed to cover two different saloons in the first two hours—and had almost no luck. The men I sat in with at the poker table either didn't work for Rust and Barrett or wanted to concentrate on the cards rather than what they had been doing all day. One garrulous old man I did get to talk by plying him with free drinks turned out to be a cleanup man at the mill who knew little or nothing about the plans of the company or the upcoming race.

By ten o'clock some of the family men had gone home, and some of the others had settled into some serious gambling or drinking. Just by chance I managed to overhear two men talking at the bar near me and I lent an attentive ear.

"The *Frances Darby* is a right scummy old scow, and I wouldn't be caught dead on her," one man with a pronounced British or Australian dialect was saying. I glanced sideways at the speaker, who was quite obviously a sailor, judging from his clothes. The man he was talking to was on the far side, and I couldn't see him well, but his voice told me he was American.

"Her bottom's covered with barnacles and sea growth all right," the American conceded. "But she's okay for these short coasting runs. If she was making a long sea passage, it'd be different. Probably slow ya down by days or weeks. We generally have enough wind off this coast, so it doesn't make a nickel's worth of difference."

"Must be a mighty cheap owner who won't haul 'er out for a good cleanin'."

"Oh, Rust and Barrett has the money, all right," the American replied. "It's just that things are in a slump right now. And besides, I'm told by some of the outfitters that the bosses are sinking a bundle into refitting the *Nellie Barrett* for a big race coming up in a month or so."

My ears perked up even more, and I hunched over my beer mug and turned my head slightly to catch the words a little clearer over the gabble in the room behind me.

"What race is that?" the foreigner was asking.

"She's gonna be a corker!" the American replied. "Our ship—the Rust and Barrett ship, that is—pitted against some little schooner from a mill down at Port Gamble. The two of 'em are gonna race, fully loaded with lumber, from Cape Flattery down to San Francisco. The winner gets a big contract to haul a lot of lumber for the next few years. Don't know all the details, but it's worth a bundle o'money and will save a lot o'jobs."

"Why, that won't be much of a race. I saw the *Nellie Barrett* out there on the ways when we dropped our hook. She's a barkentine, isn't she?"

"Right."

"And you're racing a *little* schooner, you say. How little?"

"Less than a hundred feet on deck, I'm told."

"Huh! I'd like to have a few quid on the *Nellie Barrett* myself, but the betting won't be too brisk on that match, I'm afraid. You'll waltz off and leave them."

"I hope so. Don't know why the Carlyle company is even bothering. And they're even building a special ship—or boat, I should say—just for this." He laughed. "Oh, I forgot to mention—the *Nellie Barrett* is a barkentine, right enough, but we're reriggin' her as a schooner—a little easier to maneuver and all that. They've even changed her name to the *Osprey*." He tipped up his drink.

"You don't mean it?" The tone was horrified.

I glanced sideways again. The American set his empty glass down. "Mean what?"

"That you changed her name."

"I didn't change it. The bosses did. But I like it. Sounds a helluva lot better than *Nellie Barrett*."

"Then if you're asailin' aboard of 'er, you'd best hope she's far and away a better ship, 'cause Lady Luck won't be one of your shipmates."

"How do ya figger that?"

"Everybody knows that changin' a vessel's name is bad luck."

The American gave a short laugh. "I'm glad I'm not a deepwater man. I might start believin' all them superstitions."

The foreigner nodded somberly. "Just you wait. Mark my words. She'll never have another bit o'luck until she's a rottin' hulk."

They ordered a refill and their conversation drifted into other subjects. I started toward the door, congratulating myself on my good fortune in learning as much as I had.

I only wished they had discussed the sails the converted schooner was to have.

It was almost eleven o'clock by the time I found the Blue Duck saloon. It was obviously a saloon that catered to the visiting seamen. I found Fin Staghorn waiting at the bar, but Wiley was nowhere to be seen.

"I was here right on time and I haven't seen him," Fin answered my query.

The Blue Duck was jammed with visiting sailors, and two bartenders were kept jumping to keep their thirsty patrons supplied. But I finally got the attention of one of them, a burly, barrel-chested man.

"Yeah. Yeah. I recollect a man like that. He was here maybe an hour or so ago. Said if two guys came looking for him, he was going to a couple o'places up the pier."

Before I could ask him anything else, someone yelled above the general bedlam for a fresh drink, and the barkeep went back to work.

As Fin and I left and started a quick search of the three or four saloons built out along the edge of the long pier, I briefed him on what I had learned about the Rust and Barrett entry in the race.

"Hmmm . . . So they're converting a barkentine into a schooner. Wonder how much sail area the new ship'll have by comparison? I assume she'll be using tops'ls."

I was glad I wasn't alone when we entered the first saloon we came to. Although it was not crowded, the men who were playing cards and drinking were as hard-looking a group of hardcases as I had ever seen in any boomtown on the frontier. A half-dozen women I took to be prostitutes were dancing with some of the customers to the wheezing of an accordion. Even though we were dressed in old work clothes and threadbare wool jackets to blend in, we drew stares from the patrons of this place. We didn't stay. A quick look around told us Wiley was not there.

The second place was almost a copy of the first. As we approached the third and last saloon, whose front half rested on the pier and back half was supported on long pilings that were driven into the bottom of the bay, I was becoming very concerned about Wiley. I said nothing to Fin, but I had a strange feeling in my stomach. This last emporium advertised itself to the world of incoming sailors as the Union Arms. The name was painted in large red-and-silver letters over the peeling logo of crossed muskets and the national flag. It was a place I would have hesitated to enter alone.

The draft of the door swinging inward as we entered barely stirred the heavy layer of tobacco smoke that hung just below the ceiling. A bar ran along one side of the room, and about a dozen men were in the place, some playing cards by the light of the smoky coal-oil lamps, some drinking and talking at the bar and the tables, and one or two asleep or passed out on their arms.

At first glance they all appeared to be loggers or sailors, and Wiley was not among them. We took a few steps into the dim, smoky atmosphere and slid up to the end of the bar. We generated only a few curious stares. The bartender was a big, beefy red-faced individual. He disengaged himself from a conversation with two men leaning on the bar and came toward us.

"What'll it be, gents?" He was hard-eyed, suspicious.

"Beer," I replied automatically, buying time to scrutinize the place. I didn't know what else to do. This was the last saloon on the pier, and Wiley was not in any of them. If he had come out along this pier, there was hardly any way we could have missed him.

As the bartender was drawing two mugs from a wooden keg, Fin nudged me and pointed.

"What?" I looked again. Then I saw what he was looking at. A green-topped card table, empty except for some glasses and scattered cards. Lying atop the green felt cloth was Wiley's hat! I nodded that I had seen.

The bartender slid our beer in front of us, and I put down a silver quarter. We took our mugs in hand and turned to lean our backs against the bar, surveying the room again. Wiley wasn't there, in a chair, on the floor, asleep or drunk.

"Reckon we should ask the bartender if he knows anything?"

Fin shook his head. "I think Wiley may be around here somewhere."

"Yeah. He wouldn't leave voluntarily without his

hat. If he was so drunk he forgot his hat, he would have been too drunk to walk out of here."

"But where could he be?" Fin asked quietly.

My gaze swung around the room again and stopped at a closed door, evidently leading to a back room.

The hour was late, well after midnight. The room was ominously quiet, the only sounds being the low murmur of voices and the clicking of poker chips.

While we stood there pondering our next move, I heard several loud thumps, as if someone were stomping a bootheel on the hollow wooden floor. It sounded almost as if someone were knocking. But no one had moved, and no one paid the slightest attention.

"Somebody pounding on the door?" I asked the bartender.

The big man looked up irritably. "Naw. It's none o'your concern."

Suddenly Fin grabbed my elbow and whispered fiercely in my ear, "The back room. Wiley's in the back room. I know that sound!"

CHAPTER 15

"LET'S go!" I had my gun out and was across the room in four or five fast strides. Fin was right behind me as I flung open the flimsy wooden door. My momentum carried me into a fat man leaning over an open trapdoor. With a wild yell he lost his balance and went down head-first through the hole in the floor. There was a crashing and cursing from below. But my attention swung to another man in the room. I caught a glimpse of a short, thickset body in a checkered jacket topped by a derby hat and a cigar. The man was reaching inside his coat as I lunged for him. But I tripped over a prostrate form on the floor. As I went down, twisting away from the open trapdoor, I knew the man with the cigar would have a gun out before I could recover.

But I hadn't reckoned on Fin Staghorn. I heard a thunk like the sound of a club hitting a watermelon, and the short man hit the wooden wall with a jarring crash, sliding down on his side, dazed. I untangled myself from the inert form on the floor. It was Wiley. I leaned over the hole. A whaleboat was positioned directly beneath, about ten feet down. A man in the stern was holding a torch aloft that lit up the scene and reflected off the black waters of the bay and the barnacle-encrusted pilings that supported the back room of the saloon. Four startled faces stared up at us—a man in the stern, one in the bow, and two sailors at a pair of oars amidships. Around them sprawled a tangle of bodies, among them the fat man I had knocked through the hole. He wasn't moving. Either unconscious or maybe dead from a broken neck.

"What the hell's going on up there?" the man with the torch yelled. "Your runner said you had one for us."

"Right you are!" Fin yelled back. "Got him right here." He jumped back from the opening and motioned for me to grab the shoulders of the dazed man in the checked jacket. I nodded and holstered my borrowed Colt as I caught his notion. I shoved Wiley out of the way, and we dragged the heavy man toward the trapdoor. "Give these damn crimps a taste of their own medicine," Fin grunted as we got him to the edge. Then Fin stood up and, with a heavy shove of his boot, pushed the stocky form out. "Bon voyage!"

I couldn't suppress a grin at the yelling and cursing that came up from the boat underneath. But as I turned around, the bartender was standing in the open doorway with a double-barreled shotgun in his hands.

I jumped to one side and Fin to the other. The big man, unable to cover us both at once, hesitated slightly, the shotgun wavering between us. His indecision was his undoing. As he swung the double barrels toward Fin, I jumped him from the side, rapping him soundly on the side of the head with the barrel of my borrowed Colt. He collapsed sideways, both charges of buckshot exploding with a deafening roar, tearing splinters from the floor a few feet away.

"Quick! Get Wiley!"

Fin scooped his limp form from the floor by the waist and flung him over his shoulder in one motion. I led the way back through the saloon and covered Fin as he carried Wiley out the door. No one made a move to stop us. Most of them had a wondering look on their faces, as if they had no idea what was going on. Several of them seemed indifferent or impassive, as if things of this sort were common in the Union Arms.

But I took no chances and covered Fin's retreat as he half ran down the pier with the unconscious Wiley Jenkins over his shoulder. We didn't stop until we had left the pier, turned into the street, and gone another hundred yards or so. Fin was about spent as he sagged with his burden into the doorway of a closed and shuttered shop. For a couple of minutes he didn't attempt to speak but just sat there, his chest heaving with labored gasps. It was too dark to see much, but I checked Wiley to be sure we hadn't escaped with just his dead body. The pulse was strong and steady and his breathing regular. He seemed to be in a deep sleep. Even though he smelled of liquor, I was almost certain he had been drugged. Wiley could hold his liquor better than this.

"They slipped some knockout drops into his drink," Staghorn concurred when he finally recovered his breath. "Standard practice for shanghaiing. He'll probably be out for another eight or nine hours, and then he'll be sick as a dog. Probably won't look at another drink for a while."

"We need to to get him to a hotel and let him sleep it off."

"Right," he said, pushing himself to his feet and reaching to help me lift Wiley between us. "There's a pretty decent hotel I know of up on the bluff that's not too expensive."

"I thought shanghaiing had been outlawed," I said as we half carried, half dragged Wiley's limp form down the street. The few late passersby gave us no notice. Sights like this were common in this part of town.

"Various ports have tried to enforce that law, but might as well try to outlaw drinking," Fin replied. "As long as there are bully mates to make life hell for the sailors, crews that jump ship at every opportunity without their pay, creating a constant demand for more hands, there will be shanghaiing. I saw the bark *Wanderer* anchored in the harbor when we came in. That's probably where he was bound. That ship has a notorious reputation for man driving and man killing. Can't keep a crew. Strangely enough, it's captain and half owner lives right here in Port Townsend. Has a big mansion up on the bluff. A churchgoing, charitable pillar of the community. How's that for hyprocrisy? But most sailors are looked on as barely human. The sails and running rigging are given better treatment than most of them are. Ah, well, maybe someday they'll be strong enough to protect themselves against that kind of abuse."

I made no immediate reply. This was a subject that was near to his heart and emotions, since he had spent six years before the mast on deepwater voyages to every part of the world, some of his service on just such ships as he was describing.

"How did you know Wiley was in that back room?" I asked when we had stopped to rest about halfway up the hill.

"Well, I couldn't figure out that business of his hat at first. Frankly, I had forgotten about the possibility of shanghaiing. It wasn't until I heard that thumping noise that I finally put it together. That was the butt of an oar banging the bottom of the trapdoor as a signal to open up. Then I remembered seeing the *Wanderer* and the back room built over the water."

"A few more minutes and it would have been too late," Fin added. "Instead of waking up a few hours from now in a hotel bed, he'd have been heaving his guts out in the fo'c'sle of an outward-bound ship off Cape Flattery, headed for who knows where."

"It's not the first time he and I have had some close calls since we've known each other. I hope our luck isn't about to run out."

In spite of Wiley's pleadings to let him die in peace in our hotel room, we took the next ferry back to Port Gamble the next day. Wiley was sick the whole trip, saying little, eating nothing, dozing in his chair. The alcohol and the knockout drops had produced a hangover of monumental proportions. But in spite of the way he felt, he managed to express his thanks several times to us for his rescue. By the time we debarked at Port Gamble at dusk, he was beginning to feel almost human again.

"I just wish I had been conscious," he told us. "I missed all the fun."

"Guess I should have warned you to be on the lookout for something like that," Fin said. "But really, I forgot about it."

We all ate supper and went to bed early, still tired

from our late escapades of the night before. The next morning we reported to Asa Carlyle what we had learned about the Rust and Barrett ship.

"That's good. At least now I know what we're up against and can prepare our strategy." Carlyle nodded when we had finished. "You boys had breakfast?"

"Yes, sir."

"You boys stayed out of trouble, didn't you?" he asked.

We looked at each other.

"Not entirely," Wiley finally said rather reluctantly.

"Oh?"

I proceeded to relate briefly what had happened.

"I should never have sent you up there," Carlyle said when he heard the story.

"My fault," Wiley replied. "I wasn't cautious enough. Should have known better. Anyway, there's no harm done. It just left me a little older and a little wiser, is all."

Carlyle didn't see the humor of it but dismissed us to go back into the office in his home and wrestle with problems of his finances.

As we walked back down toward the mill, Fin pointed out to us that all six of the Carlyle company ships were anchored in the harbor. There were no orders to be delivered at the moment. The industry slump was deepening, apparently, and the rumors circulating at the shipyard were that Asa Carlyle would not be able to meet his next payroll the following week. Nobody knew for sure, and the boss was not confiding in anyone, unless it was Cyrus Johnson, his mill manager.

We looked up Taps O'Neal, but he couldn't enlighten us any more than some of the others had. It was O'Neal's guess that the old man would pull an ace out of his sleeve and keep his company afloat no matter what.

"He's too experienced to let go now. Even if he has to lay off some of his workers and mill hands for a time, he'll hang on—at least until this race is decided," he affirmed as the four of us sat at lunch together that day in the mess hall.

The mill had not been entirely rebuilt but was usable. Fin's suspicions that the fire had been arson were strengthened by a strong odor of coal oil on the ground near parts of the charred building. But no empty tins had been found, no remains of a torch or oil-soaked rags. If anything of that sort had existed, the evidence had been incinerated. On his return, mill manager Cyrus Johnson had been questioned closely by Asa Carlyle, and the man had sworn that nothing flammable except wood had ever been stored in or near the mill. So the suspicions remained only that—suspicions with no proof. Even if evidence had been found to positively indicate arson, that still left the question of who. There was no motive. Asa Carlyle, as far as I had been able to tell, was the most respected and well-liked man in the area. His kindness and generosity to his employees kindled a fierce loyalty to him. This was a company town, and everything depended on his staying in business. More and more it was coming down to this race to San Francisco.

The four of us finished lunch discussing the possibilities but came up empty at the end of it. It was a puzzle with the vital pieces missing.

Before the steam whistle signaled a return to work, Taps brought up the subject of Timothy Cooper, the Secret Service agent.

"You know, that night sticks in my memory like a bad dream," O'Neal remarked. "It has an unreal quality about it that makes me wonder if I didn't imagine most of it."

"It was real enough, all right," Fin said. "All of us can attest to that. But it's just as well for now that we agreed to say nothing to anyone else about it. If it seems unreal to us, imagine what it would sound like to someone who wasn't there."

"Where'd that traveling company go when they left Tacoma?" I asked Wiley.

"Darcy said their next stop was Victoria. They had a two-week run scheduled, performing four nights a week with a matinee on Sunday afternoon."

"I wonder if Timothy Cooper is any closer to making his quarry crack?"

"Darcy told me after we wrung that story out of Cooper that the agent confronted David St. George the next day and threatened to take his story to the press if the actor didn't cooperate with him and confess to being John Wilkes Booth.''

"What happened?"

"The actor was sober and in control of himself at the time and just laughed in his face. Told him he had no proof, or he would already have produced it.''

"And?"

"Now I'm repeating only what Darcy relayed to me as told to her by David St. George, so I don't know how accurate it is. But St. George is sweet on her, so maybe he told it like it happened. Anyway, Cooper is supposed to have given him some sort of ultimatum. Darcy said he wouldn't really say what it was—more than just a threat to break his story to the press. It was more of a threat to do something to the actor if he didn't confess by a certain date.''

"What date?"

"She didn't know, but the director and producer of the Shakespearean company was becoming very aware and very irritated at David St. George's deteriorating performances and threatened to dismiss him from the acting company at the end of the tour if he didn't solve his personal problems and improve.''

"Well, if Cooper was fanatical enough to pursue this all these years, he's not going to give up now that he thinks he's got his man.''

"Ya know, that's really strange. The whole country has thought all these years that Booth was dead and buried.''

"Apparently not the *whole* country.''

The sun rose into a cloudless sky, promising a beautiful day to grace the activities. It was Saturday about a week later and a momentous day for the people of Port Gamble. It was launching day for the *Victory*. The new schooner rested proudly on the cradle near the water's edge, her copper-sheathed bottom shining dully. A few minor things remained to be done on the vessel, but these could be completed after the schooner was afloat. The sleek hull was draped with red, white, and blue bunting, and multicolored pennants fluttered from her rigging.

There would be no work in Port Gamble this day. It was a holiday that most of the town had worked toward and anticipated. The crowd began to gather near the shipyard an hour before the scheduled eleven o'clock launch. They brought picnic baskets and quilts to get the choicest spots on the greensward. Kids and dogs ran among the parked wagons and tethered teams. A small uniformed brass band of young people entertained with various lively numbers. What I guessed to be more than 90 percent of the entire community was gathered by the appointed time. And Asa Carlyle didn't keep them waiting.

At precisely eleven o'clock he climbed up on to the makeshift platform that had been hammered together next to the bow of the new ship. He was dressed in a carefully brushed black suit, white shirt, and black string tie. His heavy gold watch chain stretched across his vest as he raised his hands for quiet. He wore no hat and squinted into the midday sun at the colorful crowd of workers and their families who were spread out in front of him.

"Ladies and gentlemen! Ladies and gentlemen!"

The crowd noise gradually died until only a few distant barking dogs remained.

Carlyle greeted them and made a brief speech, thanking them for their work and dedication.

"Here is the result of your work—your long hours of labor and sacrifice—this beautiful craft we are about to christen today. This is the schooner that will carry our crew to victory over Rust and Barrett and insure the future of this company!"

While the crowd was cheering his words enthusiastically, he helped Mabel Johnson up onto the speaker's stand. A middle-aged, somewhat dowdy matron, she was the wife of his mill manager, Cyrus Johnson, and had been chosen by popular acclaim of the employees to do the christening honors. Dressed in a green dress and a wide-brimmed hat, she acknowledged the applause of the throng then took the bottle of champagne from Carlyle. Raising the beribboned bottle above her head, she proclaimed, "I christen thee *VICTORY!*" and brought the bottle down smartly across the stem of the vessel just under the bowsprit, shattering the glass and spraying the foaming liquid.

A roar went up from the crowd that pressed around close, and the brass band struck up a fast march. The chocks were knocked out from under the hull, and several workmen on either side began to pull on tow ropes. The hull began to move slowly on the inclined greased skids. Then a little faster and finally slid stern-first into the bay.

The new vessel rode lightly and easily on the water as it was towed manually over to the pier and tied up. The crowd celebrated with champagne and various other liquid refreshments of their own as they dispersed to other entertainments. The rest of the day was given over to picnics, sack races, wrestling matches between various local strongmen, foot races, horse races on the long flat course just outside town, and even a baseball game between the Port Gamble team and a visiting nine from another independent mill near Tacoma.

Fin, Wiley, and I made an inspection of the new ship, along with many other people who had not had a close look at it before. Taps O'Neal had worked on the rigging of the ship and was very familiar with it, but he wasn't with us. He was an outfielder with the Port Gamble Baseball Team and was busy getting ready for the two o'clock game.

We came out of the well-designed cabin that still smelled of new wood and fresh varnish and stood on the main deck among the workers and their families who were examining the new vessel. Fin placed his hands on the spokes of the wheel and looked forward along the clean sweep of deck.

"I'm sure itching to get her outside and try her out."

"If those sails don't hurry up and arrive, you won't have much practice time," Wiley commented, voicing a thought that had been in all our minds the past several days. "Any word from the sailmaker about the delay?"

"Nope. Probably cost Asa a few more gray hairs."

"He telegraphed them yesterday but hasn't gotten a reply," I said.

Even though the new schooner was ninety-eight feet long on deck, it seemed like a miniature compared to the

151

J. W. Brandon. Asa Carlyle had donated a ten-dollar gold coin to place under the base of the mainmast for the traditional lucky piece. The cargo hatch took up most of the deck space between the forecastle and the after cabin.

Carlyle was counting heavily on the specially made sails to help equalize the disadvantage he would have against the bigger ship. I hoped those yachtsman's sails arrived in time to allow Fin and his crew to get them set and stretched properly. They would have to be just right for the crew to extract every last knot the sails were capable of delivering to the vessel.

I could see this same thought in Fin's face as he ran a calculating eye over the two spruce masts and the tall white topmasts that extended them upward. The white-hulled vessel with its pine deck, oak keel and framing, varnished masts, and wire-cable standing rigging was the latest and best of the shipbuilder's art. The sails would give it life and the wind, breath.

As we walked down the gangway from the waist of the ship, I cast an admiring glance at the bowsprit and the beautifully curved clipper bow, with the gilt carving of the headless female figure of Winged Victory.

"I thought it was tradition, or superstition, that the figurehead was the eyes of the ship," I said. "Why a headless figure?"

"Asa wanted it that way." Fin shrugged.

"The original of that Greek statue was discovered about fifteen years ago on an island in the Aegean Sea," Wiley added. "It had no head or arms."

"How'd you know that?" I asked.

"My college education wasn't entirely wasted." He grinned. "I also happen to know she was the goddess of victory and the messenger of Zeus and Athena."

If invoking the blessing of this Greek goddess of victory would give us any assistance—even a psychological lift—I was all for it. We were going to need all the help we could get.

The sails arrived the following Monday afternoon. They had been shipped to Omaha by rail and then on the Union Pacific overland to San Francisco, where they

152

were transferred to a ship sailing with general cargo to Puget Sound. The precious canvas-wrapped rolls were unloaded by the workmen at the company wharf about midafternoon, and before dark many willing hands had unwrapped, sorted, and bent the new sails to the masts of *Victory*.

Fin Staghorn had long since selected his crew, and that crew included me and Wiley and Taps O'Neal. Asa Carlyle was also aboard as Fin ordered the bow and stern lines cast off the next morning and, taking advantage of a light southeasterly breeze, slipped away from the long pier under foresail and jib. When we were clear of the land, all sail was made and the empty schooner took the bit in her teeth as she fairly flew northward up the sound on a quartering wind.

"Wooweee!!" Fin threw back his head with a spontaneous shout of exultation, his shaggy blond hair flying as he stood at the helm like some sun-bronzed Viking. "She's alive!"

The crewmen who were near enough to hear him grinned at his boyish enthusiasm. This was something they could appreciate. I suspect they'd had their fill of serving under dour captains.

The sleek two-master ran like a racehorse, but I was more anxious to see what she would do going to windward. How much leeway would she make with no ballast but with a straight keel and considerable dead rise? We soon found out, when Fin brought her into the wind. As I watched her wake and then looked at the shoreline about five miles ahead of us, I could see that she tracked well with very little slippage to leeward. If I was elated, Fin Staghorn and Taps O'Neal were ecstatic at the performance.

For the next several hours, Fin put her through her paces on all points of sailing, with various combinations of sail as the southeast wind gradually quickened until it was kicking up some small whitecaps. After about two hours of handling the ship, he turned over the wheel to one of the sailors.

Then he paced up and down the deck, observing, sensing the rise and fall and surge of the vessel from different positions. Then he tried out various men as helmsmen, picking out the individuals with natural skills at steering.

By the time he ordered the ship back toward the Carlyle company wharf, the sun was dying, as was the land breeze. None of us had eaten since breakfast, but I'd venture to say no one even thought about it until the spring lines were being secured and the sails furled on their booms. But then my stomach told me it was long past mealtime as we stepped ashore in the long summer twilight. Wiley and I had both had a chance to handle the wheel on the ship's first trial run. Even though it was a fair-sized ship, it had the responsiveness of a yacht, just as Carlyle had hoped it would.

"It'll be a whole different story when she's carrying a full load of lumber," Staghorn told us at supper. "You won't know it's the same vessel."

The next morning the standing rigging was tightened up, and Fin had several tons of ballast added to her hold. And we went out again, with the weather staying fair, but this time the wind had shifted to the northwest. Fin took charge, shaking down the new ship and the new crew, so that at the end of the day we were all a little more used to each other.

Day followed day, and Fin pushed us from sunup to dusk, twice even taking us out at night. The weather luckily stayed clear with a good breeze each day. We gradually increased the weight of our ballast. We began to work and react as a team to the orders of the first mate, Taps O'Neal, as well as to those of Fin Staghorn. The crew was divided into port and starboard watches, based on the preferences and subtle differences of the individuals. Between Staghorn and O'Neal, they knew these men well and, with an uncanny knack, placed those men together who worked best. This may have counted for more on a long voyage, but we still had to work together quickly with no hesitation and no conflicts. We were working ourselves into a team.

Finally, four days before the scheduled start of the race, Fin ordered the schooner loaded with a full load of green lumber.

"A full dress rehearsal," O'Neal remarked as we watched the steam crane lift the lumber carefully over the rail amidships and let it down into the open hatch. Several loaders were guiding it into place and were belowdecks stowing the lumber properly. When the hull was full, the hatch cover was lifted into place and the process of stacking the lumber on deck began. More and more of it came aboard, until I was sure she could take no more. But still it was loaded.

I glanced sideways at O'Neal beside me on the pier. "Aren't they overdoing it a bit?"

He shook his head. "Not at all. It's common practice to load a lumber ship until she's almost awash, the theory being that she'll never sink with all that wood in and on her. The more cargo, the more profit per trip. Makes it tough to work around the deck, though."

Fin walked up to join us just then, watching the graceful hull settle a little deeper with every additional ton put aboard.

"The wind promises to be light and westerly today," he said. "If the *Victory* will move in light air with that kind of a load, then we have more than an even chance—provided we get some light airs during the race. Deep-loaded, she's bound to be stiff in a blow, but my concern is how she'll move in light winds. Better pray for light winds and a boring race because in anything like fifteen to twenty knots and up, that big ship of Rust and Barrett's will kill us."

CHAPTER 16

WHILE we had been busy drilling the crew, the executives at Rust and Barrett had decided, for some obscure reason, that publicity for the upcoming race would be beneficial to their company after all. It wasn't just chance or coincidence or a curious reporter, Asa Carlyle assured us, that suddenly caused every newspaper on the West Coast to run front-page stories with followups day after day on the race and the preparations for it. Reports reaching Carlyle by telegraph told him that posters were appearing on every lamppost and fence and wall in San Francisco, Seattle, and Victoria. The Puget Sound ferry had been stocked with printed handbills urging everyone to be at the start of the big race near Cape Flattery on Sunday noon September 8, or at the finish in San Francisco.

My previous efforts at a one-man publicity campaign looked extremely puny—almost nonexistent—by comparison. We could only speculate about the reasons for this sudden turnabout in thinking by Rust and Barrett. Maybe they were angry at Carlyle for his refusing to knuckle under to the cartel and take his token payment for closing down temporarily. Or perhaps they belatedly realized that this race was a means of getting free publicity and drawing a lot of attention to their company for future name-recognition. Perhaps they felt so confident of victory they wanted everyone to know about the race in advance. Most of the printed information we saw hardly mentioned the Carlyle company.

"Goliath is doing a lot of chest pounding even before David selects a rock for his sling," Wiley commented to me as we discussed this the night before the ship was to be loaded under the eyes of race officials on Saturday.

"We'll be only a few days finding out if the story ends the same way as that biblical tale," I said. "To tell you the truth, I'm nervous. The responsibility isn't mine alone, but I hate to think that the jobs and lives of so many people are resting on what I do in the next few days."

"There's a lot riding on the crew all right"—he nodded somberly—"but more weight of this thing is on the back of Staghorn and in the hands of fate and the weather than on us."

"I just wish it was over and decided one way or the other. I know I need to get a good night's sleep tonight and tomorrow night while we're being towed up the sound, but I don't feel I could close my eyes right now."

The mill hands and shipwrights had sweated most of the day moving by hand and wagon the huge stack of air-dried lumber from its open-sided shelter to the pier where it would be ready for the race officials to measure the next morning before loading. Everything was as ready as human effort could get it. The *Victory* was in perfect condition, as was the mettle of the crew. Fin Staghorn, though outwardly calm, had grown unusually quiet the past day or so as preparations for the race drew down to their final hours. No detail was too small to escape his scrutiny. Wiley and I were not professional sailors, but we had gradually gained the respect of the crew, even though they were at first curious as to why two outsiders would be included among their select number. For being chosen to crew the *Victory* was a signal honor.

The next morning the sun rose into a clear sky. The weather had been fair for the better part of two weeks, but I didn't trust it to stay that way from what I had heard about the extremely wet weather along this coast.

The two men of the race committee appointed by Caleb Hale in San Francisco were on hand just after full daylight, ruling sticks, pencils, and pads in hand, to measure the stack of lumber and to supervise the loading. There would be no light loading or empty spaces in the hold. Carlyle had been assured that the same thing was taking place in Port Townsend.

The loading went smoothly and quickly, and the schooner was fully loaded in less than three hours.

"How many board feet you reckon this is?" Wiley mused as the workmen tightened the lashings on the deck load that rose more than a foot above the rail.

"Doesn't really matter," Taps O'Neal replied. "We're loaded to capacity—or at least what these race officials consider a safe capacity. It's a much smaller load than what the *Osprey* is taking aboard. And with this dry lumber, it should be even more than proportionately lighter."

The steam tug was lying just off the pier, awaiting the signal that we were ready to heave the two lines across.

The loading of the lumber was the last thing to be done; the ship had previously been provisioned with food, water, and all gear, spare parts, and fittings, rope, sails, and tools.

Those of the crew who had family in Port Gamble said their good-byes among hugs, kisses, and well-wishes. It was handshakes all around for the crew from Asa Carlyle, who would not be aboard with us.

"I don't want to be aboard to inhibit your decisions in any way," he had told Staghorn earlier. It's best if I'm not there. I might be in the way. Besides, I'd be too nervous."

Now he gripped his young skipper's hand as members of the crew carried their seabags aboard.

"I know you'll do your best. Everyone here will be riding that ship with you. Caleb Hale will immediately notify me of the winner by telegraph."

Fin Staghorn did not reply. He just swallowed hard and nodded. I think if he had been a more demonstrative man, he would have bear-hugged his boss. But the Scotsman was also a little too formal and conservative for this.

Ten minutes later, the lines were cast off and we were taken in tow by the steam tug for our twenty-four hour trip to Cape Flattery. We moved away to the wild cheers of the crowd on the pier, the noise overlaid with the scream of the steam whistle atop the mill.

The long trip to our starting point gave everyone a chance to get settled in, including the cook Wilbur Haworth. This individual was a tall, thin, laconic man who could, according to Staghorn, whip up a tasty meal while the ship was nearly standing on her head in a blow. He could brace his long legs in the tiny galley, hang on with one hand, and work quickly and efficiently with the other. The galley of the *Victory* was thoughtfully designed for maximum convenience.

Haworth was also an experienced sailor so could lend a hand when needed. This race was a sprint rather than a long run, so we were not worried much about food. We could exist on almost anything for the few days it would take us to reach the Bay City.

Fin and Taps inspected the deck load to be sure it was well secured. It wouldn't do to have anything break loose or shift in heavy weather. The deck load was nearly even with the top of the after cabin, but it did not interfere with the access to it, since the companionway slide opened to the rear of the cabin near the wheel. The deck load was composed mostly of long, sixty-foot lengths of lumber and was held in place by chains. A walkway about three feet wide had been left down each side next to the bulwarks for passage fore and aft.

There was little else for the rest of us to do on the long twenty-four-hour tow except try to relax and enjoy the scenery, which was spectacular. It was a virtual wilderness of thickly forested slopes, towering mountain peaks in the distance. I turned in and slept fairly well in my new bunk that night. Wiley and I were bunking forward in the forecastle with the rest of the crew this trip. Fin Staghorn, Joseph Taps O'Neal, and the other mate, Hans Peterson, a quiet, bearded, muscular twenty-six-year-old Norwegian-American bunked aft. Peterson knew his job and could be depended on to do the right thing in any emergency. He was one of the two or three best natural sailors he had ever seen, Fin confided to me while we slid along behind the towline.

The next morning broke damp and very chill as the wind swept down from the snowcapped mountains and across the strait. But the sun quickly sucked up the dampness and warmed up the day. By eleven o'clock we could see the crowd of sloops, cutters, and spectator boats of all kinds scattered over the surface of the ruffled water as we approached the mouth of Juan de Fuca Strait. In addition to the private craft, two large steam ferries were jammed to the rails with spectators, steam whistles blasting. As my eyes took in the scene from the starboard side, I saw a big schooner under tow about a mile away. It was the only big ship in sight and had to be the *Osprey*. This fact was confirmed a few minutes later by O'Neal. Even from a distance and without her sails, she looked big and formidable.

The rules were these: Two bright yellow pennants would be dropped as markers about a mile apart but large enough to be easily seen. At noon a small cannon on the top deck of one of the ferries would fire, signaling the start of the race. At the firing of this cannon, both steam tugs would drop their towlines and the crews would race to raise their sails. Both ships had to pass between the markers, and the race would be on.

All our sails were bent to the booms and hanked onto the stays. Members of the crew were stationed at the halyards. Wiley and I were at the base of the mainmast. We all anxiously watched as the steam tugs for both our ships maneuvered our two vessels parallel and eased up to the imaginary line that ran between the two yellow buoys.

They brought us as even as possible, a few hundred yards apart.

The hands of my watch crept toward noon while we stood, glancing at the ferry on our left and the *Osprey* on our right. A light breeze was blowing in our faces from the open sea, and the bright, sunny day was beginning to grow a little hazy. I was staring ahead, realizing I could no longer see the horizon, when the boom of the field piece made me jump.

The race was on!

Both ferries dropped their towlines. As a sailor on our bow hauled in the line, the tug steamed off. Cheers came faintly across the water from the spectator boats, and we threw our combined weight and muscle into hauling hand over hand on the halyards. The big sail inched up the mast on its wooden hoops.

"Belay!"

The line was secured to the pinrail, and I looked around at the other members of the crew who were toiling at the headsails and the foresail.

Fin Staghorn, who stood at the wheel, put the spokes over as the sails fluttered and began to fill on the starboard tack. It was not a fast start to this long-awaited race. But at least we were moving. And the *Osprey* wasn't! We were sliding away on the starboard tack at about four knots, but the bigger ship didn't appear to be moving at all. Then I remembered what Staghorn had said earlier about the large schooners. ". . . if the wind is below fifteen miles an hour, she won't move at all. But as soon as the wind picks up above fifteen—about the speed at which whitecaps appear—she'll take off like a racehorse."

Shortly we began to dip and rise to the long swells of the open sea. The spectator boats began to fall away, and the whistles of the steam tugs blasted a final farewell.

Fin stayed on deck for several hours, as did nearly all of the crew, savoring the sight of the big, three-masted Rust and Barrett schooner growing smaller and smaller behind us.

Fin had turned the wheel over to a sailor, but he paced the deck nervously, looking up at the rigging, gauging the light breeze. I could almost read what he was thinking. He was trying to will *Victory* through the water at an even faster clip, trying to figure out how to take even greater advantage of the light wind while it was still too light to move the heavier schooner.

The wind held light and northwesterly for the rest of the afternoon. We cleared Cape Flattery, and Fin set a course that would take us straight for San Francisco Bay as long as the wind was fair. The *Osprey* was no longer in sight, but Fin kept scanning the horizon behind us with his field glasses nonetheless. Fin had made it clear to all of us that this would not be the traditional cruise where the crew bunked forward and the officers aft and only mingled while going about their duties on deck. The traditional distinctions counted for nothing here.

161

Even though we were sleeping and eating in different parts of the small ship, we were all equals, except when an order was given by the mates or the captain. In this one respect there was no change. Discipline and order were understood, but all ten of us aboard comprised a happy, informal group. If this race were to be decided by the crew, everyone's enthusiastic cooperation was going to be required. This was a youthful crew, just as Asa Carlyle had wanted it. The cook and I were the oldest two aboard, and we were past thirty-five. Most of the sailors, I judged, were from about eighteen to twenty-two. Their experience ranged from a few months to several years. If Staghorn changed course or made any other tactical move, he made known to the entire crew what he was about.

Even though Wiley and I were considered part of the crew, we both knew that the schooner could function perfectly well without us. As far as numbers were concerned, we could very well have been passengers. Since we had all been through a lot before, I think Staghorn just wanted some close friends he could trust and confide in.

But as Wiley and I stood at the starboard rail, pleasantly stuffed with our first meal at sea, and watched the sun, an orange ball through the haze, slide down into the sea, we were happy to be here and to be leading the race. Wiley and I had been on watch from noon to four and had taken the short dogwatch to relieve the others for supper. We would have the midwatch from midnight to four, but except for the evening chill that was coming on, we were looking forward to it.

Neither of us dreamed what the midwatch held for us.

CHAPTER 17

THE night was black, totally black, until shortly after we went on watch at midnight, when a blood-red moon rose through the haze that still hung over the sea. But it was another hour before the nearly full moon rose high enough to regain its normal brightness and shed some light. We had time to observe and enjoy the lunar display, since there was little for us to do. The wind held fair on our starboard quarter from the northwest about eight knots.

I had the wheel during the last hour of our watch. It was no problem keeping the compass needle steady in the lighted binnacle. I stood to one side of the wheel, resting my buttocks on the steering gear housing behind me and alternately looking over my shoulder at the shivering silver moonpath on the sea and up at the tracery of rigging and the nearly seven thousand square feet of sail drawing us along in the steady breeze, the double row of reef points fluttering along the belly of the huge mainsail above me. We had every stitch of canvas set—both big lower sails, the three jibs, the main topsail, and the two staysails. Except for the chill in the air, it was almost like a trade wind sea, I reflected as I turned up the collar of my jacket to keep the cold wind from crawling down my neck.

Wiley was up forward, and one of the men was aloft near the foremast, tightening up some rigging that had stretched and created a little slack.

I heard an exclamation from someone in the darkness,

and then what sounded like a pair of feet hitting the deck.

"Mr. O'Neal!" I heard a call from the darkness. "Come forward!" The mate made his way down the port side of the stacked lumber toward the commotion.

I wondered what was going on but dared not leave the wheel unattended to find out. I heard indistinct voices and an exclamation of surprise from Taps O'Neal.

"Fetch a lantern and let's take a look." Three or four shadowy figures came aft along the starboard side of the deck. Someone disappeared down the companionway just in front of me and reappeared in a few seconds with a shielded storm lantern.

"What's up?" I asked.

No one answered immediately.

"Let's have a look at you," O'Neal said, taking the lantern from the sailor and opening one of its shutters. A shaft of light illuminated the group of four men clustered by the deckhouse. Or I should say, three men and one girl, because the fourth figure was a slight figure, under five feet tall, with shoulder-length brown hair. I was so startled I almost forgot I was supposed to be steering. Her round, dark eyes looked frightened.

"The devil!" one of the sailors hissed, making it sound like the worst curse imaginable. "A girl!"

"Who are you, and how'd you get aboard this ship?" O'Neal demanded, his voice sounding very exasperated.

"What are you going to do to me?" she asked in a small, almost quavering voice as she looked from one to another of them without answering the question.

"It's almost time for the change of the watch. Wiley, take her below and wake Fin Staghorn."

He took the girl by the arm and escorted her down the companionway steps.

I could hardly wait the ten minutes or so until eight bells signaled the end of our watch. I turned over the wheel to the helmsman, who was still rubbing sleep from his eyes, gave him the course, and went below into the after cabin as quickly as I could.

Seated around the table in the small cabin were Fin Staghorn, Wiley Jenkins, Taps O'Neal, and our stowaway. The three other seamen from our watch were standing up. The girl seemed even smaller in the over-size coat someone had given her to ward off the chill. Her brown hair was cut in a pageboy style, and the wide brown eyes under the bangs now appeared more curious than frightened. Apparently Fin had already started questioning her as I squeezed in behind three sailors in the tiny cabin.

Staghorn's face seemed sterner than I had ever seen it. And I doubted that it was because of being awakened out of a sound sleep. Two gimbaled oil lamps fastened to opposite bulkheads had been turned up to fully illuminate the small cabin.

". . . No, sir."

"Then how did you get aboard?" Fin asked.

"I just came down to the dock when everyone was asleep the night before they loaded the wood and came onboard. Nobody was around. I brought some sandwiches and got up under that lifeboat and went to sleep."

"And you've been under there ever since?"

"Yes. When I woke up the next morning, I didn't dare come out because I could hear a lot of noise of people walking around, and I knew if I showed myself, they'd make me get off and go home. So I just kept still and nobody noticed me." She paused and licked her lips. "I sure am thirsty."

Fin motioned for one of the crew standing in front of me to bring her a drink of water.

"Go on," Fin said to the girl as the sailor edged toward the steps.

"But I forgot to bring a coat or something to wrap up in. I didn't know it would get so cold." She hugged the big coat around herself.

Apparently the lifeboat where she had been hiding was the one overturned and lashed to the top of the forecastle. The only other small boat the schooner carried was hung in davits over the transom.

Fin paused for a few moments and appeared to be deep in thought. Finally he heaved an audible sigh and said, "Tell me again why you stowed away on this particular ship. Didn't you know that we are in a very important race?"

"Yes." She looked somewhat forlorn and for the first time glanced around at the rest of us, as if seeking some moral support. No one said anything or made a move, so she continued. "School was going to be starting soon, and I hadn't done anything fun all summer. Just worked at a few little odd jobs for my daddy at the shop and ran some errands for my mother and visited with my girlfriends. Boring. I wanted to go someplace and do something exciting."

There were some mutterings among the sailors crowded into the small space.

"So you thought stowing away on this schooner would be a lark, did you? Figured we couldn't put you ashore if you weren't discovered until we got to sea, is that it?" Staghorn's tone was not as harsh as it might have been. Apparently he was just trying to clarify the situation, since there was nothing he could do about it until we got to San Francisco.

She nodded silently.

"Have you ever been to sea before?"

"No, sir, except when I was a baby. My parents came up to Port Gamble by ship. But we have been to Seattle twice on the ferry."

"How old are you?"

"Thirteen," she replied promptly and with a hint of pride.

"And your name is Liz McCormick?"

She nodded.

Fin Staghorn paused again, leaning back in his chair.

"You realize that your parents are probably worried to death about you."

For the first time she looked remorseful and dropped her eyes, failing to meet his gaze. Just then the sailor returned with a large mug of water for her. She gulped down the entire contents without stopping, dribbling some of it down the front of her coat in her eagerness.

"Well, all we can do is make the best of it," Fin said after she had lowered the mug and wiped her mouth with the back of her hand. "Luckily, we're not crowded for space. We'll shift around and give you a small room back aft here to yourself. We don't have any clothes to

166

fit you, so you'll have to make do with what you're wearing."

For the first time she looked relieved and almost smiled.

"Don't think you're getting a free ride," Staghorn continued. "You'll be working as a cabin girl, cleaning and helping the cook prepare and serve the meals. You can be of great help to us." A ghost of a smile crossed his lips. "This may not qualify as the most exciting thing you've done all summer, but it'll be done in a different setting."

"Oh, thank you. I'll do a good job and not get in the way. I've always wanted to go on a voyage in one of these big ships. But my daddy was not a sailor and my uncle Gerald had already retired from the sea and, besides, he couldn't take me with him when I was a little girl and . . . ."

"Enough. Enough." Fin held up his hand. "You may change your mind about this glamorous life at sea before you get home. But for now I'll show you where you are to sleep. You can get cleaned up and start helping the cook with breakfast in an hour or so."

He got up and she followed his example.

"Well, this race is lost with an albatross like that hanging around our necks," a sailor standing beside me muttered.

Unfortunately, his comment was just loud enough to be heard by Staghorn. Fin stopped and turned back.

"What was that?"

The young sailor, named Hoyle Rasmussen, swallowed hard when all eyes swung toward him in the sudden silence. But he didn't shrink from the captain's stare.

"I said a female aboard a ship is sure to bring bad luck."

"Stow that kind of talk!" Staghorn snapped. "I would have expected that kind of superstition from one of the older sailors but not from you. Spread the word that I don't want any of that kind of talk going around. If I hear any of that, the man who says it will be doing extra duty." He turned and led Liz McCormick out of the cabin.

I glanced at Rasmussen as I started up the steps. His face was white and his lips compressed. The girl who

167

had stowed away may not have been an albatross, but now there was a tension developing between the captain and crew that hadn't been there before.

"I was in the starboard rigging and saw someone climb down off the top of the forecastle," Wiley told me after we gained the deck. "I knew Rasmussen had gone forward to say something to the lookout, and I couldn't figure out who it was. The chills went down my back, I can tell you, when I realized it wasn't one of the crew. It was somebody a lot smaller. I slid down and hollered to stop. Still didn't know what I was approaching. But luckily, she was no threat to any of us."

"Not a direct threat, anyway."

"What do you mean by that?"

"You saw that little exchange between Staghorn and Rasmussen back there."

"Surely you can't blame that on the girl. It could have been caused by any kind of superstition."

"You're right," I answered, thinking of the statement of the British sailor in the saloon at Port Townsend about the changing of the name of the Rust and Barrett ship being bad luck. Even the coin under the mast and the figurehead were ancient superstitions, along with many others whose origins were lost in time. Superstition among seafaring men was probably older than among those of nearly any other calling.

"Let's get a little sleep while we can. I'm dead."

When we came on deck again to take the watch at eight, the sky had become overcast and the wind had shifted around and was coming at us from the east and northeast, unsteady and uncertain of direction.

Staghorn was on deck, his face set and scanning the horizon with his glasses. As far as I could see, there was still no sign of the other schooner. But light as the wind had been, I thought it virtually impossible that our rival had passed us. With the change of wind direction, the booms had been swung over to starboard, and we were taking the wind generally on our port beam, but the fluky wind made it hard to hold a steady course.

Before we relieved the watch, we had just enough time to eat some breakfast of oatmeal and some biscuits, jam and hot coffee with Liz McCormick performing her first duties waiting table.

When Wiley and I came back on deck, Fin was still there, studying the sea, and the sky and the trim of the vessel that was rolling in a rather confused slate-gray sea, nearly becalmed. Looking at him standing alone near the rail, I could almost feel the heavy responsibility weighing him down.

The way we had decided to divide up the duties of the watch, I had the first trick at the wheel this time instead of the last.

"We're in for a change of weather," Fin said as I relieved the helmsman. I glanced around to be sure he was talking to me, since he was staring off to windward as he made his comment. He stepped down into the companionway in front of me and peered at the barometer affixed to the bulkhead just inside.

"She's still going down but not as fast." He came out and pulled the slide back into place, glancing west where the iron-gray sea merged in an indistinguishable line with the dark gray overcast.

"I think low pressure is about to pass over us or maybe just north of us." He stood there with a hand resting on the cabin top and looking around at the confused cross seas that slapped at our hull. The fitful wind out of the east-southeast barely held the shape of the sails enough to give us steerageway. The loaded ship through the spokes of the wheel felt heavy and unresponsive, and the compass card wobbled in the binnacle that was recessed into the cabin wall in front of me.

"I don't like the feel of it," Staghorn muttered, just loud enough for me to hear. "All my instincts and experience tell me to claw off and get as much sea room as possible. If we weren't in a race, I'd do just that." He sniffed the damp-smelling air. "I don't like the feel of this weather," he said again.

"Think a storm's brewing?"

He didn't answer immediately but just stood still, deep in thought. He probably had not reached his twenty-seventh birthday, but already the strain of command was showing on his youthful face.

It was only 8:20 in the morning, but a strange gray

twilight enveloped us. The sea nearby was liquid pewter, but as I followed Staghorn's gaze west, I could see a distant squall line sweeping toward us. Strangely enough, the light wind still blew toward the approaching low-hanging blackness that was trailing a smoky veil. Jagged prongs of lightning stabbed downward into the sea. As far away as it was, I could still tell it was moving rapidly toward us.

Taps O'Neal noticed the heavy weather at nearly the same time. "Barker! Jenkins! Rasmussen! Get the topsail and the staysails off her. Also bring in the outer jib and flying jib. Then double-reef the fore and main. Quick! Call all hands!"

"I'll take the wheel if you want to go help them," Fin said to me.

I turned over the wheel and hurried forward to lend a hand. With the help of the other watch, it didn't take long for us to get the sails down and the two big sails reefed, since there was almost no wind pressure against them. But by the time I had a chance to look again, the black squall was nearly on us.

Liz McCormick came out of the galley where she had been helping clean up from breakfast and looked at the massive darkness rearing its head high above the ship. Her eyes widened at the sight of the hissing rain and wind churning the sea to foam barely a hundred yards away.

"Better get below," O'Neal said to her. She wasted no time taking his advice.

"I'll keep the wheel for now," Staghorn said to me as I returned to take over. I was much relieved. There was no land in sight in any direction, but I didn't feel experienced enough to handle this vessel in a hard squall. He put the wheel over to starboard, but she barely answered, we were moving so slowly.

"Slack off on the sheets and swing the booms over to port!" Fin called. "I don't want the first blast to yank the sticks out of her."

We jumped to obey him. The ship was practically becalmed now. There was a light puff from the west. It was nearly black as night. Suddenly a solid wall of wind hit the ship from the starboard side. Even though I was expecting it, the force and suddenness of it still caught me unawares. The two big double-reefed sails snapped taut with a crash, fetching up against their restraining tackles as the schooner heeled over sharply to port. I had to grab the iron rail bolted to the lee side of the deckhouse to keep from being pitched into the scuppers or over the low rail. When I dragged myself erect and squinted through the stinging, horizontal rain, Fin was wrestling the wheel and trying to brace his feet on the slanting deck.

Even under much-reduced sail area, the loaded schooner quickly responded and tore off on the starboard tack in what I guessed was a southwesterly direction, the shreds of her inner jib standing out straight from a forestay where the sail had blown away in the first mighty blast of air.

The heavy vessel was smashing the waves on her bow, still heeled at what seemed a dangerous angle, the foaming sea churning along and over her lee rail, making it impossible to walk on that side. Barker, Rasmussen, Wiley Jenkins, and I huddled in the lee of the deckhouse, since there was nothing for us to do for the moment. Taps O'Neal the mate worked his way back to Fin Staghorn at the wheel and was shouting something in his ear. Rasmussen, who had been on lookout in the bows of the ship, had been temporarily relieved. No man could see more than a few yards in that flying rain and blown spume anyway.

The wind and slashing rain held strong and steady for about an hour, and during that time Fin Staghorn kept the wheel and held the vessel on a steady course as she rushed through the sea, leaping up, over, and down, shuddering as we smashed our bowsprit into the rollers. Our lee rail scooped tons of water and flung it cascading knee-deep across the deck as the ship righted herself before the next plunge.

I hoped the storm was taking us to San Francisco. We had no way of knowing if the big Rust and Barrett schooner was also enjoying the benefits of this heavy wind. The *Osprey* would be eating up the miles in this kind of weather.

The rain finally slacked off as the squall passed on,

but the wind held strong and steady. Fin turned the wheel over to Joseph Barker, a short, muscular seaman, and went below. I was chilled through, and O'Neal directed me to go into the forecastle and bring up the foul-weather gear for all the men of our watch.

When we went off watch at noon, the sky was still overcast and the wind blew strong as ever, having shifted around a little more to the south of west. I went into the forecastle for some lunch, pleased at the thought that we were making good time. I tried not to think of our rival gaining miles somewhere behind us.

Liz McCormick struggled cheerfully to serve our food at the table, which was built around the bole of the foremast that came down through the center of the room. But a sudden roll of the schooner caught her off-balance and sent her crashing against the bulkhead with a pot of hot tea, nearly scalding her as the steaming liquid splashed out on the varnished deck.

"Oh, I'm sorry!" she cried. "I lost my balance." She was flustered as she scrambled on her hands and knees to retrieve the dented tin pot. We helped her up.

"Don't worry about it, missy. It happens all the time in rough weather. That's just the first of many spills this ship will see before she's done. Just glad you weren't burned."

"But I got all the way from the galley without spilling it!" she wailed. She took the pot and staggered out the tilted doorway to get a refill.

Thick pea soup and bread and hot tea made up the fare for our midday meal, and even though we were seated, it was difficult for us to keep the food on the table and in the bowls long enough to eat it, the way the ship was plunging and rolling. At least the rough weather hadn't yet brought on any sign of the previous seasickness Wiley had suffered on the *J. W. Brandon*.

"Feels great to be making time like this at last," Wiley commented, tearing off a piece of bread with his teeth. "Feels more like a race now."

"A mixed blessing," O'Neal said, coming in just then and sliding his tall frame gracefully on to the wooden bench. "The *Osprey* will be taking advantage of this, probably praying that it keeps up. The only way it would

172

benefit us more is if the wind hauls around so that it's coming from almost dead ahead, since with these new sails, we can probably sail closer to the wind than they can."

"Where are we now?" I asked.

"I'm not really sure. It's still overcast, so we didn't get a noon sun shot. I'd guess about thirty miles offshore and sailing at an angle away from the land just now."

"Any idea how long this wind will last?"

O'Neal shook his head. "Could be as little as twelve hours or as long as a day or two. Long enough to lose us the race in any case."

"You really think so?"

He nodded soberly. "But all we can do is take the weather as it comes and make the most of it."

The wind continued unabated throughout the afternoon from the southwest as the ship smashed and drove her way through and over the seas that came rolling in steady succession toward us. The *Victory* was getting her first real test, creaking and groaning in every joint as the tons of deadweight rolled with every passing sea and pitched into every following trough. She could take no more sail, and we drove on under double-reefed fore and main that were held as rigid as carved ivory by a wind that I estimated in excess of thirty knots. The entire main deck was wet from flying salt spray and made for very treacherous walking along the windward side of our big deck load of lumber. I was thankful that this topside load was not only lashed in place but was also chained to keep it from coming loose by even the most violent shaking.

By six-thirty that evening, the storm clouds began to show signs of breaking up. Here and there patches of blue showed through the ragged, fast-moving clouds.

About seven-thirty the sun was falling toward the western horizon. Wiley and O'Neal and I were putting our weights on the main peak halyard that had become wet and stretched when we heard a faint shout from Rasmussen, an oilskin-clad figure in the bow. We paused and strained our ears to hear over the wind roaring through the rigging.

173

"Sail ho!" came the faint shout again.

We secured the line and rushed to the weather rail. At first we saw nothing. Hoyle Rasmussen was still shouting as he came aft, pointing to windward. Shielding my eyes from the flying spray, I tried to follow his pointing finger as the ship rose and fell. But the hundreds of feather-edged combers all looked like small white sails to me. Finally a shaft of sunlight lancing through a hole in the clouds several miles away lit up the definite outline and sails of a three-masted schooner.

"Fetch Staghorn up here," O'Neal directed. "Tell him to bring his glasses."

Fin Staghorn was beside us in less than a minute, field glasses in hand. He braced himself against the roll, then focused the field glasses on the distant ship. A few seconds later he lowered them. "Too far away to make out the name, but it's the *Osprey* all right, I'm almost sure of it. There's some sort of insignia on the foresail just where Rust and Barrett always put their RB logo in red. We're moving so much it's hard to keep the glasses focused on her."

Fin passed the glasses to each of us, and we had to look for ourselves. In the few minutes this took, the larger ship seemed to move a little farther away to the south of us.

"She's not carrying topsails," O'Neal commented, lowering the glasses, "but I don't think she's got more than one reef in those lowers and she looks to be carrying one jib."

We all stared at the distant apparition across the storm-tossed ocean as it went hull-down on the horizon and gradually disappeared in the gathering dusk. It was a thrilling sight to actually *see* our competition for the first time since shortly after the beginning of the race. This made it feel more like a race.

"O'Neal, bring everyone except the helmsman below into the after cabin right away," Staghorn said, turning away and heading for the companionway.

CHAPTER 18

"I'VE called you here because we're all in this together and I want everyone to know what's going on," Fin Staghorn began when we were all crowded into the small cabin, a few of us standing. Even the cook Wilbur Haworth and Liz McCormick our stowaway were there. Barker, who was at the wheel, was the only one absent.

"We've just sighted the Rust and Barrett Schooner *Osprey* a few miles west of us and driving south past us like we were standing still." He paused, collecting his thoughts, and no one spoke. The only sound was the rushing water past our hull a few feet away and the creaking of some timbers as the room lifted and tilted.

"This is not unexpected," Staghorn continued. "I knew that any heavy wind would favor the larger ship. They have caught us and passed us. But we were lucky enough to see them when it happened. I say lucky because at least we now know where we stand in this race. Here's what I plan to do. If any of you has any objections or comments about this strategy, I'd like you to speak up when I'm through.

"Okay, first of all, my experience tells me that this wind is from a low-pressure area and will moderate and work around to the west in the next twelve hours. Then it will pick up again from the north but probably not as strong as it is now. Frankly, I was hoping for light winds and calms all the way to San Francisco because that would have favored us. As it is, we're going to have to take some chances if we expect to have a win in this race. The Rust and Barrett people are no gamblers. I'm sure Neil Brown, the captain of the *Osprey*, has had instructions to take that big ship well offshore in the event of heavy weather, especially if the wind is blowing in. They know with their speed advantage in strong winds they can more than make up the distance they would have to travel by sweeping wide. I know our approximate position by dead reckoning. If the sky clears, I hope to get a fix in the next few hours. The coastline curves west from here on down in a big bulge, so I plan to bring this ship about and drive us east by south until the coast is in sight—in other words, take the most direct line to San Francisco that I can, wind permitting. I should have done this from the beginning of this weather, but every instinct in me warns against taking a vessel too close to a lee shore in a gale. Those of you who were aboard the *J. W. Brandon* recently know what I mean. But we have to take some chances if we hope to win. It will be dangerous, and we run a risk of losing this ship and our lives on the rocks. But I'll do everything in my power to keep that from happening. And I expect every man—and woman—aboard to stay alert and ready to jump to any command of mine or the mates." He glanced at O'Neal and Peterson. "Are you with me?" he asked us.

A chorus of "Aye!" was his reply.

"Does anyone here have any questions or better suggestions as to strategy?" Fin asked.

"How far offshore are we now?" Wiley asked.

"About forty miles. We'll change course immediately. We can't afford to let them get another mile ahead of us."

He glanced around at the assembly.

"Any other questions or comments?"

Silence.

"Then get to it." He rose. "O'Neal, change course and steer directly southeast. We'll be running off the wind, so she'll ride a little easier. Station two men in the bows. Tell them to keep a sharp lookout because we'll likely close with the coast before daylight."

"Yessir."

176

I slept a lot better that night for a couple of reasons. First, the ship's running with the wind a couple of points abaft the beam lessened the pounding we had been taking when we were bucking into those big rollers, and I was able to stay in my bunk without holding on. The other reason my brief four hours of sleep was more restful was because of the knowledge that we were making a real race of it and the *Victory* was running at about her maximum hull speed. To be sure that she was, Staghorn ordered the reefs taken out of the fore- and mainsails and all three jibs set, replacing the blown-out sail with a spare. I discovered this when I came on deck to take the midwatch with Wiley, Joe Barker, Hoyle Rasmussen, and Taps O'Neal. We must have been traveling at least twelve knots—probably faster than that over the bottom—although it was difficult to tell in the blackness. Coming on deck in the middle of the night with a big sea running always gave me a momentary thrill of fear. After the relative quiet of the forecastle, the sudden roaring of the cold wind and the heaving sea in the total blackness made the world seem out of control—as indeed it probably was, as far as our small group of frail mortals was concerned. I had to pause and hold on to something until my senses became accustomed to the tumult and my eyes to the darkness.

Fin had been right. The sky was clearing from the west and the stars were showing in most of the sky, although some clouds still obscured the moon.

Sometime after two bells—or 1:00 A.M.—Wiley and I were standing in the lee of the deckhouse, out of the cutting edge of the wind.

"Land ho!" came Barker's lusty shout faintly against the wind. Chills went up my back. "LAND HO!" came the yell again, this time louder as the sailor came aft. "Port bow!"

I strained my eyes into the darkness but saw nothing at first. The wind had abated somewhat, but I estimated it was still blowing about eighteen knots. The ship plowed ahead, rolling easily as she shouldered aside the seas spreading foam, faintly white in the night, from her bows.

I looked again, and suddenly my throat constricted as

177

I spotted a line of white surf crashing against a lighter background that looked to be jagged, vertical cliffs. At this speed it would be only a few minutes or less before we would be smashed ashore.

With hardly a glance shoreward, the mate sprang out of the darkness.

"Starboard your helm," he said quickly to Rasmussen. "Steady her up on a course directly south."

In spite of the load she was carrying the small ship responded beautifully as Hoyle Rasmussen rolled the spokes up. Instead of taking the seas under our starboard quarter, we now caught them on our beam as the ship plunged directly across the waves. The wind howled mournfully through the rigging.

"Take in on those sheets!" O'Neal ordered.

We started hauling on the wet hemp that was passed through the oversize triple wooden blocks, but with the ship rolling heavily, the weight of the wind against the sail and the slippery footing, we could not move the boom.

"C'mon, put some muscle into it. Are we gonna have to call out the other watch just to trim the sheets?" the mate chided us. "Give it a heave when she rolls up level."

We did as instructed, with him lending a hand, but were still not able to haul in on the boom until the helmsman brought the bow up nearly into the wind to ease the pressure. With this help we were finally able to bring in the foresail boom a few feet.

"Belay!" O'Neal ordered.

We repeated the process on the mainsail sheet until our arms and backs ached. The long main boom protruded out over the stern of the ship and was ungodly heavy. But we braced our feet and hauled in unison, timing our heaves to the roll of the vessel until we had gained a few feet and O'Neal was satisfied that both big sails were at the proper angle to give us maximum driving force. The helmsman brought us back on course.

Only then did I look to port again. The wind was blowing the sound away from me, so I couldn't hear the thundering surf, but I could easily see the white-crested rollers spouting high against the rocks at the base of the

178

bluffs. They seemed somewhat nearer than before, but now we ran parallel to the coast instead of driving toward it. An involuntary sigh whistled through my teeth. We had escaped destruction—for the moment.

We had barely gotten the mainsheet secured to its cleat when a report like a cannon shot sounded from aloft, followed by a pounding thunder as the foresail began flogging. By the dim light of the moon shining fitfully through the ragged clouds, we could see that the long wooden gaff along the top of the foresail was at an odd angle and was thrashing back and forth. Something had carried away.

"Get that foresail down!" O'Neal shouted, leading the rush along the high side of the deck past the stacked lumber.

We got to the halyards and wrestled the foresail down in nearly record time, but from what I could see as we smothered the big sail, considerable damage had already been done. The wooden gaff had splintered in two! The long diagonal break in the spruce spar had allowed the outer end of the gaff to whip, jabbing the jagged end into the upper edge of the canvas and starting a tear that had wrenched open down to a seam at the edge of the first panel before we could collapse the sail.

"Lash it all to the boom," Taps O'Neal directed. "Be sure there are no folds for the wind to get hold of."

There was no need to call the starboard watch to help. The ship was still rolling, the seas were still high and dangerous, but the wind pressure had eased somewhat with the absence of the foresail.

We finished passing the lashings around the boom and over the shattering gaff and got the sail snugged down tight between them. Then we climbed down and inspected our handiwork. Just then Fin Staghorn appeared on deck with O'Neal. The captain's shaggy blond hair was whipping in the wind and he was rubbing sleep from his eyes. I could hear only a word here and there as O'Neal pointed to the foresail. Staghorn climbed up on the forecastle and took a closer look at the splintered gaff.

"Nothing we can do until daylight about repairing that," he told O'Neal as he jumped down. "Call all hands to get the main topsail and all staysails and head-sails on her as fast as you can. That'll help make up for some of our loss of speed. I think that gaff can be repaired and the sail, too, but it'll take some time. Must've been some weakness in the wood nobody could detect."

As he turned away to go aft, he lowered his voice to O'Neal, but I was standing near enough to catch his words and note the discouragement in his voice as he said, "This may have just lost us the race."

By full daylight the wind had moderated and backed around to the north, just as Staghorn had predicted. The wind was almost directly behind us at about twelve knots, and the main sail was bellied out full to the port side to take advantage of it. With the wind astern, the head-sails did no good, so the big mainsail was our only driver.

Our watch below was from four to eight. I was still tired when we came on deck after a hasty breakfast of oatmeal served by Liz McCormick. The starboard watch, under the direction of the second mate Hans Peterson, had the foresail stripped off the boom and mast and spread over the deck load. Two sailors wearing leather palms busily stitched up the long tear with heavy waxed thread. Fin Staghorn and two other men attempted to measure and fit some wooden splints along each side of the broken gaff. The splints were fashioned from a long piece of lumber that had been part of the deck load. The schooner was riding steady and level before the wind, so the chains were loosened just enough to slide a long heavy plank out. Then the chains were tightened down again.

One burly sailor was sawing one of the splints to the proper length, and another planed off the edges of the other, the fragrant shavings curling off and blowing across the deck. The *Victory* carried no carpenter, as most larger ships did on longer voyages. But Staghorn had selected men who were not only young, athletic, and good sailors but also were handy with tools.

The bell was struck and the watch was relieved.

"She's a bit tricky to steer with the main winged out like that," the helmsman said, turning over the wheel to

180

Wiley. "The following seas keep wanting to slew the stern around. Keep'er south by a point east."

I was stationed lookout on the bow. The morning was bright and clear, the sky having been swept clean of clouds. I could see the coast of California sliding slowly by on our port side no more than five miles distant. Staghorn had identified this as Cape Mendocino. I remembered the bulge of it from the chart he had shown me earlier. South of this cape, the shoreline curved gently east again, then back out again to a point before dropping almost straight southeast to our destination. Simple. Most of this crew had been this way and back many times before. With a clear sky and a fair wind at our back, what could be easier? But I knew better than that. I liked to think it was all a downhill slide from here, but anything could happen. The loss of our foresail meant the loss of several knots of speed for several hours at least. And how much farther ahead was the *Osprey*?

When we dropped the Mendocino Cape astern, we held our same course southeast as the straightest line to our destination, while the coastline fell away to our port side and much to my relief eventually shrank to a distant line on the eastern horizon. I felt very uneasy racing close to the coast. And I knew it made Fin Staghorn nervous, too. He was a deepwater sailor by training and liked plenty of sea room, but he was one of those young men Asa Carlyle was referring to who was not conservative, who would take some chances to attack the sea. But I had a sinking feeling in the pit of my stomach as I came off watch that no matter what our captain did, how much lighter our craft was and our lumber was than our rival's, we were going to lose this race badly. Maybe our eventual loss could be laid to the bad judgment of Asa Carlyle for deciding to enter this race with a much smaller ship, gambling that the weather this time of year would be light enough to outdistance the big Rust and Barrett craft. The more I thought about it, the more I felt as if someone had kicked me in the gut. I didn't want anyone else to think I had given up already, but as long as this wind held, our luck wouldn't.

Instead of going immediately into lunch at noon when

our watch ws relieved, I went aft into the cabin and found Staghorn putting away some potato soup and fresh bread. In the informal spirit that prevailed on this schooner, I dropped on to the bench by the table where he sat alone.

"How much farther?" I asked.

He gestured with his mouth full. "Take a look for yourself. The charts are rolled up in that rack on the bulkhead."

I got them down and unrolled them on the vacant part of the table.

"I just got a good noon sight," Fin said. "We're right there." He pointed at a pencil mark. "And this is where I had our position plotted by dead reckoning. You can see how far off I was." He gave a wan smile. "I never made any claims to being an expert navigator."

I measured off the distance with a pair of dividers. "I make it about a hundred and fifty miles to the Golden Gate."

He nodded. "That's maybe fifteen to twenty hours if this wind holds. And that's doubtful. Besides, we'll be lucky to get that gaff and foresail fixed before dark. And without it, we're running a lot slower than we should be. We'll auger some holes through the two pieces and bolt them back together and then lash a splint around that. But I don't know how strong it will be when we get it set again."

I measured the distance down the coast with my eyes, wondering where the *Osprey* might be right now. I began rolling up the large-scale chart. "What do you honestly think of our chances in this race?" I asked.

Fin Staghorn didn't reply until he had finished chewing and swallowing a mouthful of food.

"I wouldn't be here if I didn't think we could win," he replied slowly. "I can only guess where the *Osprey* is, although I'm almost certain they are ahead of us. But this race is not over until one of us ties up at the dock in San Francisco. And anything is liable to happen before we get there."

I thanked him for the information and turned to leave, thinking that he probably was putting up a brave front for my benefit, even though there was only a long chance—a very long chance—that *Victory* would throw a line on the dock first.

As I opened the door to the outside, I heard loud voices, a curse, and the thump of bodies hitting the deck. When I got around to the side of the deckhouse, I saw Barker and another sailor from the other watch rolling around, locked together on deck by the rail. By the time I got there, their shipmates were already pulling them apart.

"What's going on?" Fin Staghorn demanded, coming up behind me just as the second mate approached.

"I don't know," Peterson replied.

"I'd just had enough of his mouth," Barker spat, blood beginning to trickle from his nose. He glared across at a slightly smaller but muscular sailor who had long black hair and a black mustache. The man still wore the leather sewing palm on one hand. Both men were being tightly held by members of both watches.

"I'll not have any fighting on this ship," Fin said. "What's this about?" I could tell he was having trouble controlling his temper. The pressures inside him were about to burst.

Barker jerked his head at his assailant. "He just kept on about that girl stowaway. Says she's the cause of this accident."

The other man looked sullen. I knew his name as James Martin but knew little else about him. Being in the other watch, we seldom were in the forecastle at the same time so we saw little of each other. Martin glanced at Staghorn's face and apparently felt he had to say something to defend himself.

"Well, a perfectly good and new spruce gaff doesn't just split like that for no reason."

"So you think it's some kind of hex put on us by the girl?" Staghorn demanded, his face coloring.

"Just ain't likely it was accidental is all I'm sayin'," Martin retorted, rushing ahead, knowing he was already in trouble. "It's bound to be the girl. Everybody knows females on ships is bad luck."

"Martin, if I didn't need you aboard this schooner, I wouldn't have chosen you as part of this crew. Whatever ideas you have about luck or the lack of it you'd

183

better keep to yourself until we reach San Francisco. If you do anything further to get this crew riled up or cause us to lose this race, I'll see to it that you won't have a job with the Carlyle company when we get back," the captain said.

"Won't make no difference." Martin growled in a low voice. "Ain't none of us goin' to have a job when this is over anyhow. We'll never catch the *Osprey*. The girl's seen to that, whether she meant to or not."

CHAPTER 19

FOG was the one thing I had not counted on. That great leveler and equalizer was very common to the northern California coast. Apparently, the confidence Fin Staghorn had expressed to me the day before had not been just a facade to keep up my morale. He had expected, even anticipated, its arrival.

With the help of both watches, we had gotten the foresail sewn and the gaff repaired well enough to reset the sail before dark as Fin had predicted. The wind had begun to decrease even before the sail was hoisted, so we had no fear that the gaff wouldn't stand the strain. During the night, in fact, the wind fell off to about seven or eight knots and swung gradually around to the northeast. We jibed both booms across the deck to take this gentle breeze over the port quarter and continue making fairly decent time all night even through the cottony mist that enveloped us from shortly before midnight until about nine the next morning. It was an anxious night for all of us since we were running blind. But Fin had set our course accurately before dark, and all the helmsman had to do was steer it and hope we weren't being affected much by currents. The only danger was from other ships. Our only defense against this possibility was to have the lookout on the bow crank a foghorn once every two minutes or so throughout his watch—a lonely and monotonous job, I discovered, as I took my hour-long turn in the bow. The fog seemed to muffle the sound of the horn only a few feet from our figurehead. This was really an exercise in futility. If anything out there was close enough to hear our foghorn, we'd be too close to avoid a collision. The only indication that we were not standing still was the gurgling, swishing sound of the water under our forefoot just below me.

I had been relieved at the end of my hour of cranking the foghorn on the bow and was coming aft along the starboard side when I recognized Taps O'Neal in the dim light cast by the shielded lantern in the forerigging. Muffled by his black oilskins, southwester, and the swirling fog, he looked more like some long-dead seaman arising to haunt a shrouded ship.

"Nasty weather."

He grunted his agreement.

"Wonder how far offshore this extends? Could the *Osprey* be running in clear air?"

"Could be. But if they're in clear air, they're drifting, not running, unless they have a lot more wind than this."

His eyes were continuously sweeping around at the darkness and up at the rigging as we talked. His figure in the shiny oilskins swayed easily to the slight motion of the ship. It required no effort to picture this tall athletic man performing onstage. His calm self-confidence would probably enable him to achieve almost anything he set his mind and talents to—from sailor to rigger to dancer.

A slight moan and a movement just above my head on the top of the forecastle made me jump back, a cold chill running up my back.

"Who's there?"

No answer.

O'Neal stepped up on the second rung of the iron ladder so he could see atop the forecastle. "Looks like someone asleep up here by the boat."

The figure moved again. "Why, it's Liz McCormick!" He climbed on up to the cabin roof and shook her gently by the foot. "Wake up, Liz! Wake up."

She stirred and sat up slowly, sleepily.

"What?"

"What are you doing up here?"

She stretched and then shivered, hugging herself. She

186

was wearing only the thin cotton shirt and boy's pants she had been wearing when she stowed away.

"I came up here after I helped Mr. Haworth get the supper dishes cleaned up. I was so tired I guess I fell asleep."

Her face looked pale and wan in the fuzzy light emanating from the reflected light aloft. She had been putting in some long hours helping prepare and serve the meals, washing dishes, cleaning cabins, and making up bunks. I supected that Haworth was probably taking advantage of this unexpected help to push more of his own work off on his new cabin girl and confining himself more to the actual cooking.

I climbed up the ladder and joined them.

"It was nice and warm and sunny when I came up here," she added.

"Here, put this on." I peeled off my coat and handed it to her. She wrapped it around her shoulders and sat with her knees drawn up to her chest. She was silent for a minute.

"What do you think of this glamorous sea life now?" O'Neal asked with a hint of humor in his voice.

"I like it," she replied quickly and seriously. "I'm pretty tired, but I wouldn't be back in Port Gamble for anything. This is exciting, just like I thought it'd be."

She paused. "There's only one thing I miss, besides my friends."

"What's that?"

"I sure would like some chocolate. I keep tasting salt in the back of my throat. Ugh!"

"I think I've got something that'll fix you up," Taps said. "I'll be right back."

He slid down the ladder and disappeared.

"It took a lot of courage to stow away on this ship," I commented when he had had gone, trying to draw her into conversation.

"I was scared," she admitted. "But I've always liked the looks of those ships that come in and out of Port Gamble. They're tall and beautiful. I always wondered what it would be like to sail on one." She hesitated. "I read a lot," she went on. "All about adventures and dangerous and exciting trips. But they all happened to

187

somebody else. Nothing ever happens to me. My friend Amy and I were talking about that one day, and she dared me to sneak aboard this new schooner for this race. We were both going to try it, but she backed out."

"And you couldn't turn down a dare."

"Well, it was something even the boys were afraid to try." She half smiled. "Just wait'll I see them after school starts!"

Just then I heard a scuffling and Taps O'Neal's head came up over the ladder.

"Here's something I packed in my duffel for just such emergencies." He unwrapped a small white cloth and handed her a bar of chocolate candy. "I occasionally get a craving for that stuff myself when I'm at sea."

She bit into it eagerly. "Hmmm . . . Thanks."

"When you finish that, you'd better get to your bunk. It's late, and Haworth will be waking you before daylight to get the coffee started," O'Neal said.

She nodded, still chewing, and carefully wrapped up half of the bar and put it into the pocket of her shirt. "I'll save this for later." She got up and slipped out of my coat, handing it back to me. "Thanks. 'Night." She climbed down the ladder and was swallowed up by the fog.

"That kid'll go far," O'Neal remarked, staring after her. "I'd like to see her eventually become an actress or a dancer."

The only reply to his comment was monotonous noise of the foghorn from the bow.

The light breeze continued most of the next day after the fog had burned off, and everyone's spirits were high. No more was heard in the forecastle about Liz McCormick being an albatross.

Fin Staghorn paced the deck most of the afternoon, scanning the coastline with his glasses, sniffing the wind, eyeing the set of our new sails. The repaired gaff was holding well.

We were getting close to the Golden Gate, but there was no sign of *Osprey*. If she weren't already tied up in San Francisco, we had to be gaining on the big schooner. This light breeze would not be able to move her. In fact, she might be losing ground if she happened to be caught in the north-flowing currents along this coast, while we were sailing south at an easy five or six knots.

I could read nothing from Staghorn's face, but I didn't want to ply him with a lot of questions. If he wanted us to know what was on his mind, he'd tell us. Everyone in the crew knew generally where we were, since our progress had been discussed in the forecastle, and we mingled freely with the captain and the mates. Even Liz McCormick, who had become a favorite of most of the crew members who didn't regard her as a bad omen, had gotten into the spirit of the race and was just as eager as the rest of us for a sighting of our rival.

After the supper dishes had been cleaned up by Liz and the cook, both watches stayed on deck, mingling and talking, two or three of them smoking pipes, but mostly just scanning the horizon and the coastline that was just visible about fifteen miles off. Staghorn even sent Joe Barker, who had the sharpest eyes among us, up the ratlines to the top of the foremast with the field glasses to see if he could see anything. About fifteen minutes later he descended to report that he had spotted a full-rigged ship and what appeared to be a couple of sealing schooners outward bound from San Francisco several miles ahead. But nothing could be identified as the Rust and Barrett schooner. I had a sinking feeling in my stomach that they were already inside but said nothing.

We had altered course a point or two to starboard to give plenty of clearance to Point Reyes, and it was several miles behind us by the time the sun slid into the sea. The wind was dying with the day, but it was hardly noticed in the excitement generated by the sighting of the *Osprey*. The last rays of the sun picked out her sails for the good eyes of Barker, who had again ascended into the foremast rigging. He reported her becalmed about twenty miles offshore.

As dusk settled in and the wind was still nonexistent, our own progress stopped also, and the two vessels lay becalmed about fifteen miles apart. Fin Staghorn called a strategy council in the cabin for all hands just before dark.

All of us, including Liz, eagerly crowded into the after cabin to hear what he had to say.

"Okay, it's come down to this," he began with no preliminaries. "It's going to be a sprint to the finish."

"A sprint with no wind?" someone asked. There was a chuckle of laughter from two or three of the men.

"As soon as it cools down after dark, a light sea breeze will begin blowing toward the land. We need to be ready to take advantage of it. Unfortunately, it will also bring a heavy fog. Fog is almost a nightly occurrence along this coast at this time of the year, as you noticed last night. Many of you are familiar with this coast. Maybe more familiar than I am. Rasmussen, I believe you and Barker know this area better than anyone aboard. Is that right?"

"Yessir. We sailed out of San Francisco as fishermen on the same vessel for about two years, before we went with the Carlyle company."

"Good. Then I want you at the wheel or standing by to help me navigate tonight. Barker, the same thing for you. We're going to try to get in as close as we can before the fog gets too thick to see. How soon will the fog really begin to form, Hoyle?"

"Hmmm. About two to three hours after dark, sir."

"All right. The sea breeze will bring us to within about five miles of the entrance to the Golden Gate by that time. Here's what I plan to do. It's all or nothing now. My tide tables indicate that the tide will turn and start running in at about ten-twenty. It'll be at full flow about one-thirty. If we can get into position before the fog completely obscures the view, we'll feel our way inside with the light sea breeze and the strong ingoing tide. I plan to be at Caleb Hale's dock by daylight— first—*before* the *Osprey*!"

"Or on the rocks and drowned first," someone mumbled in the back.

"I know it's extremely dangerous," Fin said. "That's precisely why we'll be stealing a jump on the *Osprey*. Neil Brown would never attempt anything like that. But the best we can hope for is a tie if we wait and try to signal a pilot and a steam tug in the morning. And we could very well lose it. Do all of you want that now that we're so close? Or after all this, have the race decided by the fastest steam tug?"

The rhetorical question hung in the air for at least a full minute as Fin looked around at the packed assembly, searching each of our faces briefly. The looks on the youthful faces ranged from surprise to somber traces of fear. Someone standing behind me shifted his feet. I could only guess at what mental images they were forming of this hazardous night passage. I sensed they felt they were not being given all the available options but were hesitant to question the judgment of their skipper.

Finally one of the men spoke up. "Since we're a lot closer in, wouldn't it be better to wait until daylight and signal for a tow? We could still beat them."

"The fog normally doesn't lift until midmorning, and then it might be too late," Staghorn replied. "For all we know, they may already have a pilot aboard and be waiting for a tow. I'd guess with all this publicity the steam tugs have been on the lookout for us since shortly after we cleared Cape Flattery." He glanced around. "Barker, did you see any tugs when you were aloft?"

"Not that I recall, sir," the stocky sailor replied.

"Well, if we can't get one right away, they can't either. And it would take longer for a tug to reach them," Fin continued. "We're both becalmed. A light breeze will move us, but it won't help them. They'll have to depend on a tug. And I plan to use whatever breeze I can get to steal the jump on the *Osprey*."

He stopped talking.

"Is it too late for us to signal a tug now?"

Fin nodded. "Afraid so, even if there were one within sight. It would be a lot easier if we could, but no tug operator is going to run in a dense fog. And any harbor pilot we bring aboard would refuse to let them try."

The meeting broke up, and we went back on deck. Before I went to my bunk in the forecastle to get what sleep I could before coming back on watch at midnight, I borrowed Fin's field glasses and climbed the foremast for a look around. Dusk was rapidly coming on, but the view from about eighty feet above the water was magnificent. I could see about a half-dozen sails scattered across the slightly ruffled gray surface of the gently heaving sea—fishing boats, small trading schooners, and pleasure boats—all more or less becalmed as we were. I finally picked out the sails of what I took to be the *Osprey* almost hull-down on the western horizon. She had beaten us to the vicinity of San Francisco by taking an outside route and using the strong winds we had encountered. But now she drifted helpless offshore, while we had hugged the coast most of the way and now stood a better than even chance of beating the bigger schooner to the dock in the bay.

"The race is not always to the swift, nor the battle to the strong." I muttered the quote from Ecclesiastes to myself, smiling at the thought.

But my attention was suddenly arrested by a movement I caught out of the corner of my eye. I brought up the glasses and focused on a powered vessel that was already several miles offshore and was heading across my line of sight out to sea. It was a steam tug! I watched her as she crawled on away from us, trailing smoke, her glowing lights only specks in the twilight. She never altered course but plowed on past the few becalmed sailing craft and continued west—directly toward the *Osprey*.

I scrambled down the ratlines and hurried into the after cabin to find Staghorn. He looked up curiously from the table where he sat alone.

"What's the hurry? I didn't need the glasses back that fast."

"There's a tug going out. Looks like she's headed for the *Osprey*."

He jumped from the table and, grabbing the field glasses out of my hand, bounded up the companionway steps.

It was nearly totally dark by now, and he had trouble picking up the faint moving light that marked the tug. He looked for a few seconds then slowly lowered the glasses and turned away from the starboard rail to go aft.

"Too far away to signal. She may be headed for the *Osprey*, anyway. Our plan to sail in on the tide still stands."

I was so keyed up I didn't think I could sleep, but I was wrong. I hit my bunk fully dressed and was asleep

192

almost immediately. The next thing I knew, someone was rousing me in the dark to go on watch. I came awake quickly and was out on deck with Wiley and the other members of the port watch a few minutes before midnight.

The air felt chill and clammy. I looked aloft at the lantern placed high on the foremast. Its light was shielded from below, but it was only a dull glow in the thick mist that swirled around the ship. I heard the bleating of the hand-cranked foghorn on the bow where the lookout was stationed.

As we came aft, I saw Staghorn's face, dimly recognizable in the faint glow from the binnacle. He was steering in the very light breeze that we had picked up since sundown. He motioned Rasmussen to take over the wheel from him and stepped aside, giving him the course.

"We're making about three to four knots," he said. "The wind's over our starboard quarter, and the tide is going in, so she's easy to keep dead on course. but stay alert. We're running blind, and we're running toward shore.

"How far out do you make us to be?" I asked as Staghorn stepped toward me, the collar of his foul-weather jacket turned up and a wool cap covering most of his unruly blond hair.

"If my dead reckoning is correct, less than two miles," he replied. "But the problem with dead reckoning in this situation is that there is no way to accurately estimate how fast the current is running. The tide sucks in and out of the narrow slot of the Golden Gate with a lot of speed."

We walked over to the port rail by ourselves, and he stared into the thick fog as if trying to see through the impenetrable murk. "We're taking a terrible risk," he confided to me in a lower voice. "Even more than I let on to the crew. If we're not dead on course to that opening in the shoreline, then this ship will be piled on the rocks at the base of the bluffs on either side of the gate and we'll probably die. It's as simple as that."

"Its a scary, helpless feeling running in the fog like this," I agreed, looking over the side at the black water I could hear swishing along the side of the hull. Beads of

193

water hung in rows on all the rigging and lines and along the bottom of the foresail boom. Now and then the light breeze shook off some of the condensed moisture from aloft and sprinkled us. Staghorn was strung tighter than the wire rigging and just needed a good friend to talk to to relieve some of the tension.

"Still using that method of attacking whatever frightens you," I commented, referring to a technique for conquering his own fears while growing up—a technique he had confided to me and Wiley last year when we had first met and shared some experiences with him aboard a Mississippi River steamboat.

"That's right. I just hope I haven't carried it a little too far this time. What bothers me is that the fate of a lot of other people is riding on this venture. And I'm not at all sure of the outcome."

I put my hand on his shoulder. "Don't worry about it. You made the right decision. Everyone is here of his own free choice. Even the girl stowaway. We chose to trust you as our skipper."

"They have confidence in my expertise. And my own confidence is wavering right now. The *Western Shore*, a full-rigged clipper ship built in '74, recently hit Duxbury Reef off San Francisco while she was sailing at twelve knots—and *not* in the fog, either. Tore the bottom out of her. Total loss. Several crewmen lost. And that's just one recent example. Can't get my mind off those wrecks."

"Well, even if something happens, and we hit the rocks or a reef or another vessel, we could all take to the boats and be picked up as soon as the fog lifts in the morning." I tried to sound cheerful. "Even if the worst happened and we lost both the race *and* the ship, we'd still save our lives." Even as the words left my mouth, I realized how naive they sounded. Yet his answer was patient. "Don't bet on it. This is no small inland lake. These waters are ice-cold and filled with sharks. Shipwrecks don't often happen by the book. You can expect the unexpected. That's one reason I had the lashings taken off the lifeboat on the roof of the forecastle and had it turned right-side up, just in case we needed it in a hurry and maybe won't have time to launch it. It'll float

194

free. The davits on the boat hung off the stern are ready to let go quickly also.''

Fin couldn't seem to stand still as we spoke. He kept turning and moving, pacing a few steps forward and back, continually looking out into the darkness. He needed an outlet for his nervous energy, but there was none. It was only a matter of waiting and watching and hoping now. It was like running a silent canoe down a dark river with a swift but smooth current. The periodic bleat of the foghorn on the bow was the only sound to break the silence. We were isolated and muffled by the thick white vapor. Even though the light breeze was pushing us, I had the sensation we were standing still, wrapped in the thick fog.

Barker was on the bow, operating the foghorn, while Rasmussen was still steering, and Fin excused himself and went back to stand near the helmsman. Another thirty minutes, he estimated, would decide the fate of our gamble. While I had been talking to Fin, Taps O'Neal had positioned the men of our watch far forward along the port and starboard rails as lookouts in the hope that any obstacle might be seen in time to avoid it. We didn't fear any outbound ships, Fin explained, since any sailing vessels would be waiting to catch the outgoing tide and a more favorable wind or at least a thinning of the thick fog or daylight or all four. Steam tugs or ferries might be a different story.

A sudden, shuddering bump threw me off-balance as the schooner slowed, followed instantly by a shout from forward, ''Rocks on the port side!''

My stomach balled into a knot and my throat constricted. I heard an exclamation behind me as Rasmussen spun the wheel down. Even though we were right on top of it, I could barely make out something big sliding past the ship. Or did I just imagine I saw something? Our keel bumped twice, but the ship had been slowed by the first blow. Then I felt rather than heard a long, scraping grinding as we slid over some submerged boulders or jagged rocks, and I could hear a sucking and gurgling of water somewhere near. Unconsciously I held my breath, knowing instinctively it was a small surf breaking over some unseen rocks or nearby cliff base.

Then the sound receded until it was suddenly gone and only the beating of my heart in my ears and the steady swish of water along the hull and a quiet creaking of wooden blocks could be heard. The straight, heavy keel Asa Carlyle had designed had taken a hard blow, with tons of deadweight on top of it, and had apparently withstood the underwater rocks. We were again alone in the thick fog.

Five agonizing minutes crawled by, then ten and fifteen. Then I heard a distant tinkling of a bell. The sound grew louder, and I identified it as the clanging of a bell buoy. But in the fog I could never tell for sure from which direction the sound was coming. It seemed to move around. Or was it the ship's movement that made it seem that way? We must have cleared the Golden Gate and be just inside the Bay, I guessed. The fog was as thick as wet, shredded wool, but I began to breathe a little easier in the chill dampness. We must be out of danger now. But we would never find the pier in this pea soup fog and darkness. And there was also the danger of ramming Alcatraz Island.

Fin was in and out of the cabin checking his charts, trying to identify the bell buoy, estimating, calculating our set and drift, gauging the breeze.

Finally shortly after 2:00 A.M. he gave the order for Rasmussen to round up into the wind and told O'Neal to have an anchor let go. This was done smoothly and with a will. All the men of the watch were eager for some sort of physical activity to break the tension. Three men from the other watch had also remained on deck all night, unable to sleep, watching, assisting when needed.

"Douse all sail. Leave only a deep reef in the foresail," Fin directed the mate.

The water was deeper than Staghorn had estimated, and we had to let out considerable scope to get a good grip against the swirling tidal current. I knew we were ahead of the *Osprey*, but the race was not over until we reached Caleb Hale's pier. At least we were inside and a hook was down. If we didn't get run down by another vessel, we were safe until daylight. The lookout was still cranking the foghorn on the bow, and Fin had another lantern sent into the rigging.

I drew a deep breath of the cool, damp air and blew it out, running a hand across my brow. Judging from the dampness I felt under my oilskins, the moisture on my face could very well have been cold sweat as well as condensation.

Even though we were at anchor, Fin kept the crew on the same watch schedule. By the time I stumbled fully clothed into my forecastle bunk a few minutes after 4:00 A.M., I was exhausted. I had been on deck through my own four-to-eight stint and also through the harrowing eight-to-midnight watch as we felt our way into San Francisco Bay and then had stood my own watch again from twelve to four.

Tired as I was, nervous excitement had me out of my bunk a little more than two hours later. I poured a cup of coffee from a pot slung on its overhead hook by a sleepy-eyed Liz McCormick and stepped from the forecastle door into the chilly, clammy morning. Dawn was just graying the enveloping fog. A slight breeze blew droplets of moisture off the rigging, and the ship pulled back steadily on her anchor line. With the hazy, uncertain light, I couldn't tell if we were still facing toward the sea. We may well have swung around our anchor with the turn of the tide or wind. The compass was aft by the wheel.

The other watch was on deck. One sailor was cranking the foghorn on the dim bow, and the other three, including the second mate, were standing idly by the aft cabin near the wheel. The oilskin-clad figure of the captain stood apart at the port rail, steaming cup in one hand. He was staring off into the dull gray blanket of fog as if he could actually see something.

I went along the narrow walkway by the wet lumber and leaned on the rail beside him. He didn't move or acknowledge my presence as I sipped at my hot coffee. I knew he must be watching for any sign of the misty shroud beginning to lift or burn off with the early sun, which probably hadn't yet made its appearance above the hills to the east. He hadn't slept in at least twenty hours that I knew of. I was very anxious to get this race over with, so I knew he must be churning inside. The victory was not official until we were tied up at Caleb

Hale's pier, and there was absolutely nothing he could do until we could see where we were going.

I could think of nothing to say so just leaned there in silence for a few minutes, staring down into the oily looking black water alongside, and listened to the low chuckles of the men behind me as someone told a joke.

"Don't worry," I finally ventured in a voice just loud enough for the younger man beside me to hear. "We'll all be drinking champagne for lunch."

He turned a pair of bloodshot eyes in my direction. "Let's hope so."

"Smile," I continued. "It's all over. We've done it."

His face relaxed into a tired grin. "You're right. But I can't help worrying. I just wish this damnable fog would clear so we could finish this."

But the fog didn't lift right away. After exchanging a few more words with Staghorn, I left him to his thoughts and went back into the forecastle, where the cook had left some oatmeal and brown bread for breakfast. I had a second cup of coffee with Taps O'Neal and Wiley Jenkins, who had also rolled out earlier than necessary. When we came back on deck, we still had more than a half hour to kill before our watch. And the fog continued to hang heavy around us, smothering sound and sight.

Time crawled, and Fin Staghorn took to pacing the deck, hands jammed into his jacket pockets, tufts of blond hair escaping from the edges of his black stocking cap. He spoke to no one. The fog grew white as the sun rose, but it wasn't until one bell into our watch, or about eight-thirty, that the sun and the light breeze began shredding the thick fog into patches of white cotton.

At the first sign of breakup, a quick, spontaneous cheer went up from the men on deck. Fin ordered the anchor winched up and the reef shaken out of the foresail. Everyone was on deck, including Liz, who was dressed in an oversize jacket one of the men had lent her. Haworth appeared in the forecastle door wiping his hands on a greasy apron.

Fin took the wheel himself. A fast glimpse then another as the fog parted before thickening again showed we had anchored only about a mile off the waterfront. Fin spun the wheel to port, the foresail fluttered lazily and then filled as the bow fell off, and we started moving in the general direction of Caleb Hale's company pier. An outward-bound fishing boat materialized close off our port bow but quickly luffed to let us pass.

Within the space of only a few minutes, the fog began to dissipate quickly. We were only about a half mile away from the line of wharves marking the waterfront.

"Aauugh!"

The strangled cry from Staghorn wrenched my attention aft. Then sudden shouts and curses were going up from the crew all around me.

"Damn! They beat us! Those SOBs beat us!" Rasmussen was incredulous.

Then I saw it. The *Osprey* was snugged up alongside a pier directly ahead of us. I felt as if someone had kicked me in the stomach. My knees went weak and I staggered over to sit down on a bitt. I stared ahead again. My eyes must be playing tricks on me. It must be some other ship! Yes, that was it—a lookalike. But no, there was the name *Osprey* emblazoned in tall letters across her counter. The big Rust and Barrett schooner had somehow slipped in ahead of us. But how? It just couldn't happen. Maybe I was asleep and having a bad dream. There was no way that ship could have gotten in ahead of us in the fog. The last we had seen of her, she was becalmed several miles offshore at dusk last night. The steam tug. Somehow the captain of the steam tug must have been persuaded or bribed to tow the schooner in through the treacherous Golden Gate in the dark and fog. Even if a captain was very familiar with this harbor, it had to have been a remarkable feat of piloting.

I felt sick.

After the initial shock, the crew fell silent, staring at the sight we were approaching. The light sea breeze from the starboard side carried us closer, and Fin let *Victory* slide off astern of the *Osprey* toward an open section of pier. As we got within a hundred yards, we could see a few figures moving around on the dock, but no one appeared on the deck of the *Osprey*. Some folds of maroon-and-white bunting—the Hale company colors—still decorated the pier and were fastened to high stacks of boxes and barrels that had been moved back to form

199

a large open space at dockside. The litter left by a large crowd became visible as Staghorn spun the wheel expertly and the ship swung her stern around. Our bow pointed into the wind, the foresail flapping as we lost way and settled in, port side to the barnacle-encrusted pilings in a perfect landing.

Two stevedores caught the bow and stern mooring lines that were heaved across, while two crewmen positioned the fenders over the rail. Except for small sounds of the foresail being lowered and furled on its boom and the shrill cries of a few seagulls overhead searching for food, a dreadful silence prevailed. No one spoke. The watch went about their duties numbly. The celebration for the winners had evidently taken place several hours earlier, and the crowd was gone. Second place was last place. No one was here to cheer a loser. The workmen who secured our lines had gone back to sweeping up the trash, taking down the bunting and moving the boxes. Not even Caleb Hale was here to meet us. The sparkling morning sun was nearly dimmed by an almost palpable gloom that hung over the ship.

All the preparations, the cost, the effort, and the work that had gone into this race had been for naught—from Asa Carlyle's planning and vision to the men who had built the schooner to the men who had sailed her, and especially to her captain who had plotted her strategy and taken the chances to bring us here. Even the faraway sailmaker in Maine had contributed much. But to no avail.

I swallowed a lump in my throat and glanced furtively at Fin, who still stood with one hand on the wheel, as if unsure what to do next. He had not spoken a word since his first anguished cry. Maybe he was in a state of shock, or perhaps he was trying to set an example for the crew by clamping an iron will on his emotions.

Among the men who were stuffing their gear into seabags in the forecastle and preparing to go ashore, there was some muttering and shaking of heads and a few quiet oaths, but I don't think the full impact had yet hit them. The Carlyle company was ruined, and all of them would shortly be unemployed.

Wiley and I took Liz under our wing as we prepared to leave the ship.

An open carriage came bouncing along the quay, and the driver pulled his team to a stop while his passenger jumped out and came running down the wooden pier toward the ship. Fin stepped across the gangway to meet the fat well-dressed man who was puffing mightily when he finally stopped and mopped the perspiration from a high, balding forehead. I caught a few words of the conversation—enough to know he was a one-man welcoming committee representing Caleb Hale.

"Yes, yes. The *Osprey* . . . about an hour before daylight . . . big celebration . . . brass band . . . helluva crowd at that . . . surprised you didn't hear . . ." The voice trailed off as he and Fin walked away.

We followed down the gangway to the deserted pier. I was glad no one from the *Osprey* was about. Our loss was hard enough to take without any gloating from the opposing crew. At least there would be no fights here this morning.

I wondered idly how many people had shown up to greet the conquering heroes. Had mere curiosity brought out a large crowd to see the outcome of a race they had no stake in? Maybe many of them were Hale employees. The race had been highly publicized. But I suspected that some fresh chicken bones and the empty champagne and beer bottles strewn around on the wooden planks and stuffed into the big trash barrels probably had a lot to do with the size of the crowd. Caleb Hale would have made sure that ample refreshments were supplied for all those willing to brave the predawn chill to cheer the winners. The blackened torches that were still affixed to the pilings would have provided adequate light, even in the fog, to brighten the watchers during what appeared to have been a night-long vigil and picnic.

I glanced back over my shoulder at our little lumber schooner. My eyes alighted on the headless figure under the bowsprit. Winged Victory she may have been for the ancient Greeks, but no doubt she had a head then. Some of our more superstitious crewmen would probably say her sightlessness had prevented her from leading us to victory. The way I felt now, I wouldn't even argue with such an assertion.

CHAPTER 20

FIN Staghorn, as the ship captain representing the Carlyle company, accepted defeat with official good grace by appearing briefly at a victory dinner hosted by Caleb Hale the night of our arrival. He shook hands with William Rust and read a congratulatory telegram from Asa Carlyle. I admired the courage Fin showed in performing this duty, since he was such a fierce competitor. I suspect this was the hardest job he had done in many a day. Being a gracious loser was not something he was well-trained for.

"Condescending little slick-haired . . ." Staghorn was gritting his teeth as he entered our hotel room that night. "It was all I could do to keep from grabbing that skinny Adam's apple and shaking him like a rat!"

"Who?"

"Rust."

I laughed. "C'mon in. Let me get my shirt on. We'll go get a beer and let you cool down," I added, noting his red ears. "Did they at least feed you at that dinner?"

"I could have eaten, but I didn't have much appetite."

Liz McCormick was ensconced in a small room adjacent to the one shared by Wiley and me. Taps O'Neal and Fin Staghorn were across the hall. All of us except Fin had been resting in our rooms, waiting for his return before going out for a late supper.

The five of us went downstairs and out into the chill air of the San Francisco night.

"They've got some great halibut at a place about two blocks from here," Taps O'Neal said when we had reached the street.

"I'm for some hot chowder," Wiley replied. "Along with some salad and fresh bread. Uuummm! Sure am hungry. Must be this sea air. Is San Francisco always this cool in the summer?"

Fin nodded. "And mostly free of bugs. That's one reason it's becoming a favorite place to live."

I wanted mainly to get Fin's mind off the loss of the race and the humiliation he had just been through at the victory dinner for the crew of the *Osprey*. The headline of a newspaper I had seen someone reading in the lobby was blaring the news of the Rust and Barrett triumph in bold, black type. If Fin was aware of the press coverage, he didn't mention it.

But apparently Fin did have the failure of the company on his mind, because after we were settled in the restaurant and he had a foaming mug in his hand, he remarked, "I feel very sorry for Asa Carlyle. He has the most to lose in all this."

I nodded. "But at least he's a bachelor. He can start again. What about all those families in Port Townsend? What will they do? That's a company town."

Fin gave a slight groan and shook his head. "I don't even want to think about it."

I was suddenly aware that Liz McCormick's father was one of those merchants dependent on Carlyle company workers for business. She was staring at us, wide-eyed and solemn.

"Well, something will work out," I finished lamely. "Things are never as bad as they seem. Even if Rust and Barrett buys him out, they'll probably keep the mill open."

"I found out it *was* that tugboat pilot who brought them in last night," Fin remarked, harking back to the subject of the race.

"Was he bribed?" Wiley asked. "Surely those steam tug captains don't take risks like that routinely."

"I could never get anyone to say so. I mingled with a few of the crew before the dinner. Most of the sailors claimed they didn't know. They did say that as soon as the tugboat came within hailing distance, Captain Brown got out his speaking trumpet and shouted for the tug skipper to come aboard. As soon as he came over the rail, the two captains rushed below. Only a few minutes later, the tug captain went back to his own vessel, a towline was secured, and they got underway, even though it was totally dark and the fog was already settling in heavy around them. A couple of the sailors admitted to me their hair was practically standing on end, they were so scared. It must have taken a helluva nerve on that tug captain's part, bribe or no bribe. There's no law against running in those conditions, but no seaman can get away with it very long without losing his vessel and maybe his life." He shook his head sadly. "If I had only gone for the pier right away instead of anchoring! Damn!" He slammed his fist down so hard the silverware jumped on the white tablecloth.

"There's no way we could have found Hale's pier, even if it had lighted torches all around it. That tugboat captain has lots of experience in this bay. And he had better control, since he was under power."

Fin looked disgusted but only replied, "Maybe so."

Asa Carlyle had sent a brief telegram earlier in the day commending Staghorn and the crew on a valiant effort and authorizing all of us to stay four nights at our hotel at his expense. ALSO LIZ MCCORMICK, the telegram had read.

"Oh no!" the girl had wailed when she heard this. "My folks are going to *kill* me. Daddy will be in a bad mood anyway after this race. I'd better enjoy my stay here while I can. I'm almost afraid to go home."

"Oh, they'll get over it." O'Neal laughed. "I'm sure they're grateful to know you're safe. But if I were you, I think I'd do something special for them to show you're sorry for running off like that and causing them all that grief and worry. You know they didn't deserve that. I'm sure they love you very much."

She nodded. "I will." She looked like a proper young lady in a very feminine dress the crew had chipped in and bought her earlier that afternoon. Gone was all the talk of her being an albatross. If two or three of them were still harboring superstitions about her being bad luck, they were keeping the thought to themselves. Or they were so despondent they didn't care. At least two of them had mentioned using their few days in the Bay City to look for other work. Even though none of the crew had been officially terminated, there was a unanimous feeling that it was only a matter of time. Their loyalty and high regard for Asa Carlyle was also unanimous, but each had his own welfare and livelihood to consider first.

It was a rather subdued but otherwise pleasant evening, and we all returned to our hotel and went to our beds very tired shortly after midnight. And I'm sure not one of us dreamed what was coming two days later.

"If I had only hugged the coastline all the way, I think we would have beaten them," Staghorn bemoaned for about the tenth time as we turned into our hotel lobby about midafternoon two days later. He had grown increasingly moody and preoccupied since our arrival in town, and when he spoke, it was nearly always on the subject of the race as he ran it over and over in his mind, picking out flaws in his strategy. I felt very bad about our loss, too, but his constant harping on the subject was beginning to grate on my nerves. Nothing I could do seemed to distract him for more than a few minutes. He was dragging the full responsibility for the loss down on himself.

Taps and Wiley were conducting Liz on a tour of the city, riding the cable cars and seeing the sights. They had taken to her like two older brothers, and she was loving every minute of it. Fin and I were alone as we crossed the big lobby to get our room keys at the desk. The slim clerk with the high stiff collar reached into the pigeonhole for Fin's key.

"Two messages for you, Mr. Staghorn." He handed over the key along with a folded slip of paper and a yellow Western Union envelope.

Fin flipped open the folded sheet first.

"Hhhmmm."

"What?"

"Caleb Hale wants to see me in his office right away."

"What about?"

"Doesn't say."

"What time is it?"

"He'd still be there. It's only two-thirty," he said, glancing at the big wall clock over the honeycomb of pigeonholes.

He inserted the tip of a finger under the flap of the yellow envelope and ripped it open as we walked away from the desk. It was a telegram from Asa Carlyle. Fin unfolded it and scanned it quickly. His eyes opened slightly and his jaw dropped.

"Well, I'll be damned!"

I moved around to read over his shoulder.

THREE MEN ARRESTED HERE FOR CONSPIR-
ACY TO MURDER US IN CHINATOWN STOP ALL
THREE ARE RUST AND BARRETT EMPLOYEES
STOP ALONZO BOGGS IS RINGLEADER STOP
NEWSPAPER STATES BOGGS ALSO CONFESSED
TO BURNING MY MILL STOP MORE LATER STOP

A CARLYLE

We looked at each other.

"But those were Chinese who attacked us," I said.

Fin shrugged. "I don't know. Maybe they were hired to do it. This says they were arrested for conspiracy. Who's this Alonzo Boggs? Carlyle sounds like we should know him."

"Boggs . . . Boggs . . . ?" The name sounded vaguely familiar to me, but I couldn't place it. "Alonzo Boggs?"

We looked blankly at each other.

"Oh, I know!" The recognition hit me in a rush. "Don't you remember? He was that loud-talking guy who buttonholed Rust in the saloon where we were eating."

Fin still looked puzzled.

"Early summer. The day we had the meeting with Caleb Hale and he proposed the race. Boggs practically demanded that Rust reopen some mill where he worked."

"Ah, yes. Now I remember. Big, rough-looking guy. Short hair."

"Right."

He refolded the telegram and slid it into his shirt

pocket. "This is beginning to come together, but it still doesn't make complete sense. Maybe Caleb Hale can shed some light on it. Let's go see what he wants."

The white-bearded Hale rose from behind his desk as we were shown into his paneled office.

"Ah, you got my message. Good, good. Have a chair. One moment."

He went out the door and closed it behind him. Fin and I glanced curiously at each other and then around at the office. The room was not large, and the dark heavy desk and armchairs made it seem even smaller. One window high in the wall behind the desk did not admit much of the afternoon light, so the green-shaded coal-oil lamp on the desk was burning to throw a pool of yellow light over a sheaf of papers strewn about. Shortly the door opened and Hale reentered, followed by William Rust. I felt my stomach tighten. What was going on? Caleb Hale's face gave no clue. But he was not smiling.

Hale waved Rust to an upholstered chair opposite us and went to sit with one leg on a corner of his desk. He picked up a piece of paper.

"Gentlemen, I'll get right to the point. I have here a telegram I received earlier today from Asa Carlyle. He tells me that three men who are employees of Rust and Barrett have just been arrested and jailed in Port Townsend. They're accused of trying to murder Carlyle and a few of his people—including Captain Staghorn here. It happened in this town the very day of our meeting last spring. I checked this report with the newspaper here, and they verified it with one of their stringers in the Puget Sound area." He turned to William Rust. "Do you have an employee named Alonzo Boggs?"

"Yes. He was the manager of our Spruce Point Mill."

"*Was* the manager?" Hale furrowed his brow.

"Well . . . technically, still is, but the mill has been shut down more than it's been open this summer because of the slump. Why?"

"He's reported to be the leader of the three men who were arrested. And I'm told he also confessed to setting fire to Asa Carlyle's mill." He stood up, leaning his buttocks against the front edge of his desk, and folded his arms across his chest. "Do you know anything about this?"

Rust looked bewildered and then annoyed. "Of course not. These men will be immediately discharged, pending a trial. If found guilty, I presume they'll be punished for their crimes. I can't imagine why they might do such a thing. But I fail to see what you're driving at. What concern is this of yours?"

"My only concern is this—if it turns out these men were interfering with the Carlyle company while they were in your employ, then this race will be forfeited. You of course remember our agreement."

I saw Rust's jaw muscles work, but he quickly regained his composure. "Must I remind you that we now have a legally binding contract?" He grated.

"If you'll read the fine print, you'll see that the contract is contingent upon fulfillment of all our verbal agreements concerning the race. And these agreements are spelled out. If it turns out that our verbal agreement of no interference was violated, then the contract is void."

"My company cannot be responsible for anything my employees do on their own time," Rust said with a wave of his hand, as if to dismiss such a ridiculous notion. "If they're guilty, their motives probably had nothing to do with the race between our companies."

"You heard what I said!" Caleb Hale retorted. He did not sound like a man who was used to being contradicted. "A conviction means the contract reverts to the Carlyle company. Pending the outcome of the trial, our lumber orders will still go to Rust and Barrett."

Rust knew enough to clamp his mouth shut then. It was obviously painful for him, but he was at a disadvantage and knew it. Caleb Hale was holding all the cards in this game, and Rust preferred to throw in his hand and wait for a better deal. We had only preliminary reports. Anything could happen yet.

"That's all, gentlemen." Hale dropped the telegram on his desk and walked around behind it. "My secretary will show you out. I'll be in touch with both of your companies later." Rust's face reminded me of a thunderhead as he passed us going out the door. This proud, wealthy, and powerful man was not accustomed to being dismissed like an errant schoolboy from the headmaster's office.

Late in the afternoon the following day, Wiley and I were in our room, shaking the wrinkles out of the only suits we had brought along in our seabags preparatory to dressing for the theater. In all the excitement of the race and the crushing defeat following it, then the strange events of the previous day, I had completely forgotten about the actor David St. George, his pursuer Timothy Cooper, and the touring Shakespeare company.

But Wiley had not forgotten. He reminded me that he had made a date several weeks earlier with Darcy McLeod to attend the opening night performance of *Macbeth* here in San Francisco. The company of players had finished their tour some weeks earlier and had returned here to their homebase to begin rehearsals for *Macbeth*, which was opening tonight.

"About ready?" Wiley asked, adjusting his tie in the mirror.

"Rap on Liz's door there, and see if she's dressed. Taps and Fin are meeting us in the lobby."

A few minutes later we locked our rooms and went down to the street. It was only five-thirty, and we had plenty of time for a leisurely dinner before the theater. Since the restaurant we had selected was only two blocks away, we bypassed the hacks standing in the street and started walking.

"Paaapper! Get yer evenin' paper right here!" The newsboy was doing a good business among the strollers and supper crowd. O'Neal dug into his pocket for some change, hailed the boy, and bought a paper.

He waited until we were seated in the restaurant and had placed our order before Taps opened the paper and began scanning the articles.

"Ah, here's something on it," he said, folding the paper back and smoothing it out on the table where the overhead lamplight was better.

We all crowded around to get a look at the article, trying to read over O'Neal's shoulders.

MAN ARRESTED IN CONSPIRACY TO MURDER
Drunken Boast Leads to Charges
PORT TOWNSEND MAN AND TWO
COMPANIONS JAILED
CONFESSION INCLUDES ARSON AT MILL

We were each reading at our own pace, but Taps still read parts of it aloud. It seemed Alonzo Boggs, faced with eyewitness testimony from two former associates he had recently fired for being drunk on the job at the mill, had made a full confession. He was quoted as saying that while his mill was closed, he had gone to San Francisco checking on future job prospects. According to this story, Boggs and two Rust and Barrett mill hands were drinking in a saloon when they overheard William Rust and two company officials discussing the race that Rust had just agreed to. Rust did not see or recognize Boggs. But Boggs determined on his own that the Carlyle company would not be competing in any contract race. His two drinking companions had some underworld acquaintances. They were able to put Boggs quickly in touch with a network of outlaws whose tentacles stretched even into Chinatown. This well-organized gang jumped at the chance to get their hands on some gold and currency from wealthy travelers. In return for Boggs's tip as to time, place, and description of victims, they were more than happy to slit a few throats in the process of relieving Carlyle and friends of their money. This would also insure the robbers against any embarrassing testimony later.

"That's it!" Wiley shouted. Everyone in the room turned to look at him, but he didn't even notice. "That means the race is ours by forfeit and the contract goes to Carlyle!"

"I hope you're right," I said. "But I wouldn't be celebrating quite so soon. Hale said yesterday it would take a conviction to forfeit the race. Besides, newspaper articles are written more to sell papers than to be dead accurate. I ought to know; I was in the business for a few years. It says here that Boggs overheard Rust and his friends talking about the race. Says Rust didn't recognize or see him. We know that isn't so. We watched and heard their first meeting."

"But if Rust met him later, as he promised, he could have told him about that race."

"Yes."

"Well, if you can put any stock in this story at all, it explains about that phony hack driver and the attack in the Chinese quarter," Wiley said, looking up from the paper.

"That explains a lot of things—like the arson at the mill. With Carlyle out of business, there'd be no competition for the contract, and Alonzo Boggs would keep his foreman's job."

"Helluva way to go about it. Why would anyone go to such lengths just to keep a job?"

Staghorn shrugged. "Who knows? He was virtually in sole charge of a mill in an isolated area. Maybe he was pilfering money from his employer and didn't want anything to interrupt his setup. Rust and Barrett has had to fire two company executives in the past year for that very thing."

"Even if they close one or two of their mills or even have to sell off all but the largest one at Port Townsend, the Rust and Barrett company will survive. They've got enough resources to make it. Besides, before this latest market slump hit, they were working on consolidating sales to several overseas markets like Hong Kong, Australia, and South Africa."

"I'd like to attend their trial," I said. "Boggs didn't even know me. I guess maybe it was an impersonal thing as far as he was concerned."

"Does it say anything in that article about Boggs and his boys trying to shanghai me?" Wiley said.

"Nope." I grinned.

"Probably coincidence," Fin said. "That sort of thing happens all the time. You just happened to be in the wrong place at the right time."

"I guess I'll never know."

Two hours later, pleasantly stuffed, we settled ourselves into the plush theater seats at the Gilbert Hall. The house was rapidly filling up, and I was glad Wiley had purchased our tickets the first day we arrived in town. The opening-night patrons were formally dressed

211

for the most part, making us appear rather plain in our slightly rumpled traveling suits.

Liz McCormick was looking around wide-eyed at the very plush surroundings, the rich red damask upholstery, the beautifully coifed women entering the carpeted hall and finding their seats amid a soft rustle of satin gowns.

"Do you see Timothy Cooper anywhere?" I asked Wiley in a low voice.

He shook his head. "He's probably long since given up and gone home."

"I don't think so. He didn't seem like the type who would quit this easily. Did Darcy say anything about him when you saw her at dress rehearsal yesterday?"

"She said she hadn't seen him for about two weeks. She said she was very grateful that he hadn't been hanging around rehearsals because David St. George was beginning to relax and concentrate on his acting. And she was thrilled to death to get the role of Lady Macbeth. Says it's the most challenging she's ever tried. In fact, she's nervous about playing the lead opposite St. George because he's so moody and so talented. But she said he's been much easier to work with since Cooper has been dogging them. Even though his nerves were about shot, he's been distracted and at least wasn't throwing fits of temperament whenever things didn't go his way."

"That's a strange thing," O'Neal said, shaking his head. "I still can't decide in my own mind if that man *is* Booth. He certainly looks like the man I remember from Washington, and that limp makes it even more likely."

"Or more coincidental," Staghorn added, leaning forward to talk around Liz McCormick.

The hum of voices subsided, and I looked up to see a portly bald man in formal evening dress step through the curtain and stand in the middle of the stage as the limelight was increased to illuminate him.

"Ladies and gentlemen, may I have your attention please!"

The buzz of voices subsided. The man waited patiently for silence to reign before he continued.

"I have an announcement to make. I regret to tell you

212

that the wonderful actor David St. George who was scheduled to play the part of Macbeth has been taken suddenly ill and is unable to appear this evening. . . ." He held up his hands as a wave of discontent rolled up from the packed house. "Don't worry; it's only a throat problem that temporarily affects his voice. I am sure you will enjoy the performance of Mr. Sidney Blackwell, who will be Mr. St. George's stand-in. . . ."

I didn't hear the rest of what was said because a man in a tweed suit jumped up from the front row, climbed clumsily over the other patrons, and literally ran up the center aisle toward the door. It was Timothy Cooper!

We looked at each other.

"David St. George has finally made his move," I said. "And what a time he picked to do it. Opening night. Cooper figured his pride would never let him run out on a big role like this."

"If St. George *is* Booth, I don't think Cooper will ever find him again," Wiley said. "St. George was at dress rehearsal yesterday," Wiley added, "so he couldn't have much less than a twenty-four-hour head start if he's running."

"Obviously, Cooper thinks he is. Was anything wrong with St. George's voice yesterday?"

"Not that I noticed. But this cold, damp climate could sure give a person some throat problems," Wiley said.

"If St. George isn't Booth, he's probably sitting in his hotel room this minute gargling salt water for his laryngitis," I laughed.

"And if he *is* Booth, he's probably long gone," Wiley said.

"Well, it took Cooper about twelve years to locate the man he's convinced is Booth. It may take him another dozen years to catch up again. But he's as tenacious as a bulldog."

"He wasn't able to break him in the few months he had him in his sights. I'll bet if he ever catches up with him again, he'll use some different tactics."

"My money's on Cooper," I said. "He's a professional at this sort of thing."

"Well, I'm not going to worry about it now," Wiley

said in a lower whisper as the gas jets in the wall sconces were dimmed and the footlights went up on the opening scene. "The beautiful Lady Macbeth is the one I'm after from here on in."

CHAPTER 21

SINCE the robbery of our belongings and the attempted murder had occurred here, the trial of Boggs and his two conspirators had been moved to California from Washington. The charge of arson was still pending in the Territory.

"Gentlemen of the jury," said the judge, "have you reached a verdict?"

"We have, your honor," the jury foreman replied. "We find the defendant guilty on all counts."

I gripped Carlyle's hand. "Congratulations! The contract is finally yours."

He shook my hand, grinning broadly, and made some reply that was lost in the buzz of excitement among the spectators around us. A heads-together consultation was taking place between Alonzo Boggs and his lawyer.

The judge rapped for quiet.

"Gentlemen of the jury, you are dismissed." Swiveling back to face front, he said, "The defendants will please rise."

The three men sitting at the table with their attorneys stood, facing the judge. Boggs was a rawboned man with rather short hair and a weatherbeaten face who looked out of place in the dark broadcloth suit that had obviously been purchased for his court appearance. His two codefendants were shorter, one of average build and the other lean and sallow-looking.

"Inasmuch as a jury of your peers has found you guilty of the charges, there is nothing left for this court to do but pass sentence. Thirty years! Through no fault of yours, these four men are still alive, but that doesn't lessen the gravity of your crime— conspiracy to murder. Do you have anything to say before sentence is passed?"

"I didn't do it, your honor." Boggs spoke up in a strong voice. Just as the judge was about to rap his gavel, he was interrupted.

"Wait! I've something to tell this court!"

He angrily shook off his lawyer who was trying to pull him back to his chair.

The judge rapped for order. "Have you consulted with your counsel about this?" the judge asked as the lawyer continued to urgently argue under his breath with Boggs.

"Lemme alone! Thirty damn years! You think I'm gonna stand for that? You promised I'd get a light sentence!"

"We'll appeal!" the lawyer hissed in a stage whisper. "Sit down and be quiet!"

"Hell, no!" He yanked his arm loose. "If I'm going to prison for life, I'm not goin' alone. Judge, I admit I arranged for those men to be robbed and killed. But I didn't do it on my own. Nossir. I was *hired* to do it. My boss, Mr. William Rust, paid me ten thousand dollars in gold to get rid of these men so my company could get the lumber contract without having to compete for it!"

The courtroom erupted.

"It's a lie! It's a lie! He's just trying to save himself!" I could barely hear Rust's strident voice above the tumult. He had jumped up on to a bench and was shaking his fist at Boggs.

"It's true!" Boggs screamed back. "And you paid for this big-shot lawyer. You said he would get me a light sentence! Thirty years! I'll never get out to spend your damn money!"

The judge was pounding his gavel for order, but no one heard him in the chaos that had broken loose when Boggs hurled his thunderbolt. From where I sat I could see the back of William Rust's slicked-down black hair as he was on his feet in the spectator section, facing his accuser across three more rows of spectator benches and the wooden balustrade. The backs of his prominent ears were turning red as he shook his fist and yelled something about Boggs being a liar. "You ungrateful cur. If you think you're going to drag me into this sorry affair, you're crazy!" He looked toward the judge, who had quit pounding the gavel. "Can't you see, your honor? He just admitted he perjured himself during this trial and now he's changed his story and is lying again! It's just the tactic of a desperate man."

"I have the proof!" Boggs yelled back.

"Silence in this court!" the judge bellowed above the din. His voice had more of an effect than the gavel. Two men managed to pull Rust and Boggs to their chairs, and the rumble of spectator voices gradually subsided.

"This court is adjourned!" the judge said in a hoarse voice when he had regained control. "Bailiff, remove these prisoners and detain Mr. Rust for questioning."

"That's a helluva development," I said to Carlyle, wiping the perspiration from my face as we adjourned to the cooler hallway outside.

"You reckon there's anything to it, or is he just trying to take someone down with him?" Wiley asked.

Carlyle looked somewhat shaken, and he moved back next to the wall as the crowd streamed past us.

"I don't know what to think." He shook his head. "I've known William Rust casually as a business acquaintance for several years. He's a humorless stuffed shirt, and I enjoy putting a burr under his saddle now and then. I've also heard he can be a hard-nosed bastard with his employees, but I wouldn't have thought he was capable of murder."

"I've seen the desire for money make men do strange things," I said.

"Rust is a very conservative type," Carlyle mused. "He's definitely not a gambler. He would bet only on a sure thing. And the only way his company could be assured of that lucrative contract was to make certain the Carlyle company was not able to compete in the race.

"It'll be interesting to see what proof Boggs has."

"What would he have to gain by such an accusation if it were false? He's going to prison, regardless."

"Just the satisfaction of revenge, I guess."

"Will you be staying around to see the outcome of all this?" Carlyle asked me and Wiley. "You two have jobs at my mill if you're interested. Since I've won that contract, there will be plenty of work. And this time I'll pay you," he added with a chuckle.

"Thanks, but I think we'll be going back inland," I answered for both of us.

"Darcy McLeod and that traveling troupe of players are working their way east," Wiley said. "They're scheduled to open at the Denver Opera House next week."

"Ah hah!" Asa Carlyle smiled, his eyes twinkling. "So it's not just the desire to see some new country that's taking you east."

Wiley grinned self-consciously but did not deny it.

"Good luck with that story," Staghorn said, turning to me and shaking my hand.

"I think *Leslie's Illustrated* is interested in my account of this race," I replied. "If not, I'll try *Harper's Weekly*. I've written a number of things for them in the past. Selling one of these eyewitness stories to a big-circulation magazine now and then sure helps pay the bills."

"With a little more time and practice, I could have made some top-notch sailors out of both of you," Staghorn said.

"I believe I'll keep my feet on dry land for a while," Wiley said. "Matt may miss that wild sea road, but I won't."

"A man in love is not interested in anything else," I put in. "And this infatuation could turn into something serious."

"Well, who knows what you may run into in Colorado besides your ladylove?" Carlyle said. "A lot of new country opening up back that way—gold and silver mines in the mountains. Railroad's abuilding along the base of the Rockies and down toward Santa Fe, I hear."

But his reply was fading in my ears as my mind slipped back to relive some of the scenes aboard the Carlyle company ships—the quiet of a moonless night overlaid by a blanket of a billion stars that seemed just out of reach above the masthead, hauling on a sheet while a gale drove stinging rain and spray into our faces, the sudden sinking feeling in my stomach as a rocky shore loomed up out of the gloom to leeward, the taut feel of the wheel as the tall schooner heeled to a fresh breeze, the shudder as the lumber-laden vessel buried her bow in a foaming sea, the roaring of the night wind through the rigging, the smell of the salt air, the shrill cries of the gray-white gulls wheeling over an anchorage.

I could still feel it, smell it, hear it. The vivid scenes would live long in my memory.

I dragged my gaze and my attention back to Carlyle and Staghorn, who stood near me.

"If the salt in my blood gets a little diluted, I'll be back," I said. "I've been told the sea is like the desert—if a man spends much time on it, he'll never be satisfied anywhere else."

About the Author

Tim Champlin was born in Fargo, North Dakota and grew up in Nebraska, Missouri, and Arizona. He lives in Nashville, Tennessee with his wife and three children where he is employed in the federal Civil Service. He is the author of SUMMER OF THE SIOUX, DAKOTA GOLD, STAGHORN and SHADOW CATCHER.